DOUBLE

The gunman looked th[...] scope mounted on the [...] of his expensive Sharps rifle. His friend sighted along the iron sights of his Spencer. The target of both men was the large, buckskin-shirted scout who rode a black-and-white paint toward them. A woman and a boy rode to Colt's left, but Colt would take the first two bullets.

The gunman smiled menacingly at his friend. "I want to make sure I don't miss. This job has been too difficult for too many, when it should have been so easy. Both of us aim at Colt first. When he goes down, take the woman, and I'll shoot the red nigger."

The gunman returned to his scope and held steady on the center of Colt's chest. The Chief of Scouts was just entering the Sharps' range. . . .

COLT

CHIEF OF SCOUTS

COLT

by
DON BENDELL

Chief of Scouts, Volume 3

A SIGNET BOOK

SIGNET
Published by the Penguin Group
Penguin Books USA Inc., 375 Hudson Street,
New York, New York 10014, U.S.A.
Penguin Books Ltd, 27 Wrights Lane,
London W8 5TZ, England
Penguin Books Australia Ltd, Ringwood,
Victoria, Australia
Penguin Books Canada Ltd, 10 Alcorn Avenue,
Toronto, Ontario, Canada M4V 3B2
Penguin Books (N.Z.) Ltd, 182–190 Wairau Road,
Auckland 10, New Zealand

Penguin Books Ltd, Registered Offices:
Harmondsworth, Middlesex, England

First published by Signet, an imprint of Dutton Signet,
a division of Penguin Books USA Inc.

First Printing, March, 1994
10 9 8 7 6 5 4 3 2 1

DEDICATION

This book is dedicated to my children: Don, Jr., a good solid man and businessman who would rather kayak and "eat water" in a white-water river than do anything else; Brooke, a classy, beautiful lady who inherited a ton of the Bendell artistic talent and has worked hard to develop it; Brenna, another beautiful lady who is destined for stardom in the entertainment business; Britt, a tall, good-looking, intelligent, and fiercely independent person who is a success at anything he tries; Brent, a muscular, quiet "hunk," karate champion, and perfectionist who is headed for the top; and Josh, another good-looking karate champion who won't be satisfied unless he breaks an NFL record for vicious tackles and who would take on King Kong for the sake of defending a principle. I love and am very proud of each and all of you.

Dad

A Warrior's Prayer

Keeper of Dreams, please hear our words,
Which fly to you like soaring birds.
This prayer now comes from many tribes
From concrete caves and bison hides.

Please grant us freedom, hear me sing.
Let our hearts soar on eagle's wing.
Please give us courage, this we pray,
To face the storms that blow our way.

Your words have iron, let them ring.
We seek the key to everything.
We want fine husbands or good wives,
A love to carry through our lives.

Our wills are soft like cougar's feet.
Without your strength we'll cry, "Retreat!"
Our tongues are forked like crawling snakes.
What weakness all our lying makes.

Your breath now blows through prairie grass,
And sings through canyons lined with glass.
Please send your whispers to our souls
And help us reach some useful goals

Oh, give us mountains lined with gold,
And grant us grace while growing old.
Then dignify our spoken tongue
And hear the songs of love we've sung.

We ride our mounts with spotted hides
With lance and bow upon our sides.
We seek white bison, this we pray;
Please help us make this a great day.

Forgive the times we have not tried,
And dropped our spears, sat down, and cried.
Please grant us rabbits for our stew
And give us strong-hearts, counting coups.

If we should fall on Mother Earth,
They'll take us to our place of birth,
Then place us on a funeral pyre,
And burn our flesh with roaring fire.

For we have followed tribal ways
And chased the great bear many days.
Please stack the fire with wood and coal,
With flaming tongues to warm our soul.

Please take our souls to eagle's lair
And find our father hunting there,
In teeming woods and mountains high,
Where we are born the day we die.

Then we can ride in hunting lands,
With noble warrior spirit bands.
We'll hunt great bears and deer and boar
And live in peace forevermore.

—From *Songs of the Warrior*, by Don Bendell

A good soldier, like a good horse,
cannot be of a bad color.
          —Oliver Wendell Holmes

chapter 1

>>>>>>>>>>>>>>>>>>>>>>

Homes

Colonel Rufus Birmingham Potter felt strange lying in ambush behind the boulder, overlooking the road between Denver and Colorado Springs. He always hired others to do his killing for him, but most of his hired guns had been murdered or scared off. The target of his ambush was the one who had frightened away or killed all his men, the one who was on his way south from Denver right now.

Pike's Peak, clearly visible to the left in front of the colonel, was wearing a fresh cap of snow, glistening in the afternoon sun, on its fourteen-thousand-foot head. At its feet, to the east, lay the growing town of Colorado Springs. The Rampart Range lay just to the west of Colonel Potter's ambush site, which was at the highest point between Denver and Colorado Springs, Monument Pass. At an elevation of almost eight thousand feet, it rose two thousand feet higher than the Mile High City of Denver and over one thousand feet higher than Colorado Springs, a short ride south and within sight now.

Pike's Peak, named for its discoverer, Colonel Zebulon Pike, who had charted and mapped most of this area more than a half a century earlier, was a 14,110-foot mountain standing on the edge of the high prairie. The highest mountain for miles, it stood as a silent sentinel guarding one of the gateways into the dangerous and unforgiving, albeit majestic, Rocky Mountains.

Potter felt a little more secure, too, because he had Curly Shanks, his top gun, with him. Curly also wanted to kill this man, and Curly was a real shootist. He didn't like trying to set up an ambush. He wanted to stand up to the man who had killed his friend, the giant Will Sawyer, up in the Yellowstone. He wanted to face him down and shoot it out, one dying and the other living. Shanks had killed some good gunfighters and had had face-offs with other men on ten different occasions; he would rather die in a shoot-out than most other ways anyhow. Curly was a hard man, and he didn't like this ambush idea one bit, but he rode for the brand and Potter was his boss. That's the way it was, so he'd put up with it, but he'd try to convince the colonel to let him shoot it out with the man.

He had gone ahead toward Denver and waited up around the bend about five miles north of the ambush spot on Monument Hill. Seeing the man and his two companions coming, he jumped on his blood bay horse and made it quickly back to the selected dry gulch spot. Right at the highest point of the hill, the stagecoach and wagon road went through a wooded area with small evergreen trees, then started downhill slowly toward the springs.

Curly had a Spencer rifle, and the colonel had a Sharps buffalo gun. The rocks they were on overlooked the wagon road, and the shot would be less than a hundred meters—a simple matter of squeezing the triggers for these two. There was no way they could miss.

They also couldn't miss seeing and identifying the approaching riders. The man they were after was tall, several inches over six feet, and whipcord lean. He was all sinew, with shoulders that made men jealous and women stare every time they could get away with it and a washboard stomach that was crisscrossed with scars like the rest of his upper body. He had piercingly honest green eyes and brown hair. His high cheekbones, like the rest of his face, were a little bit windburned, showing that he was a man who spent all his time outdoors.

He wore a floppy leather scout's hat, a porcupine-quilled and fringed buckskin Lakotah (Sioux) war shirt, yellow-striped blue cavalry trousers, high-heeled cowboy boots with large roweled Mexican-style spurs, and a bone-hair pipe choker necklace (a gift from the famous Chief Joseph). A brown leather gunbelt with twin holsters held two mother-of-pearl-handled Colt Peacemaker .45 revolvers with engraved scrollwork on the metal. A hand-carved eagle, grasping a serpent firmly in its talons, was carved on each pearl grip. Behind the right holster was a large beaded and fringed sheath containing a horn-handled Bowie knife, sharp enough to shave with. Hidden on the man's body were numerous other weapons.

He was mounted on a tall black and white paint horse, a gift from his blood brother, the late Lakotah war hero Crazy Horse. The stallion, who was named War Bonnet, was prancy and proud in his carriage. He had three red coup stripes painted around each foreleg, red handprints on each rump, and eagle feathers braided into his long white mane and tail.

The rider sat in a black saddle, covered with silver conchas and tapedero stirrup covers; it was a wedding gift, presented the day before by his new wife. One of the two saddle scabbards contained a brass-tack-and-feather-decorated Winchester eighteen-shot carbine. The other scabbard held a Colt revolving twelve-gauge shotgun. Behind the saddle, in the bedroll, was a short Cheyenne bow and a quiver full of steel-tipped arrows.

The woman sat on her wedding gift—a solid, stocky, and well-muscled golden palomino gelding she had named Buttercup. The woman was incredibly beautiful, with bright auburn hair and a figure that made men dream dreams and smile in their sleep.

Next to her was a teenaged Nez Perce warrior who looked much older and bigger than his fifteen years. He was clad in traditional dress, except that he also wore a low-slung holster with a brand-new walnut-handled classic Colt Peacemaker .45—a gift from the man on the paint horse.

The object of the ambush was no ordinary man. He had already become a legend in the West, like Hickok, Hardin, the Earps, Doc Holliday, Cochise, Crazy Horse, Sitting Bull, Chief Joseph, Geronimo, the James brothers, and so many more. Christopher Columbus Colt, chief of cavalry scouts, nephew of the late Colonel Samuel Colt, and gun handler extraordinaire, was an expert tracker and scout, military strategist; but more important, he was outraged by the treatment the American Indians had received from the United States government. That was the main reason he was a scout, so he could watch over the operations between the military and the Indian nations and do what he could to protect both sides from atrocities.

Colonel Potter, ruthless money grubber and landgrabber, had had a land-fraud scheme of his foiled in Oregon and had taken refuge in Colorado, where his men had been chasing prospectors away from new gold and silver strikes. When Chris Colt and his fiancée, Shirley Ebert, had shown up in Denver to get married, Potter happened to run into them and Colt's new sidekick, a young Nez Perce warrior named Man Killer, as they stood outside the office of the justice of the peace.

Potter was convinced that Colt was following him, and he decided right then to ambush the famous scout and his wife and friend so they would never haunt his dreams or his waking moments again. It didn't matter to Potter that he had hired the best guns he could find to kill Colt, and they had all been defeated. The crooked colonel was one of those men who just felt that he was smarter and tougher than anybody else.

Potter looked down the long telescope mounted on the top of his expensive Sharps gun. Curly sighted along the barrel of his Spencer. In the sights of both guns was the large, buckskin-shirted man now riding the ambush point. The woman and the boy rode to Colt's left, but the scout would take the first two bullets. From their position at the height of the pass at Monument Hill, Potter and Curly could see a good distance north. There were hills and prairie with some dips, but the wagon road was clearly visible for over two miles, until it finally wrapped to the right around a hill covered with trees. Several large herds of antelope and mule deer grazed in the large meadows of long green grasses.

Potter put the cross hairs on the center of Colt's chest, but then he relaxed. They were still a little too far away.

Looking at Curly, he said, "I want to make sure I don't miss. This job has been too difficult for too many when it should have been so easy. Both of us aim at Colt first. When he goes down, you take the woman, and I'll shoot the red nigger."

"No, sir," Curly said. "I ride for the brand and am

totally loyal to you, Colonel, but I ain't shootin' no woman."

Potter cleared his throat and nonchalantly replied, "Very well, then. I'll kill the woman and you take the red nigger. The main thing is to shoot Colt first. This Sharps will blow a hole in him big enough to push my fist through, but I want you also blasting a hole through the scoundrel's black heart just for insurance. When you do a job, do it right."

"Yes, sir," Curly said, "but I'd druther put a couple .44's in the sumbitch."

Potter said, "They're close enough now. Fire when ready."

The colonel was proud that he sprinkled his normal conversation with expressions such as "fire when ready," suggesting military background. In fact, he was not a former colonel; he was a cowardly deserter from the Civil War. The man he was now aiming at had been a hero in that same war as a teenager, even lying about his age to enlist in the 171st Regiment of the Ohio National Guard.

The two men carefully sighted along their guns and pointed the deadly weapons at the center of Colt's chest. The Sharps's loud report had not even started echoing when it was followed by the explosion of Curly's Spencer. The buffalo gun hit its target in the center of his chest and sent his body flying backward five feet over the horse's rump, and the bullet from Curly's gun literally tore the scout's left arm half off. His body hit the ground like a rag doll.

The two men started to switch their sights to the other two targets, but spun around when an arrow from behind snatched the beaver hat off the colonel's head. The two dry-gulchers were shocked by the sight before them. Colt wore only an Indian breechcloth, a pair of moccasins, and his double Colt .45 Peacemakers. In his left hand was his short Cheyenne hunting bow.

Potter couldn't swallow, his throat was so dry, but Curly just smiled and stood up in a gunfighter's crouch. Colt smiled, too, and dropped the bow and quiver of arrows, his hands relaxed and hanging down at his sides.

Colt said, "Well. Colonel Potter, I presume. Guess you put a big hole in my buckskin shirt and destroyed one of the mannequins I spent so much money and time on fixing up before we left Denver."

Potter said, "One of the mannequins?"

Colt said, "Sure. You don't think I'd expose my wife to ambush from crawl-on-your-belly snakes like you two dry-gulchers, do you? She's taking a bath in a pond miles from here while we take care of you two."

In a quivering voice Potter said, "How did you know?"

Colt laughed. "Potter—or whatever name you're really wanted for—people like you are easy to figure out. You can't go out and seek honest labor. You want what others have and you want power. Now I just need to know, What do you want on your tombstone?"

Potter said, "That's many years off, Mr. Colt."

His words came out bravely enough, but inside he wanted to vomit. He had never been frightened by any man like this. Just looking at the scout was terrifying.

Colt's build made him look like he had started throwing boulders just for fun when he was still in diapers. On his large pectoral muscles were scars from the torturous Sundance Ceremony. After fasting and steams, Colt had had his pectoral muscles pierced by eagle's talons held by a Lakotah shaman. The man then pushed wooden awls through the holes, and Colt had to dance in circles with leather thongs attached to the awls pulling at his breast muscles. The thongs went up over the center pole in the sundance lodge, came back down, and were attached to heavy buffalo skulls. Colt had danced and danced until he was hauled up toward the ceiling by the thongs, finally falling into a faint and experiencing a vision.

Amid a number of bullet and knife scars, four large claw marks ran down his right bicep, obviously left by either a bear or a mountain lion. A fresh bullet scar stood out on one of his large thigh muscles, a remnant of his journey leading Chief Joseph's Nez Perce on the nationally famous 1,700-mile flight and fight for freedom from the U.S. Cavalry.

The recently unbandaged scar was still pink around the edges, but he didn't seem to favor the leg.

Colt spoke. "You were spotted in Denver. It didn't take a schoolmarm to figure out you would try to ambush me when I left town. I cannot believe that you would have killed my wife, too. You're a real piece of work, Potter."

Curly interjected, "He's my boss. Only way to him is through me, Colt."

Colt said, "You sure don't have much taste in bosses, mister. You can lay your guns down, and I'll promise you'll get a fair trial. You don't have to do this."

"Hell, I don't, Colt!" Curly said. "I ride fer the brand. Jest tol' the colonel here. Live or die, that's me. Besides, you kilt my friend Will Sawyer up in the Yellowstone."

Colt chuckled. "Whooee, you don't have good taste in friends either."

Curly sneered, then his eyes opened wide and he clawed for his .44. I've got him, he thought as his gun cleared leather. Something slammed hard into his stomach, knocking him back. Just cock the hammer back and squeeze the trigger, he told himself. But something was wrong. He looked at Colt and saw a smoking gun in his right hand and flames shooting out of the gun in his left hand. Something smashed into the left side of Curly's face, and then he couldn't see out of that eye. He was spinning around. He couldn't feel anything, but he didn't know what was going on. He only hoped his uncle wouldn't catch him smoking the corn silk in his cob pipe again. He wondered where the privy was; he always hid behind it to smoke. But he was looking at Pike's Peak. Curly was confused. What was happening?

In the distance, or through a rock wall, he heard a voice. It was Colonel Potter's.

He was saying, "Damn! You blew half his head off!"

Reality struck and Curly knew Potter was talking about him. He had been shot twice. He saw the ground rushing up at his good eye, and he felt it slam into his face. Curly tried to apologize to his uncle for running away and breaking the old man's heart, but he couldn't form words. He couldn't move any part of his body. He tried to scream. They would bury him alive like this. He couldn't even blink or shed a tear. What could he do? he wondered in abject fear. He died with that his last thought.

Rufus Potter stared at Curly's body, then at Colt, and tried to decide what to do to escape this horrible nightmare. Did he dare try for his pistol? No, he couldn't. He would have to use his wits against the famous shootist.

Chris Colt spun his pistols backward, and they slipped comfortably into the worn holsters. Potter thought, He's baiting me, the wretch. I have no chance. No chance at all against the likes of that demon. Something—I must think of something.

He heard the sound of hooves behind him and turned his head. The young Indian boy led two horses. In the saddle of one was a mannequin dressed like a woman in a red wig. The other saddle was empty. The boy hopped off his horse and walked toward Potter, his teeth bared.

"Great Scout," he said, "this is mine to do. His men murdered my brother."

Colt stared at the boy and understood the look in his eye and the meaning of his words.

This boy had spent his entire life being trained as a warrior, and this man standing in front of him had hired the killers who murdered his ten-year-old brother in cold blood. He had taken a blood oath to kill Potter, and Chris Colt could not stand in his way. The scout just watched.

Potter looked at Colt and then at the Nez Perce with a look of astonishment on his face.

"Why, you little red nigger," he said with disdain. "You dare say that you'll kill me. You—"

Suddenly he grabbed for his gun. The boy's hand dropped to his gun and came out of the holster in one fast, fluid motion. As his hand thrust forward, the web of his thumb pulled the hammer back, and his mind automatically responded to the words Colt had told him over and over: "Squeeze the trigger, squeeze the trigger."

The gun went off, and Potter clutched at the lower left part of his rib cage, looking at Colt with horror. He stared wide-eyed at the boy, then back at Colt.

Barely able to speak, Potter said, "He's just a boy!"

Colt grinned. "Why do you think he was named Man Killer?"

The good colonel turned his attention back to the Nez Perce boy, who, imitating the words he had heard from his hero, said, "If you're going to shoot a man, shoot him. Don't talk."

Potter's eyes rolled back in his head, and he tasted bile in his throat. He saw blackness and heard muffled voices. A hand pushed on the side of his neck.

He heard the voice of Chris Colt say, "He's a goner, kid." Then he heard nothing at all.

An hour later, Colt and Man Killer rode up to the little grove of cottonwoods and found Chris's new wife, Shirley, sitting by a small but well-built campfire. Steam came from the spout of a blue coffeepot, and part of a deer's hindquarters had been well browned on a spit over the flames from the burning green wood. Shirley was frying apple slices in a black pan, but stopped and poured two cups of coffee when she saw the men ride up. Smiling broadly, she greeted them with the coffee when they dismounted. Colt also got the additional treat of a long, passionate kiss.

"Afternoon, Mrs. Colt," he said.

"Welcome home, darling," she replied. "Won't you come in with your friend and have supper?"

Man Killer smiled, gulped some coffee, mounted

up again, and said, "Potter and one man are dead, Shirley. The road before us is much safer now, but I must scout the trail to Colorado Springs. I will meet you there tomorrow."

Without waiting for a reply, he kicked his horse into a lope and headed back the way they had come.

"This is our wedding night," she said, her arms around Chris's neck.

He replied, "Sometimes I swear that kid is going on thirty years old. I got to take care of War Bonnet, honey, and I'll be ready for as much food as you want to shovel into me."

When Chris returned to the fire, he carried his saddle with one hand and his saddlebags and bedroll over the other. He set them down and was greeted with a plateful of hot food and a fresh cup of coffee.

After a sip of the coffee, he said, "Now, Mrs. Colt, I am going to have to teach you how to make a proper cup of trail coffee. You are indeed the finest cook west of the Mississippi, but cowboy coffee is a specialized art."

"Whatever do you mean, Mr. Colt?"

Chris said, "Watch."

He set his cup down on the ground and picked up a stone by his foot. Colt held the stone over the cup of hot liquid and dropped it into the cup. Coffee splashed onto the ground around it. Shirley laughed, but she had a questioning look on her face.

Chris said, "Honey, if that had been trail coffee the stone would have bounced off the surface."

"Oh," she said coyly, "I'll remember that, sir."

Shirley said, "Ready for dessert?"

Colt nodded. "The rest of the food was wonderful. What's for dessert?"

She got up, heading for the darkness, saying, "I'll go get it. I left it by the pond to stay cool."

Colt wondered what it could be, but he was glad she had stepped away. It gave him the chance to dig into his saddlebags quickly and grab the items he had bought in Denver. He set them on the ground in front of him and partially hid them with his legs.

"Shirl," he finally called, "you coming?"

He heard her say softly, "Yes, I've got your dessert, Chris."

She stepped out from the darkness, and he gulped as he stared at his beautiful new wife, standing in front of the fire, totally nude. He reached down between his legs and turned on the music box, and she looked at it, tears welling up in her eyes. Colt was out of his buckskins in seconds.

They came together and danced, staring into each other's eyes.

"Oh, Chris, darling," she said, "I'm so happy."

"I plan to spend the rest of my life trying to keep you that way, Shirl. I love you," he replied and kissed her softly on the forehead while he waltzed her around the campfire.

Several days later, Chris Colt led his wife and his young friend across the deeded property he had purchased for their ranch. The buildings were weathered, but very well constructed.

Colt had bought the land on his way from Arizona Territory to North Dakota Territory when he was to become chief of scouts for George Armstrong Custer and the Seventh Cavalry. It was owned by a man who had been a shipbuilder back east in the area called New England.

Chris was greatly impressed by the construction of the main house and the outbuildings. All the logs had been carefully notched and fitted together, almost to the point that no chinking at all would be needed. Each building was set on a solid foundation, and the main house had a wood-plank floor. The windows and doors had heavy wooden shutters, each equipped with firing slits. There was a barn with a hayloft, and a small blacksmith shop was built onto it. Near the end of the barn was a bunkhouse with wooden bunk beds that would accommodate eight men. There were two outhouses, one for the main house and one for the bunkhouse-barn area. Additionally, there was a well-built native-rock fruit cellar, and the foundation had been laid for a large addition on the main house with a flat rock floor, the rocks meticulously chipped and fitted like a crossword puzzle. With the size family Shirley and Chris hoped to have in the years ahead, this was a welcome sight.

The two windows on the front of the house faced toward the south, so the winter sun passing from east to west across the sky would help warm the log structure. A porch had been started as well, and there one could rock back and forth while looking at one of the most pristine and magnificent views in the world.

Facing south, Chris and Shirley could look off to their right at the Sangre de Cristos mountain range, and along the right front as far as they could see was what was being called Wet Mountain Valley. Their land was at the base of the Sangre de Cristos, which had already been described as the most beautiful range in the Rocky Mountains. Named the "Blood of Christ" by Spanish conquistadores for the red hue on their snowcapped peaks when the sun shone just right, most of the peaks were fourteen-thousand-footers with heavy timber going up their sides. On the Wet Mountain Valley side, the slopes were more gradual, while on the western side of the range the San Luis Valley, the largest high mountain valley in the world, had slopes that were almost straight up.

Colt had chosen his ranch property well. Although the winters were harsh, cold, and short on the San Luis Valley side of the range, the Wet Mountain Valley side had relatively mild winters, with many storms getting trapped up against the western slope of the high, steep range. Consequently, the angry winter clouds would spill their bowels on the western side. Colt's property had two different streams running through it, coming down out of the big range and spilling into Texas Creek, which ran the length of the valley, eventually emptying two thousand feet and ten miles lower into the churning Arkansas River.

The east side of the long valley, which ran down to New Mexico Territory, had a shorter, gentler range called simply the Wet Mountains. Sometimes these mountains were called the Greenhorns because of Greenhorn Peak, the tallest of them, which stood guard over the growing town of Pueblo, thirty miles out on the big prairie but clearly visible from just about anywhere on the eastern side of the Greenhorn Range.

Colt's ranch was about ten miles or so north of the booming mining centers of Westcliffe and Silver Cliff in the center of the Wet Mountain Valley. A stage also ran from Westcliffe down through Copper Gulch to Canon City, a longtime center for trappers and fur traders as well as the winter hunting grounds of the southern Cheyenne and Utes. Other tribes came to Canon City as well, to trade with fur trappers, although the fur trade had pretty much played out by this time, with buffalo skins taking the place of beaver and such back east. Canon City was farther down, right at the edge of the prairie where the Arkansas River ended its angry, churning white-water journey down out of the mountains and started a more orderly, albeit fast-flowing, traverse through the high prairies sloping gently down toward the Big Muddy. Canon City was at just over

5,200 feet elevation, and Colt's ranch was at over 7,000 feet, but the winters were still comparatively mild. Canon City was now providing miners and wagon trains with supplies, especially locally grown fruits and vegetables. Its abundance of water, its great climate, and the fertile soil made it an ideal spot to grow hay, crops, fruits, and vegetables, even though it got less than one foot of snow annually.

Colt's ranch got maybe three times as much snow. Large herds of elk, mule deer, and antelope grazed on his grassy pasture lands. The streams teemed with brook and rainbow trout, and a tremendous amount of game could be found starting in the scrub oak thickets due west of the ranch and sloping up into the big range and its thick forests. The valley was full of cinnamon-colored black bears, as well as grizzlies and wolves, especially up on the big range, and there was a thriving population of mountain lions, which helped keep the deer from overpopulating and overgrazing the area.

Chris and Shirley's plan was simple. He would continue to work as a chief of cavalry scouts, always returning to his lovely wife and his beautiful ranch between assignments. Man Killer would stay with them and work on the ranch, living in the bunkhouse and learning both the ways of the white man's world and everything there was to know about owning a ranch. Using the animal husbandry practices he had learned under the tutelage of his tribal leader, Chief Joseph, Man Killer would raise the

Appaloosa mountain horses made famous by his tribe and sell their offspring to those who needed them for hard riding and mountain ranch work. He would send telegrams as soon as they made their first trip to Westcliffe and arrange to have some relatives who were "treaty Nez Perce" Indians on the Lapwai Reservation near the Idaho-Oregon border bring him a good stallion or two and a small herd of mares to start with. With Colt's help, he would also occasionally round up wild mustangs, cull out those with good confirmation, and crossbreed them to his Appaloosa studs. He would break the tough mustang-Palouse crosses when the horses were two years old and, again with Colt's help, sell the tough critters to the Pony Express, as well as to working cowboys.

At Shirley's insistence, Man Killer would accompany Chris whenever he got a new contract with the U.S. Army to work as chief of scouts. It would be easy for Colt to have Man Killer hired as an additional scout. It was the young Nez Perce's idea to be at the side of his hero and learn how to grow into such a man himself. He was smart enough not only to honor and revere his roots but also to learn how to survive and be successful in the white man's world.

One of the first orders of business, after cleaning up the ranch and its grounds and making immediate structural repairs, was to buy livestock and hire hands—most importantly, a good tough foreman to run the ranch and watch over Shirley whenever Colt had to leave. To make the ranch pay for itself, Colt intended also to raise, train, and breed horses, but he would raise American quarter horses, so well loved by just about all westerners. He would look for some Hereford cattle and Texas Longhorns and cross-breed the two to see of he could come up with some good beef cattle. Livestock here could graze all over the mountainsides as well as the pastureland, rich with gramma and other green mountain grasses.

Colt and Man Killer both would scout for wealthy industrialists from back east who came to this area in search of magnificent trophy elk, deer, and bears. Colt would keep a string of well-broken horses and some pack animals to take such "dudes" up into the high lonesome after the animals, maybe packing in to one of the many almost-inaccessible high mountain lakes. The scout had heard that many of the rich easterners had paid a good many double eagles for the pleasure of downing a large stag in the western wilderness, and he reckoned that those double eagles may as well go into the coffers of his ranch or Man Killer's account.

As soon as they arrived at the ranch, after hugs and ceremonial smiling and wonder at the spread, Shirley began sweeping and cleaning out the inside of the main house. Colt and Man Killer inspected and took a mental inventory of all the other buildings and rode the perimeter of the large mountain ranch. It was just after dark when the two rode wearily back into the yard. They put their horses in the barn and gave them a fresh bait of corn and hay. Water running from a tributary of one of the two creeks had been diverted to feed a constant supply of clear, cold mountain water into several watering troughs around the ranch buildings. This was doubly good, because the ground around the full troughs stayed muddy, which helped keep the horses' hooves from cracking and chipping during the winter months.

After Colt and Man Killer finished putting their horses up for the night, Colt led the way to the front of the main house, where they found a towel and a full washbasin and soap. When the two men cleaned up and walked into the large cabin, they were shocked. A fire roared in the native-rock fireplace, and the whole place was spotless. The rough-hewn cedar-slab table was set with three plates full of steaming hot food, and one of Shirley's famous apple pies was cooling at the edge of the table.

Colt gave her a long kiss, and the trio sat down to a hearty dinner of elk steaks, wild onions, cooked carrots and peas, biscuits, and hot coffee. After consuming several large helpings and devouring the pie, the two men sat back and smoked cigarettes.

Colt said, "Shirley, you are remarkable. How did you even come with enough stuff to clean and prepare and serve a meal like this? I remember what we packed."

"I build nests. You scout and hunt, Colt," she said, grinning. "How do you tell the track of a grizzly is five days old just by looking at it? You're good at your job, and I try to be good at mine."

"Yours tastes better," Man Killer added.

The statement's timing and the awkwardness of it struck Chris and Shirley both funny, and the two started laughing so hard they held their sides. Man Killer joined in.

Finally Chris spoke. "Darling, if you don't mind, tomorrow we'll head for Westcliffe and buy some supplies and a buckboard and see if we can get a line on some cattle and some ranch hands."

Shirley said, "I would love it. I want to get some material to make curtains for the windows, and I need all kinds of supplies."

Money would not be a problem. Shirley had owned a very successful restaurant in Bismarck, North Dakota Territory, and she had sold it and her house to a banker and his wife for a good amount. Traveling to Oregon to find Chris after she heard that he had been blinded, she lost her wagon and all her supplies during an Indian attack in which she had been captured. Fortunately, she kept her funds in the bank and drew on them by bank draft when she needed money.

Shirley continued, "Chris, I want you to promise me one thing."

Colt said, "Anything."

She said, "Whoever you hire to be foreman has

to be someone good and totally loyal to us. I have to feel confident that he can help handle any emergencies when you're not here, and you will be gone for long periods of time when you're on a major campaign."

Chris said, "Shirley, you are the most important thing in my life, ever. It is even more important to me to hire the right man for that job. You are never going to worry about being captured or kidnapped again. You've had enough adventure for ten people."

"Being the wife of Chris Colt is an adventure, sir."

Man Killer stood up, stretched his arms, and yawned, saying, "I am sleepy. Good night."

Chris and Shirley grinned at each other privately.

The trio left the ranch shortly after daybreak, and Colt and Man Killer ate "bear tracks" while they rode. Bear tracks, or bear sign, a popular food among cowboys, was a doughnut-type pastry shaped like bear claws or long teardrops and nicknamed by some unknown cowboy in the mid-1800's.

Man Killer didn't usually do a lot of talking, but he could not keep quiet about the bear tracks. He complimented Shirley all the way to Westcliffe. She had discovered the food that would eventually be used to lift the young man's spirits when depressed, heal him when wounded or sick, and make him quite selective about whoever he eventually picked for a wife. The woman would definitely have to know how to make tasty bear tracks.

By mid-morning they arrived at the bustling little mining town. Gold had been discovered in the area in 1858, but there were still plenty of active gold and silver mines in the area, as well as some copper mines closer to Canon City.

The mercantile was well supplied with products, and Colt was able to make a good deal on a large buckboard wagon and team of matched black bay Percherons. The man who sold it to him even included a set of runners that could convert it to a sleigh in the wintertime. The wagon wheels could be tied and fit into grooves chiseled into the framework of the sleigh runners. It was a neat little invention and a solid wagon, so Colt felt quite lucky to get it for a fair price.

The word had already gotten around that he had bought a spread north of town, and his arrival helped some of the residents, especially those with riches from the mines, sleep easier. Colt's stature was such that townsfolk in Westcliffe and Silver Cliff felt as safe with him in the area as if Hickok or Earp were the local constable.

Shirley enjoyed shopping in Westcliffe but told Chris that she would prefer to take the buckboard down to Canon City occasionally to buy supplies, as it was much larger and had more to offer in the way of shopping.

The Colts had decided to do their banking at Fremont Bank of Canon City, named for the famous Major John C. Fremont, who had explored the area a few decades earlier with Kit Carson. Carson probably had more to do with making Fremont famous than old John C. himself did. Frontier Fremont was a vainglorious explorer and self-promoter who was intelligent enough to hire the legendary Kit Carson to scout for him, thereby helping to put himself in the history books.

From Colt's ranch, the ride to Canon City was fairly easy, if there was no snow or rain, by stagecoach down Copper Gulch about thirty miles. Since Westcliffe was less than half that distance, Shirley and Colt realized that they would be doing most of their shopping in the little mining center.

While Shirley shopped for material and supplies at the mercantile, Chris took Man Killer to the nearest saloon to pick up the latest news about the unsettled West. Saloons were like news stores; a person could buy a beer or whiskey and listen to conversations about what was happening all over the untamed country. Colt even overheard three different stories about himself and his own exploits. He also kept hearing about a tragedy he had just been deeply involved in: the plight of Chief Joseph and the "nontreaty Nez Perce," who had fled 1,700 miles. They were currently being held in Nebraska, but Colt knew they would get shuffled around everywhere and never be able to return to their beloved homeland in Oregon's beautiful Wallowa Valley.

Colt sometimes felt like a fool, because he used his expertise to work as chief of scouts for the U.S.

Army. He wanted to try to make a difference in the Indian problem. He wanted to watch out for the native peoples and do what little bit he could to protect them and their interests.

The big problems were that Colt was a man of freedom, not of a military order, and he always seemed to be in conflict with Army commanders like Custer and Howard; he had no respect for their dealings with the red man. He also was just one man against an Indian Ring, a group of unscrupulous white men who were stealing and shortchanging supplies and cattle meant for the tribes. The ring originated right in Washington in the Indian Bureau and Congress itself, and its membership spread all the way down to crooked agents at many of the reservations. Sometimes the Indian Ring was just too powerful for Colt to fight. He had to be careful about approaching its members, because they had millions to lose and were very strong in both numbers and political import.

He also heard in the saloon about more Apache trouble down in New Mexico and Arizona Territory. Geronimo and Victorio were on the warpath, having split off from their major tribes with their own groups of followers. He heard enough stories about the Apache trouble to believe that he'd better get his ranch in order as quickly as possible, so he could leave Shirley without too much worry and fuss. He would also have to find a very good foreman and crew.

Colt had another reason for going to the saloon. He wanted people to see Man Killer with him and to know that the young Indian was Colt's friend. That would probably cover him in case he ever came to town by himself.

Colt sipped an ice-cold beer while Man Killer had a refreshing glass of sarsaparilla. The saloons in Westcliffe and Silver Cliff were never wanting for ice, thanks to an enterprising young man by the name of Johann Gruber who had a small string of pack animals and made several trips for ice per week up into the Sangre de Cristos. He would take the winding cutback trail up above timberline on Hermit Peak, due west of town, and chop large blocks of ice, which he packed down to the two towns below. Gruber had a standing order at each saloon and restaurant, as well as several homes of affluent miners. He also hauled firewood, hiring some boys to cut it for him and often making several trips up the mountain each day. He loaded the wood into a big freighter wagon at the base of the mountain each trip, then returned for more. At the end of the day, he drove the wagon, with his pack string trailing behind, the several miles across the west side of the valley to Westcliffe, where he delivered to his regular customers.

With the success of so many gold and silver mines in the area, Wet Mountain Valley was a bustle of activity, but Chris and Shirley Colt knew that the mines would eventually peter out. But their family would still prosper with their hardy cattle and horses fed on the rich gramma and mountain grasses and the abundant supply of water. Eventually they would pick up more range down near Canon City and Pueblo, where the winters were comparatively mild. Colt would have a thriving family business to pass on and a safe home for his wife and children. It would be a place he would love to come home to after his scouting expeditions.

Colt and Man Killer turned from the crowded bar at the sounds of the commotion behind them. For a moment, Chris Colt thought he was looking into a dirty mirror.

There was much racism throughout the United States, but on the other hand, only one-third of the cowboys in the Old West were white. The rest were black, red, Mexican, and half-breed. Even though various races of cowboys were pretty much expected, racial incidents occasionally did break out, especially in this area. Canon City was the headquarters for the Knights of the Ku Klux Klan in the newly admitted state of Colorado.

The man seated at the table in the corner had a grin on his face, even though three tough-looking gunslingers stood over his table, all holding six-shooters in their hands. What was amazing was that the rough-looking man at the table had light-brown skin and very curly black hair, but other than that, he looked very much like Christopher Columbus Colt.

He was definitely a man of the range. Colt could spot that immediately. The man wore a beat-up, but clean and oiled, classic walnut-handled Colt .45 Peacemaker. His light-brown holster and gunbelt were scuffed and scarred from many days and nights on the trail. His batwing leather chaps looked the same. Like Colt, he wore fancy big-roweled Mexican spurs, but each had two tiny brass bells which made tinkling sounds when he walked or rode. He wore a faded red western bib shirt, which did little to hide the bulging chest muscles and shoulders, developed by many hours of hard work. A large cowboy's scarf was tied around his neck with a slip knot, the kind of closure favored by wise western working men who didn't want to be accidentally lynched when their horse passed under a low-handing tree branch. The left side of his gunbelt held a large Bowie knife. The black man had an ivory toothpick sticking out between his white teeth, and Colt could see that the end of it had been carved into the shape of a Colt .45. It looked very familiar.

Man Killer stared wide-eyed at the man, then turned and stared at Colt.

Man Killer said, "Colt, he is your brother!"

Colt was astounded and his voice showed it. "Nonsense!" he fumed. "I don't have any brothers. Besides, he's a nigra."

Man Killer said, "I do not care, Great Scout. He is your brother."

Colt said, "Man Killer, have you ever seen other Indians who look a lot like you?"

Man Killer said, "Yes, sometimes. But this man is your brother. I can tell."

There was going to be trouble, and Colt was not going to spend time worrying about an incredible resemblance. He was a man of the frontier, a man of action. Here in front of him three men held cocked pistols on a man seated at a table. They looked like they had been riding the owl hoot trail, and the black man looked hard, but he had honest eyes. Chris Colt didn't like bullies, bushwhackers, or braggarts. The odds morally dictated that he should get involved.

His mind flashed back to his first experience with bullies, back in Ohio when he was a strapping young boy. He had gotten into a fight with two brothers whose family owned a farm just outside Cuyahoga Falls. Their family and his attended the same church, but the two brothers were about as far as you could get from walking the Christian walk of life. They were simply troublemakers who beat up everybody. Finally Chris's turn came. Everybody backed down from the bullies, because they were so brutal; they would chase their target down and beat him senseless. When one of them started picking on Chris, he tried everything he could to avoid getting into a fight. Then one of the two made some disparaging remarks about a girl in Chris's church whose father had been arrested for public drunkenness, and Chris finally snapped. He was very scared, but he was beyond caring at that point.

Chris was so ferocious in his demeanor alone that the two bullies started to look a little unsettled. He had heard somewhere that a man who uses his head has a much better chance in a fight than one who just uses his muscle, so he tried to think his way out of the trouble. The first punch landed square on Chris's temple and sent him reeling to the ground. His right hand closed around a smooth egg-shaped rock lying on the ground, and he grabbed it without anybody noticing.

The two brothers ran up and kicked him in the rib cage, knocking the wind out of him and severely bruising his ribs. Most boys would have crumpled and cried, but Chris simply got furious. He leapt off the ground and tore into both brothers. His fists were swinging so wildly and quickly that his opponents didn't notice the rock in his right hand. The faces of the bullies, however, showed that they had made contact with the rock. Within a minute, both brothers were lying on the ground unconscious, sporting black eyes and broken noses. Chris dropped the rock behind his back, and nobody saw it.

He became a hero to the girl he had defended and the community. His repute grew, and the story of the fight was embellished with each telling. In actuality, part of the reason he went off to fight in the Civil War was that he was worried that the two bullies would try to get retribution. It bothered him to leave like that, but as he grew and gained confidence, he realized how smart he had really been. But he never forgot the butterflies he had felt in his stomach when he faced the bullies and the great fear that clutched at him. It would have been so easy to start his life out as a coward back then. Instead Chris Colt chose to act like a man. That decision made him a hero.

Chris Colt also developed a great disdain for bullies. Now he held back to see what the man at the saloon table would do. He knew it would be useless to try to send Man Killer away. The Nez Perce boy was not a boy any longer, despite his age. He was a man and a warrior, a very good one. Chris felt his presence next to him and was even comforted by it, as he had seen enough of the young man in tough situations to know that he could count on him. There were very few men Colt felt that way about.

Finally one of the gunslingers spoke. "Stand up, nigger, and take yer medicine! I got some lead pills yer gonna swaller."

The man remained seated and relaxed, saying, "Mister, I don't appreciate being called a nigger. That's not what I am. I am a man. Now, I know why you boys are here, but your friend got what was coming to him. Why don't you let me buy you all a beer, and then you can head back to Texas? We'll all put this behind us."

"My friend!" the speaker fumed. "You lynched my brother back there on the trail!"

The black man said, "Sorry, mister, but your brother and his two amigos cut my herd. They rustled two hundred head of prime longhorns that I had driven all the way from San Antone. That happens and there's no law around, a man dies of hemp fever. Now, first of all, it's going to take a better sawbones than you to make me swallow any lead pills, and I can promise you one thing. I'm not a gunfighter, but I am a man. Unless you get a lucky head or heart shot on me out of the holster, I'm not going down with just a few bullets in me. I'll have time to take at least two of you to hell with me."

He shut up and stared at the man.

The man had salt, Colt thought, and he was smart. He probably wasn't going to do too much shooting with a bunch of .45 slugs in his brown hide, but he was making them think, making them nervous, slowing their reaction time. He needed an edge, a big one. This man had shot a few men, but he was a cattleman, not a shootist. Chris Colt was. He would give the man an edge.

Colt raised up his glass of beer and walked slowly over to the table. He was cataloging and judging each of the three men. The black man would shoot the speaker, but which one would Colt take first? The one on the right had three notches carved into his gun grip. The habit of a dude, not a real gunfighter. He would take the other one first. The whole place was quiet now. Colt was smiling when the speaker turned; he was obviously shocked to see a white man with such a similar-looking face.

Colt said, "Mister, I heard him offer you gents a beer. Why don't you take him up on it? I'll drink with you."

"Butt out, scout man!" the speaker fumed. Colt just grinned, taking a sip of his beer.

Colt said, "I just have a big problem with these odds, boys. Lemme show you a little trick I've enjoyed doing a time or two. Mister, will you please open that back door and make sure no one's behind the saloon?"

A nervous poker player in the corner opened the back door of the saloon and looked outside into the bright sunlight. He turned back around and shook his head from side to side.

"Much obliged," Colt said.

Colt faced the door and stuck his right hand straight out, waist high. He placed the beer glass on the back of his hand and held it steady.

The speaker said, "You can balance a damn beer on yer hand. So what?"

Suddenly, with a blur, Colt's hand dropped and came up with his right-hand .45 in it. Before the beer mug had dropped more than two inches, the gun exploded, sending pieces of shattered beer mug and gold liquid flying everywhere. He heard someone near the door give out a loud whistle.

Another man said, "I never seen shootin' like that

in all my born days. Shot the durn glass 'fore it could even drop."

Another man, a black-garbed gambler, said, "Monsieur, do you not know who zat man is? N'est-ce pas? He ees zee great gunfighter and scout Colt."

Chris turned to face the three killers and said, "Gents, now we got a problem. My guns are pointed at your belly, mister, and your guns are pointed at the cowboy. One of us better put our guns away, and it sure isn't going to be me."

The speaker said, "Colt, this ain't yer damned business. Yer makin' a big mistake."

Colt said, "I've made them before. I'm willing to die making a mistake. How about you, mister?"

The man was clearly aggravated.

He said, "What's your stake in this, Colt? What's this nigger to you?"

The black man said, "I'm his older brother."

The speaker snapped his eyes to the cowboy and, totally shocked, said, "What?"

At the same time, Colt also snapped his head toward him and said, "What?"

The man said, "Tell you later."

Colt couldn't think about it now. He had work to attend to, maybe killing work.

He stared hard at the speaker, and the man finally slowly placed his gun back in the holster. The other two reluctantly followed suit, and Colt spun his gun backward into the holster.

He said, "Why don't we all go outside and have a parley, boys, where there's more room?"

The small group walked outside into the bright sunlight. Man Killer, followed by Colt and the black cowboy, walked out into the middle of the street. The three gunslingers faced them side by side and shifted nervously, uneasily. People started rushing out of the street, and many saloon patrons peered out the windows and above the batwing doors of the saloon.

Colt grinned and said, "Now it's a little more even, three against three. Wanna try your luck now, boys?"

The speaker said, "You might have the upper hand now, Colt, but yer damn shore gonna pay fer this. We'll leave, but you ain't heerd the last of me. You either, nigger boy."

Colt said, "Tsk, tsk, tsk. Now you just said the wrong words. I'm a little tired of being threatened and having people trying to kill me lately. Since you have announced your intentions and my wife is with me, we will just get it over with now. I don't want any more yellow bushwhackers shooting at me on the trail."

The black man whispered, "I appreciate yer help, but this was my party. You weren't invited. No need for you two to risk gittin' shot at."

Colt said, "We invited ourselves. I'll take the big mouth. You take the one with the notches on his pistol. Man Killer, take the one with the red bandanna."

The three gunslingers faced the multicolored three and felt their knees shaking. Suddenly each of them wanted to be anywhere but here, fast. It was a desperation draw, and the speaker tried it. The movement made the other two go into motion.

Colt felt both guns jump into his hand. The speaker's body flew backward, hitting the ground in a heap. Chris turned his guns and attention to the other two and saw one, Man Killer's, drop to the ground clutching at a big red splotch on his right thigh. Another one of the Nez Perce's bullets slammed into his belly, and he doubled over. The one with the notches had been hit by the surprising quick shooting of the black cowboy, but he spun all the way around, shoulder bleeding and gun coming up in the other hand. Both of Colt's guns belched smoke again at the same time as the cowboy's, and three holes tore into the man's chest. He was literally lifted and tossed backward through the air. He landed on his feet, stumbling backward. He turned and screamed, running away as fast as he could, but he only made ten steps before sliding to a stop on his face. He was very dead.

The chief of scouts heard Shirley's scream down the street. "Chris!"

Ignoring her for now, Colt walked forward, carefully watching the three corpses for signs of life while ejecting his spent shells and reloading the empty cylinders. The black cowboy walked next to him and did the same. Man Killer stayed back and watched for signs of any unexpected partners of the dead gunmen. The cowboy knelt down and picked up the gun of the man he and Colt had killed and his own six-shooter. Pulling out his Bowie knife, he quickly made another notch in the grip and dropped the gun on the man's body.

Colt looked down at the body and said, "It's a man's work and not a game, sonny boy."

When the three were confirmed to be dead, the crowd rushed forward around the scene. Shirley, packages in her arms, ran up and threw her arms around Chris, kissing him and holding him tightly. She suddenly noticed the face of the black cowboy and jumped back with a gasp. The cowboy grinned and tipped his hat.

"Mrs. Colt," he said. "Howdy, ma'am."

She nodded, still thunderstruck by the amazing similarity.

The cowboy looked at Colt. "Thanks for the help. I really . . ."

The punch came from Colt's hip and hit the cowboy flush on the jaw, flinging him backward into the dust. He started to stand, and Colt hit him under the chin with an uppercut. Totally dazed, he lay on his back as Colt, in a complete fury, stood over him.

Teeth clenched, Chris pointed down at him and said, "Stay away from me and don't ever say that again. You . . . you nigger!"

Shirley cried, "Chris!"

He stormed toward the buckboard, and she struggled to keep up. Man Killer stayed behind and helped the black cowboy to his feet. The cowboy stared after Colt and chuckled, rubbing his jaw.

Man Killer said, "I have seen him almost shoot men for calling Indians red nigger."

The young man ran after Colt and jumped into the back of the wagon as Colt started whipping the horses into a canter out of town. Shirley didn't speak. They were back at the ranch in less than an hour, and Colt was gentle with Shirley, helping her down from the bench seat, but he hadn't spoken the whole way home, and now he headed toward the barn. He stopped and came back to the wagon.

He gently said to Shirley, "Honey, I need some time to myself right now."

"Of course," was all she said.

"I will unload the wagon, Colt," said Man Killer. "You go."

Chris said, "Thanks," and resumed walking toward the barn.

He saddled War Bonnet and rode out toward Spread Eagle Peak, which towered above him to the west. Within minutes, he was trotting in and out between groves of scrub oaks. The big paint finally stopped and pranced, while Colt turned and looked back at the ranch house and the buildings far below.

Colt headed up into the black woods, where the elk liked to bed down during the afternoon. In fact, he rode right into a herd of elk, which quietly rose up out of their beds and moved higher up, circling above and heading northward along the range toward Nipple Mountain.

He and the mighty stallion climbed higher and higher, while his thoughts turned to the events that had happened earlier. Chris Colt always headed for the "high lonesome" when he was troubled with something. It was up high, where the air was clearer and thinner, where every step brought difficulty in breathing, where few men had dared travel before and eagles made their homes, that Chris Colt could do some hard thinking. And so he did, until just before dark.

He was ashamed of himself. He had called this man a nigger, a derisive term he had never used, one that he despised. He did not understand discrimination and had spent most of his adult life fighting against it on behalf of the American Indian. He had even lied about his age to fight for the Union in the Civil War because he wanted to abolish slavery. Now this man had shown up and claimed to be Colt's brother, no less. Maybe the man had run into someone who told him about his amazing resemblance, and he figured Colt had inherited part of Colt Firearms when his uncle Samuel Colt had died. Chris could get all the weapons and ammunition he wanted from the factory, whenever he wanted, but he had not inherited any part of his uncle's fortune.

Colt, however, had felt something when he met the black cowboy, and the scout had learned from his red brothers to listen to his heart, because it was more honest than his head. There was something about the man's character. Colt could sense it. He was an honest, hardworking, stand-up man. Chris Colt felt this strongly because he was the same way himself.

Colt looked up at a rocky crag and saw a bald eagle fly off its cliffside aerie and wing its way eastward out over Wet Mountain Valley. Far below him, he could see the ranch house and outbuildings of his new home. They were all like little boxes in his vision now.

As he watched the eagle make lazy circles thousands of feet above the valley floor, Colt thought back to the story he had heard in the lodges of the Minniconjou, his first wife's people. Chantapeta was Lakotah, and her name meant "Fire Heart." Their little girl was named Winona, which meant "First Born." She was to be the first of many, but a party of five Crow renegades cut their family life short, assaulting Colt's wife and murdering her and his daughter.

Colt had spent much time with Chantapeta's band and had heard there the story of the eagle and the prairie chicken. A mighty eagle flew off from its cliffside aerie, like the one Colt had just seen, and searched for more branches to make the nest sturdier. While it was gone, a gust of wind suddenly appeared over a ridge line and blew one egg out of the large nest. Miraculously, it rolled unhurt all the way down the cliffside and out onto the prairie at the base of the steep mountain.

It landed squarely in the nest of a prairie chicken. The prairie hen didn't notice the extra egg, which was larger than the other five eggs all combined. The hen sat on the nest each day until the eggs all hatched, and then started raising the young eaglet as her own. It didn't matter to the rooster and hen prairie chickens that, within a few months, one of their offspring was twice their size. They raised their brood as best they knew how.

One day the male prairie chicken led his young offspring single file through the sagebrush, creosote bushes, and mesquite. The eaglet was last in line, and he happened to look up into the blue sky and spot his real father, the mighty bald eagle, soaring around above him in big circles.

He cried, "Oh, Father, oh, Father, look up at that mighty bird. He is so beautiful and strong and free. He is truly blessed by Wakan Tanka, the Great Spirit. What kind of bird is he, Father?"

The prairie chicken father looked at the big eagle and said, "He is an eagle, my son."

The father started to go on, but the eager young bird said, "Oh, Father, I must meditate and speak to the Great Mystery and ask him to make me like such a bird. It would be wonderful."

The father looked at his adopted son and said,

"No, forget it. You can never be like him. He is an eagle, and you are just a prairie chicken."

Colt watched the big bird, far out over the valley, swooping down toward the earth, apparently diving after prey. Then Colt lost sight of the bird below the tops of the trees. He smiled to himself and thought of the young black cowboy while he was growing up. He tried to picture in his mind's eye how many times the boy must have been told he was just a prairie chicken. He tried to picture the man as a boy, fighting and struggling to be an eagle. He would have had to. It ran in his veins, Colt thought, then grinned at himself.

He mounted War Bonnet and headed straight down the mountain. It was time to go home. The sun felt the same way. It didn't take Chris long to get down the mountain and soon he was at the bottom of the thick tree line and overlooking his ranchland.

In the distance Colt saw a rider on the road from Westcliffe, headed toward his place. The man was on a big dappled-gray quarter horse. Colt could tell, even from afar, that the man was the black cowboy. The scout's trained eyes were sharp, and his memory had automatically filed away the cowboy's description.

The scout touched his heels to the great stallion's flanks, and they were off like the wind. Chris wanted to meet the man and talk to him. He had things to say and questions to ask. He had an apology to offer.

Just before sunset, Colt rode into the ranch yard

and dismounted, leading War Bonnet into the barn. The cowboy had arrived just minutes before and was now speaking to Shirley, who fidgeted nervously on the front porch. Man Killer was busily moving around the area between the ranch house and barn, doing chores, finding a place for equipment long since just dropped in various places.

Colt unsaddled War Bonnet, rubbed the horse down, and gave him a pail of oats and several squares of alfalfa/grass hay mix. He petted his friend, then went to join Shirley and the black cowboy.

The black man had a serious look on his face as Chris Colt walked forward and stretched out his hand. Shirley had a look of extreme relief on her face.

Colt said, "Mister, I owe you an apology for that stunt I pulled."

Colt didn't get the next word out of his mouth, because he was suddenly flying backward. The only thing coming out of his mouth was blood from split lips. As he started to stand up, he was met by an uppercut which sent him flying again, over the hitching rack in front of his porch. The small of his back hit the rail with a thud, and Colt spun over it, landing on his face. Shirley clapped her hands over her mouth and stared at the two men.

Colt spit blood out of his mouth and grinned at the other man, while pushing himself up with a moan. He stepped over the railing and again stuck his hand out.

"I deserved that. I still owe you an apology for what I said and for hitting you. I don't ever say things like that."

The man said, "I know."

Colt replied, "Why are you here?"

The man said, "I've heard about you. I brought a herd up to Beaver from Texas and heard you'd bought a spread here. I thought I'd finally meet my kid brother after all these years."

Shirley interrupted. "It's obvious that you two have a lot of serious talking to do, but it doesn't need to be done standing out here. Get your hands washed, both of you. Chris, tell Man Killer to do the same."

The black man said, "Man Killer, huh? Nice name. S'pose he got it for his expertise at huntin' doves?"

Colt laughed and led the way to the outside pump, hollering at Man Killer, who was in the barn.

Colt said, "What's your name?"

"Joshua," he said.

"Colt?" Chris asked.

Joshua replied, "No. I took the last name of Smith."

Still totally skeptical about the story he would hear, Colt asked, "Why?"

Joshua looked down at his brown hand and replied, "You have to ask, Chris?"

Colt dried his hands on the towel hanging by the pumps. "Why are you here? What do you want from me?"

Joshua said, "Not a damned thing, Chris Colt. I just wanted to meet you at last. We are brothers, whether you like it or not."

Colt said, "Well, this is going to be a story I need to hear."

Man Killer didn't say anything, but he stuck his hand out and shook Joshua's, saying, "I am Man Killer."

The man replied, "Joshua Smith."

The supper was, as usual, delicious. Shirley had prepared mashed potatoes and gravy, fried chicken, corn on the cob, and fresh bread. The meal was followed by apple dumplings, and everything was washed down by several pots of hot coffee.

After dinner Colt offered Joshua and Man Killer cigars, and they talked while they smoked and drank coffee. Shirley joined them and had several cups of coffee herself.

Joshua began his story. "Do you remember the Carlsons and their maid Lulubelle?"

"Sure," Chris said. "Their family was so wealthy, they were always having my father make them new shoes or boots for someone in the family. The Carlsons sometimes came back to visit—twice, I think, while I was growing up—but they went off when I was young."

Joshua said, "Yep, they moved back to their family

home in Georgia. Old Man Carlson's pa died and left him a big old plantation covered with cotton and peach orchards, and plenty of slaves."

"What about them all?" Colt asked.

"Lulubelle was my mother," Joshua replied. "You recollect her little boy?"

Colt said, "Yeah, vaguely. A little bit older than me. That was you?"

Joshua nodded. "Your father was my father."

Colt stared at him, not knowing what to think or say.

Joshua went on, "He and my mother fell in love. They lived next door to each other, and my ma used to go down to look at the falls while he was there fishing. They talked a lot and thought the same way on most things. Many colored women were just used by white men, but this was different. They loved each other, but nothin' could ever come of it. She was colored and she was a slave. He met yer ma and married her half a year later."

Colt looked up at the ceiling, then at Shirley. He finally looked at Joshua.

Colt said, "One time . . . the only time I ever saw my pa cry was a year after my ma died of consumption. I was about eleven, and I wanted to go fishing with him down at the gorge. I walked in his room to ask him, and he was holding a tintype of your ma and tears were running down his cheeks. I was really surprised, and I asked why he was crying over her picture and why did he have it. He told me that she gave it to him before, because they were friends before, and he was thinking about fun they had fishing just above Cuyahoga Falls. Then he showed me your ma's picture and said kind of matter-of-factly, gee, she was awful pretty for a colored girl, wasn't she?"

Joshua gave Colt a knowing grin.

Colt went on, "I was a boy with a boy's curiosity. I asked a question and my pa answered it. I was satisfied and never thought about it anymore, until now."

He poured more coffee for everyone.

Finally Chris said, "You can put your horse up in the barn and bunk in the bunkhouse tonight. Man Killer'll show you. Breakfast will be just after daybreak. Shirley and I got a lot of talking to do, and I have a lot of digesting to do."

The two men left the house.

chapter 2

》》》》》》》》》》》》

Coyote Run

The next morning the four ate a hearty breakfast of apple flapjacks, ham, maple syrup—and coffee, of course. Before Chris and Joshua had a chance to talk again, a rider came up to the house.

A deep voice outside boomed, "Hallo the house!"

Colt hollered back, "Coffee's hot and the food's getting cold. Hurry and wash up before it's gone."

The voice laughed and yelled back, "Dadburn, you drive a hard bargain, feller. Ya talked me into it."

The sheriff was big and gruff-looking, with a salt-and-pepper handlebar moustache and a twinkle in his eye. His belly hung down over his gunbelt, and his six-shooter looked like it was used only once a decade or so.

He stuck out a meaty hand. "Sam Dearborn, local law."

Colt shook. "Chris Colt. This is my wife, Shirley."

The sheriff smiled and tipped his dirty Stetson.

Colt continued, "And my friend Man Killer."

The sheriff looked nonplussed and offered his hand to the Indian. "Howdy, youngster."

Colt went on, "And this is Joshua."

They shook, and the sheriff got a very strange look when Colt added, "Joshua Colt, my brother."

"The hell you say?" Sam replied, but that was it.

He did keep staring at the two men, apparently intrigued by the resemblance and the obvious differences.

The widest-eyed stare came from Joshua, though, who looked at Chris Colt with wonder. With the introduction and the use of the last name of Colt when identifying Joshua, Chris had spoken volumes.

Sam wondered why he saw tears welling up in Shirley's eyes, but he figured she was a woman, and he didn't "understand them nohow." Mebbe, he figured, it was that time each month when women and mares start acting funny and crying if you so much as spit on the ground. He also couldn't understand why she was smiling at the same time she had tears in her eyes. Then she walked over and wrapped her hands around Colt's big arm and stared up at him from the side, like he had just won the Civil War all by hisself.

The next day Colt and Joshua rode the borders of the Colt Ranch property. Walking the foothills and discussing digging ditches with little wooden gates to irrigate the pastures better, the two occasionally talked again about their backgrounds.

Finally Colt asked, "How is your ma, Joshua?"

"She's dead," he replied sadly. "She passed on about two years ago, as I understand. Pox took her."

Chris said, "When did you leave home?"

Joshua said, "Civil War. Fought in an all-Negro unit, 'cept our officers were all white. After that, picking cotton and harvesting peaches would have been a bit boring, and whenever I visited Ma, I had some close calls with the Klan. They didn't really like the fact that I had been a Union soldier. So I headed west, just to see what was beyond the horizon, but I kept finding a new horizon to check out."

Colt grinned. "You, too, huh?"

Sitting on War Bonnet and looking out over the high mountain valley, Colt pulled out two cigars, handed one to Joshua, and lit both. The two men enjoyed the view and the taste of the tobacco.

Joshua went on, "I worked a riverboat for a few months on the Big Muddy, worked the docks in New Orleans, did some prizefighting, and finally signed on with a cattle outfit. Now, that was an education. A man took me under his wing, by the name of Callihan, James C. Used to be a schoolmarm. Sat for the bar back east. He taught me how to read and speak a little. The boss, Jess Chapman, taught me about cattle. So did a lot of years of chokin' dust, meadow muffins, bad coffee, saddle sores, twisters, blisters, and stampedes."

"How long you been punchin' cows now?" Chris asked.

Joshua said, "My whole adult life. I worked two

drives as a puncher, then it got around I had a way with men, so I started getting hired to ramrod drives. Been doing that for a decade, about. Got two good men who always work for me, too. They're down in Canon City with my herd."

"Herd?" Colt said, "What herd?"

"Last year Jim Callihan looked me up again and asked me if I wanted to go into business with him. We started picking up range cattle down in south Texas that had been running wild and were un-branded. We put them in with a bunch of longhorns we picked up off two ranches that had gone belly up and needed money bad. We would drive our gather together and split the money in half. Callihan liked the money and decided to sell to a buyer down in Trinidad. I wanted to drive them up here and see if I could get a better price from one of the wealthy mining concerns or the railroad maybe."

"How many head you got?" Chris asked.

Joshua replied, "Little over five hundred."

Colt said, "Maybe they'll fit in with our plans. I want to know if you would like to own a piece of our ranch. You will run the whole thing."

Joshua was shocked. "What are you talking about?"

Colt said, "Look, you and I are brothers, and we might have a lot of differences, but the same blood runs through our veins. I am a chief of scouts. That's what I do, and it will take me away for long periods of time. Number one, I need someone here

I can trust—totally, all the time—to watch over my wife and the ranch. Number two, I am not a cattle rancher or a horse breeder. I also need someone here who knows how to run a ranch, profitably, and it has to be someone I can trust with my business. Shirley and I will buy your cattle from you at fair market value and hire you to run the ranch, or you can contribute the cattle and be one-fourth owner of the ranch. It will become what we make of it, but you will be totally in charge of the entire ranch operation."

Joshua dismounted and stared out over the ranch, holding the reins of his horse and puffing on his cigar.

"Totally in charge?" Joshua asked.

Chris said, "Totally."

Joshua said, "You don't owe me nothing. Why are you offering me this?"

Colt said, "You're my brother. Way life is, way people are, it's just not fair. I know I don't owe you anything, but maybe our pa did. There were certain things in this life that probably just came easier to me because of the way folks think and act. Besides that, I don't know women very well, but I can tell about a man by a few words, the way he carries himself, and the look in his eyes. Even if we weren't kin, you'd be a man I could trust to protect my wife and ranch, and I think you've probably learned a lot about the cattle and horse ranching business."

"Think so, huh?" the black cowpuncher said.

"Why'd you hit me when I offered my handshake and apology to you? You've heard stories about me, haven't you?" Chris said, puffing on his own cheroot.

Joshua said, " 'Cause you had it comin'. Simple as that."

Colt replied, "That's the point. You didn't worry about stories or anything else. You did what you figured was right, period."

"So?" Joshua said. "That's how a man ought to do things."

"One thing is damned sure right, brother," Colt said.

Joshua replied, "What's that?"

"I did deserve to get hit. What I called you back there in Westcliffe. Well, I don't believe in calling folks by names like that. I was dead wrong, and I apologize."

"Never happened," Joshua said.

"Let's get back to the house," Chris said. "Tonight we'll work out our agreement on who owns what. Tomorrow, you, Man Killer, and me can head for Canon City and pick up your cattle."

Joshua said, "Can we afford to hire the two men I have with the herd?"

"Yes, if you want to keep them on. Shirley owned a restaurant in Bismarck and got a good dollar for it, and I got a little inheritance from Pa. It's all in the Fremont County Bank in Canon City. We also want to invest in some horses. I favor the American quarter horse and Man Killer plans to raise Palouses."

Joshua responded, "Appaloosas will go great in these mountains, but I still favor the quarter horse. That's 'cause I work with cattle. No better horse for cattle, 'cept for a few of the mustangs occasionally."

The next morning, the men left at daybreak, headed toward Canon City. Chris's saddlebags were loaded with bear tracks freshly made by Shirley, and the three ate while they rode. Instead of taking the stage road south toward Westcliffe to hit the Copper Gulch turnoff, Joshua led Colt and Man Killer cross-country. They went off over one ridge line, covered with rock and piñon trees, and dipped down into a shallow, nondescript gulch, then back up over another rocky ridge line and down into Turkey Gulch. Colt made mental note of this place, as the sand in the bottom of the gulch showed him that the canyon had been properly named. He had never seen so many turkey tracks in one small area.

The men rode up Turkey Gulch, crossed a smaller ridge line and a high mountain meadow area, skirted a peak called Deer Mountain, and took a canyon leading to Indian Springs, a well-known watering hole for outlaws, miners, trappers, and Indians. They watered their horses there, letting them graze a little while they put together a quick fire and heated a pot of coffee. Finishing the rest of the pastries, they mounted up and continued their journey to Canon City.

Along the angry, churning Arkansas River, the trio spooked a herd of bighorn sheep watering late in the afternoon. Then they forded at the place called Parkdale at the western mouth of the Grand Canyon of the Arkansas, as Zebulon Pike had named it. The water swirled and roared through the long, narrow canyon whose solid-rock walls went straight up for over a thousand feet and ran that way for close to ten miles.

A little over an hour later, they rode into Canon City, and Colt told Man Killer and Joshua that he and Shirley had agreed to put them all up in a hotel on the west end of town along the Arkansas. The hotel advertised hot natural mineral water baths, and the trio took advantage of them, each letting months of tension, hard work, trail dust, and gunpowder soak out of their bodies and float away in the hot, refreshing water.

The next day Joshua led them to the herd, grazing on the sparse grass and sagebrush northeast of Canon City in the foothills where the mountains met the high prairie. The site was just beyond the mouth of Phantom Canyon, close to the settlement named Beaver. Phantom Canyon and Eight Mile Creek wound uphill for miles to the booming mining towns of Cripple Creek and Victor on the western slope of Pike's Peak.

Chris met the two hands he had hired unseen to work and live on his ranch. One was old, wrinkled, wiry, and tough as old leather, with a constant twinkle in his eye that Chris liked. The other was big and solid, the type of man who could grab hold of something, anything, and it would always move.

Joshua said, "Tex, Muley, I want you to meet my half brother, Chris Colt. He owns the ranch you two were just hired to work for."

The four men turned their heads at the sound of something coming through the mesquite. Two coyotes flashed right by them. One was chasing the other, and he must have been tough, because the one in front was hauling the freight.

Joshua said, "Look at that coyote run."

The old man let out a whistle. When the canines were out of sight, they turned their attention back to each other.

Joshua indicated the old man and said, "Chris, this is an ornery old coot named Tex Westchester, who has forgotten more about cows than we'll ever know."

Tex nodded his head and lit a smoke. "What's the name a yer spread?"

Colt looked over to where the two wild dogs had disappeared into the brush and said, "Coyote Run."

Then Chris said, "This is my compadre Man Killer of the Nez Perce. Joshua wasn't quite right about the ranch, though. He owns part of it and will be running it as foreman."

Joshua said, "This is Muley Hawkins. If a twister comes up, he'll wrap his arms around us, the herd, the chuck wagon, and the horses and keep it all from blowing away. He doesn't talk much, but when he does, folks listen. He'll work any other man into the ground, start earlier and finish later."

Colt nodded at Muley and smiled.

Muley asked, "What's our brand look like, Boss?"

Colt dropped off his horse and drew the outline of a revolver on the ground. He looked up at Joshua and smiled as his half brother said, "The Colt brand."

They pushed the cattle across the Arkansas on the west end of Canon City, just beyond First Street bridge. The bridge was noted for being a good spot to stretch the necks of unruly rustlers who had no respect for brands of cattle in the county of Fremont. Instead of heading up Copper Gulch, they went up Grape Creek and made camp for the night at the mouth of Pine Gulch, in the shadow of Iron Mountain.

It was there that a wild young war chief and thirty-six just as wild Ute warriors thought that they would take the big herd away from the Colt crew. The men had just broken camp and finished their last cups of coffee, when Man Killer's words turned everyone's heads.

"Enemy comes," he said simply.

The men all turned to look at the group of warriors, painted for war, riding proudly down the rocky ridge to their west. Side by side the Ute fighters rode their mounts down the side of the ridge, figuring that their show of force would cause the white eyes below them to take flight and abandon the herd.

Back east, dime novels of the West would portray killers taking over towns and terrorizing frightened citizens until some hero like Wild Bill Hickok or Wyatt Earp rode in to take them all on single-handed. People didn't realize that most of the men in the West were from very hardy stock. Just to live in the mountains, a man had to learn to fight outlaws, blizzards, blistering heat, drought, gulch-flooding thunderstorms, grizzlies, rockslides, avalanches, and Indians. And there was very little law enforcement. A man who faced all those dangers and more usually wasn't the type who would just stand by, knees shaking, while someone came along and took his herd or land away from him.

The Ute leader was a large man with big muscles all over his body. He had a proud uplift to his chin, and Colt could tell that he would have no give to him.

The leader said, "I am Dying Wolf of the Ute. Want cows. You give. No kill you."

Chris Colt sat his horse, which the chief admired, between his half brother and Man Killer. The two new ranch hands rode up and sat alongside the others.

Colt said, "I am Chris Colt. This is my brother, Joshua Colt."

He saw hands gripping rifles tightly and saw the muscles in Dying Wolf's shoulders and arms tense.

He knew that words would not get them out of this situation.

Colt said, "Our uncle Samuel Colt said you cannot have our cattle."

Dying Wolf looked puzzled and said, "Your uncle?"

Colt said, "Yeah, he made these guns."

Having already picked up on his signal, the others drew and started firing into the assembled braves. The fire of Man Killer and Chris Colt alone was enough to unnerve the Utes, who had never witnessed such rapid and accurate shooting with pistols. Warriors flew off their horses. Chris and the young Nez Perce emptied the backs of ten ponies on their own, and Joshua, Tex, and Muley shot seven more. It was all accomplished in seconds.

Colt shoved his Peacemakers in his holsters and yanked his Colt revolving shotgun from his left saddle scabbard.

He emptied three more saddles with the scattergun, and the young Nez Perce already had his rifle out, sending more Utes on the spirit trail.

The accurate and deadly fire from the Colt crew was too much for the remaining braves, and they dashed helter-skelter back up and over the ridge.

"Whooee!" Tex hollered. "We got us a outfit! I ain't seen sich shootin' in all my born days. We shore sent them redskins a scurryin'. Ah, no offense meant there, Sonny."

Man Killer laughed and replied, "None taken, Grandpa."

The young Nez Perce followed the route of the retreating Utes up over the ridge line while reloading his guns.

The old man chuckled and winked at Colt. "I like thet youngster. He'll do ta ride the trail with. Got spunk, and looks like he's got him some larnin' on handlin' a six-gun from Chris Colt his own-damned-self."

"What about the cattle?" Chris asked, remembering the herd, which had been headed up Pine Gulch when the attack started.

He reached into his saddlebag and pulled out a piece of jerky, tossing it to a moaning Ute warrior, lying ten feet away with a broken arm and a bullet through his left calf. The man gave Colt a strange look.

Joshua smiled, "Don't fret about the herd, Chris. They're from Texas, and we must be at about seven thousand feet elevation right now. They won't run far. Can't breathe. Got to get used to the altitude."

Just then sounds of shooting and yelling erupted from over the ridge line, and suddenly Man Killer appeared at full gallop at the top of the ridge, firing back at someone who was chasing him. Seconds later, a line of fifty or sixty Ute warriors, along with the survivors of the earlier attack, swept over the ridge, firing and whooping at the Coyote Run ranch group.

Colt yelled, "Follow me!"

He kicked the big paint into a lope up the draw after the cattle, and the rest of his group swept after him, with Man Killer bringing up the rear. Colt had noticed that in this area the piñon- or cedar-covered hills seemed to have rocky caps all over the tops, with boulders scattered here and there. Hoping that the rocks would impede the attackers' movement, he headed up a hill to their right. The Utes followed easily on their surefooted mustang ponies.

Chris went down a little gulch and back up onto the next hill, where he found more than he expected. The hilltop was covered by a large outcropping of rocks, with numerous boulders. He rode right into this natural rock fortress and dismounted, pointing to the several openings for each man to fill and cover. There were four openings into the tangle of rocks, and he and Man Killer blocked two of the entrances facing back toward the attacking Utes. As the braves swept up the hillside, Chris and the young Nez Perce started spilling more braves out of their saddles, while they heard the others occasionally picking off attacking warriors sweeping below the crest of the hill. It took only a few minutes of their deadly fire for the Utes to retreat out of sight back into Pine Gulch.

The men all sat down and looked at each other while they reloaded and kept a watchful eye out for another attack.

Man Killer climbed on top of the tallest rock and

looked down at Colt. "Rest, make coffee. I can see them coming from anywhere."

Chris nodded and backed into the rocks with the others. He got out his coffeepot and coffee, and Joshua poured water into it. Tex and Muley gathered up pieces of piñon branches.

Man Killer, from atop the big boulder, yelled down, "Great Scout, I read that the Utes were great allies of the white man."

Colt laughed and said, "These warriors never bothered to read the same book. Besides, I read the Nez Perce were great allies of the white man, too."

Tex said, "Yer an Injun and ya can read? I cain't even read."

Man Killer fired his rifle at some unseen target in the trees and laughed. "You're a white man, and you can ride a horse?"

Tex chuckled and said to Colt, "Yes, sir, I like that kid."

Joshua pulled out some cigars and handed one to Muley and another to Colt. He offered one to Man Killer, but the lad shook his head. Within minutes, Tex poured out cups of steaming coffee for each man.

Chris sipped the hot brew and said, "So, where you from in Texas, Tex?"

The old man answered, "Ain't. I'm from Massachusetts."

Chris laughed, "So they decided it would be easier to pronounce if they just named you Tex, huh?"

Tex chuckled. "Naw, my given name is Sedgewick, but they started callin' me Tex when I was still a young pup, on account a I tol' one and all thet's where I was headed, soon's as I could git growed."

He reached up and winced as he squeezed his left shoulder, then took a long puff on the cigar. Colt noticed a growing spot of crimson on Tex's shirt.

Tex ignored it. "Ain't the same as fightin' Comanche," he said. "Too durned many hidin' places up here in these mountains. Down there on the plains, ya can take a look at the sky and see Tuesday's weather on Monday. Look a little farther out an' see Wednesday's weather. Ya' kin even look at the horizon and see next week's storms formin' up."

Colt shook his head and laughed. "But here, you'll be able to climb any big peak and look at all the weather over the plains. Don't suppose you noticed that your shoulder's bleeding, did you?"

Tex looked to his left and stared at his shoulder. "Sumbitch. Guess someone up and put a bullet hole in me again. Durn, that gits under my hide."

He laughed loud and hard and tapped a barely grinning Muley on the arm, saying, "Git it? Bullet, gits under my hide? Ya git it, ya big galoot?"

Muley smiled and shook his head affirmatively.

Still chuckling, Tex fell over sideways in a faint. Chris and Joshua ran to him and turned him on his back. They stripped away his dirty, worn brush jacket and homespun shirt. The bullet had passed through the back of his shoulder and come out the front. Colt ran to his saddlebag and grabbed the flask of whiskey he carried for just such emergencies. He also pulled out clean white cloth to make bandages. Colt cleaned the wound with some water, then poured the alcohol into the bullet hole. The burning of the astringent made Tex come to. He sat up, chuckled again, and looked around, assessing the situation.

He said, "Wait a minute. Quit wastin' good red eye. Pour it down my throat. Thet'll git me better than anything."

Colt and Joshua both laughed and continued bandaging the wound.

Joshua said, "When did you get shot, Tex?"

"Hell, Boss," Tex said, "I don't know. Sometime when we was bein' shot at, I s'pose. Didn't notice."

Joshua laughed. "The hell you say."

Tex chuckled and winked, picking up the cigar he had dropped when he fainted. He relit it with an ember from the fire. The old cowboy then replaced his shirt and jacket and poured himself a fresh cup of coffee. His face was very pale, Chris noticed, but he knew it was better to keep quiet.

Finally, the old man asked, "Clean wound?"

Colt said, "Yep."

"Bleedin' stop?"

Joshua said, "Yeah. You were lucky, Tex."

Tex said, "I'll live, then. Nurse myself now. Be good as new in a couple a days. 'Member oncet when me and some boys from West Texas was holed up like this in a big fight with some Comanches. Them buggers got tired a tryin' to wait us out, so they up and set the brush afire. Durn, it was hot."

Colt said, "What happened?"

Tex got the now-familiar twinkle in his eye and said, "Well, this ol' boy with horns and a hay fork, an all dressed in red, just comes up outta thet fire. He says to us, Boys, ya wanna git away from here? Wal, we up and says shore. Ol' Satan says, Follow me. Well, we hopped on our mounts an taken off after him, and he leads us right into the fires a hell."

Colt laughed. "That's it?"

Tex said, "Nope, we kept ridin' deeper an' deeper into Hades, and the next thing ya know we was in the hottest deepest worstest part a hell. Lucifer turns to us and says, Well, here ya are, boys, the fiery depths of hell. We look around, and he was right. We was right smack dab in the middle of Colorado."

Colt, Joshua, and even Muley started laughing heartily. The laughter stopped, however, when Man Killer jumped off the boulder and landed right next to the little fire.

"They have set fire to the trees!" he said.

Colt jumped up and said, "Come on. We have to ride! Maybe we can use the fire to help us."

He led the way, and the others followed as he rode out the entrance toward the fire. The smoke was thick and would quickly kill them if they were not careful. The chief of scouts tried to stay right at the border of the swirling black stuff, carefully walking War Bonnet along the edge of the thickening cloud. Colt knew that assembled warriors were waiting for them to charge blindly down the opposite side of the hill from the fire. As they eased along the front line of the fire, they traversed the western crest of the hillside, and Colt angled down toward the thicker trees. He finally was able to lead the group into the woods and circle around behind the fast-burning fire.

Now safe from the fire, Colt went through one trail of thick smoke and ran headlong into a small party of painted warriors. The lead brave brought his rifle up, but Colt spurred his paint and the big horse leapt forward, slamming his shoulder into the Ute's pony and knocking the smaller mount off its feet. The warrior hit hard on some rocks. Chris heard Man Killer's Colt exploding behind him while he was still drawing his left-hand gun and pumping two rounds into the two braves closest to him. The rest were shot off their mounts as they spun and tried to run.

With Chris leading, the group charged off into the trees and wound their way back toward Pine Gulch. Within an hour they caught up with the herd, which was still heading up and had been funneled into one tight group by the terrain. The little hills and the ridges along the side slowly gave way, and the herd and men came out on a high mountain prairie. As they climbed up to where the ground leveled out, they saw the Sangre de Cristos Range fifteen miles in front of them, and soon they were looking at the entire Wet Mountain Valley. Herds of antelope dotted the wide-open greenery.

Colt knew that the Utes were not finished with them yet, and now their small group was out in the open. The chief of scouts could look five to ten miles south and west and see several thousand acres of his own ranchland, but none of the ranch buildings were visible yet.

Suddenly the Utes rode out of the trees to their right rear. Colt was fighting mad now. He wondered why these people couldn't learn.

Joshua rode up and sat next to Colt, his own six-shooter in one hand and his belly gun, a Colt Russian .44, in the other. His teeth were bared as he said, "Little Brother, I'm getting tired of this. You don't keep smacking a grizzly with a cattle prod, and that's what they're doing."

Just as angry, Chris nodded at Joshua. He held a Peacemaker in each hand and had his reins between his teeth. War Bonnet was a war horse and knew what to do. Besides, Chris could control him with his legs alone.

Joshua said, "The rest of you keep the herd headed toward the ranch, and I'll hold the Utes off for a bit."

Chris removed the reins from his teeth and said, "Joshua, I think *we*."

Joshua interrupted. "Chris, you said I would run

the cattle operation. You're in charge of fighting, but I don't want these critters scattered to hell and gone now that we're out on the open prairie. Go on. I'll hold them."

Chris said, "Fine about the cattle, but I am in charge of fighting, and I'm staying with you."

He replaced the reins in his teeth and was ready to charge ahead, when they saw the whole line of warriors stop. A small group rode out carrying a white cloth on a coup stick. Man Killer spotted this and led the others back to Chris and Joshua.

Colt said, "Rest of you boys sit tight. Come on, Joshua. Let's parley."

They rode up to the small party, and Colt could see that the leader had wise eyes. The man was a mature warrior and had several impressive battle scars on his torso. Colt held up his right hand, palm out. The leader of the Utes did the same. The two parties rode up to within ten paces of each other and eyed each other suspiciously.

Colt signed as he spoke. "Do you speak my tongue?"

The other said, "Yes. You are Colt, the mighty scout and warrior, blood brother to the Sioux and Nez Perce?"

Colt said, "Yes, and this is my brother, Joshua Colt."

The leader said, "He has the blood of both white and brown."

Chris said, "Many of us are made of two races or more. I wear white skin but have red in my heart."

The chief said, "I have heard this. I have heard you are a mighty warrior, and today you and your brother have proven you are indeed mighty warriors. You have made many of my men take the sky trail."

Colt said, "They did not ride up to our fire and ask for coffee or food. I would have shared it with my Ute brothers. They tried to tell me they would take what was ours. First, warriors red, white, or brown would have to take our lives before they could take what is ours. We are not rabbits. We are stronghearts."

The chief smiled and said, "This, all can plainly see. Where do you go, Colt?"

Chris pointed across the valley and said, "That is our ranch there in the shadow of those peaks."

Colt pulled a bullet from his gunbelt and tossed it to the chief. The man examined it.

Colt said, "Our sign burned on each cow will be shaped like that. It means Colt. Whenever a hunting party of Utes crosses our land and wants a steer or two to eat, you may kill and eat them. Leave an arrow sticking in the ground so we know it was the Ute who stopped for a meal. You can leave us a gift in trade for each cow, too."

The chief said, "We can just take all the cows."

Colt grinned. "You can try."

The chief grinned also and said, "I am not like

the young warriors who always want to stab the grizzly with a sewing awl."

"No, you have brains."

The chief replied, "No, I have years. As the mighty
scout has said, so it shall be."

He rode forward, and the two shook hands, gripping each other's forearms in the Indian fashion.
Then this was repeated with Joshua.

The chief turned his horse and glanced back, saying, "We will bury our dead."

Joshua said, "Send three men with us. Fighting
makes a man hungry. They can cut out three steers
and take them with you to eat."

The chief said, "Take this," and walked his pony
back to Joshua, handing him a bone-handled knife
and a war club.

Joshua glanced at Chris, who nodded almost imperceptibly, letting his older brother know to accept
the gifts.

The chief said, "I am Runs Ahead of the Herd."

Colt said, "Runs Ahead of the Herd will always
be welcome at our fire. Our tobacco is strong, and
our coffee is good. We warriors have too many stories to share over a smoke and a coffee. It is wrong
to kill each other, for we kill more good stories to
hear."

Runs Ahead of the Herd smiled and gave the pair
a wave. Within seconds, three braves ran up and
rode beside Chris and Joshua, escorting them back
to the herd. When they reached their party, the

three Indians went on and cut out three close steers, pushing them back to the assembled warriors.

Tex turned his horse and swayed a little in the saddle, catching his balance by grabbing the saddle horn. Chris and Joshua pretended they didn't notice. The man was tough as nails, and he didn't want anyone to detect any weakness. Colt knew that he would indeed recover fully from his wounds and would keep all suffering to himself. He was the type.

The wrinkled cowpoke chuckled again and said, "Appears to this old bugger that the Colt brothers kin talk about as good as they kin shoot."

When the small group and the large herd reached the newly named Coyote Run ranch, Colt was surprised to see a cavalry patrol waiting there. Shirley had served them coffee, beef stew, and biscuits, and was just giving them all some of her delicious bear tracks when Colt and the ranch hands appeared with the cattle. Chris gave Shirley a kiss and introduced her all around.

Next, she introduced him to the cavalry patrol commander.

"Honey," she said, "this is Lieutenant Wiggins. Lieutenant Wiggins, my husband, Chris Colt."

The lieutenant clicked the heels of his shiny boots together and gave Colt a snappy salute.

From the corner of his eye, Chris noticed the patrol sergeant making a face.

Colt said, "Lieutenant, your gig line is crooked."

The young spit-and-polish officer got a shocked

look on his face and looked down to see if the flap of his fly, edge of his belt buckle, and edge of his tunic were all in a straight line—something drummed into the head of every good West Point cadet. Colt laughed and heard the lieutenant's men chuckle quietly as well.

Chris said, "Tricked you, Lieutenant. Don't worry. You look as neat and proper as a sky pilot's wife on a Sunday morn."

The military leader stiffened up even more and seemed to adopt a condescending air toward Colt. In actuality, though, he had heard many stories about the legendary chief of cavalry scouts, and his stiff and starched demeanor was simply a front to hide behind. The notoriety of Chris Colt intimidated the frightened young officer. The young man was not a coward, but he was afraid that he could not lead a group of men and make life-and-death decisions regarding their lives. He was worried about not being correct, about making mistakes—not about facing death, just about being wrong.

Chris knew this, and so did the veteran enlisted men on the patrol. The younger ones were like the lieutenant, except they didn't have the responsibility or the schooling. They were still wide-eyed and full of wonder and worry, awe and fear. Would a screaming young painted brave hold their scalps on the end of his lance? Would they die of thirst on a desert patrol or freeze to death in a mountain blizzard trying to rescue some stranded settlers? Would they go out on a wave of glory in an Indian massacre? These were the thoughts that went through their young minds. Some of them indeed would die. Some would become less cautious as they spent more time in the military and would eventually be killed because they let their guard down. Most would end up like the veterans on the patrol, a lot wiser and experienced enough not to take either young lieutenants or the military too seriously. One could drive you crazy, and the other could get you killed.

Colt and Joshua had cups of coffee while they explained about the Indian attack to the cavalry leader and his noncommissioned officer.

"Mr. Colt, we'll get out dispatches immediately about the Utes, but I have different orders," the commander said. "The U.S. Army would like to enlist your assistance, sir, in New Mexico Territory in the tracking and capture or death of Apache renegades Victorio and maybe Geronimo. If you will come to work again as chief of scouts, we are to accompany you, Mr. Colt."

"Right now," Colt said, "I would like to eat some of the delicious supper made by my wife. Afterward, she and I will discuss it and sleep on it and I'll give you my answer in the morning."

The lieutenant said, "But, sir, time is a-wasting and we need to proceed."

Joshua interrupted, "Lieutenant, you might line up all your men and threaten to shoot my brother to force him to give you an answer tonight to satisfy your impatience, but the results will be the same. Even if you succeed in shooting him, he still will not give you his answer until the morning, as that is when he said he would."

Chris continued, "Just so we know where we stand, Lieutenant. This is my protégé and close friend, Man Killer of the Nez Perce, nephew of Chief Joseph. If I work for the Army in New Mexico, he will work for me as a scout. He is not named Red Nigger, Injun, Redskin, or Chief. His name is Man Killer."

"Of course," the lieutenant said. "Mrs. Colt, thank you for the wonderful food and my apologies if my crude language offended you, ma'am. I will be turning in and will await your answer in the morning, sir."

Colt said, " 'Night."

The young cavalry officer had grown up on a bluegrass thoroughbred farm in Kentucky. His prized possession when he was a young lad had been a proud chestnut thoroughbred gelding named Charger. Charger had been the foundation stallion at his father's stables, but he had a distended testicle, so his father had him gelded and made him a gift to the youngster. The retired cavalry officer knew that giving the fine horse to his only son would encourage the boy to follow the same military career as he and his father before him had.

Charger ran up to the fence and whinnied loudly as the boy held out the carrot to him. This had become a daily ritual, and both young man and horse looked forward to it. Charger stomped his foot and whinnied once again, and Wiggins opened his eyes.

It was barely dawn and Lieutenant Wiggins looked up at the head of War Bonnet, standing directly over his bedroll. Mounted atop the big paint was Chris Colt, and just beyond was Man Killer, mounted on a tall black Appaloosa with a white rump covered with black spots. Colt didn't even look at the cavalry officer, who tried to shake his head clear of the cobwebs of sleep. Colt stared out at the valley to the south.

He said, "Lieutenant, if we're going to catch Victorio, we better get a move on it. Head south down this valley, while we scout ahead. I'll meet you around high noon."

Wiggins asked, "Where?"

"Wherever you are."

The officer closed his eyes and laid his head back down, covering his nose with his bedroll against the wet smell of the early morning dew. Suddenly his eyes opened and he sat up, then jumped up off the ground. In the distance he saw the backs of Man Killer and Chris Colt, as the two men rode south.

"Sergeant! Sergeant!" he yelled.

"Yes, sir," the voice came from behind him, and the lieutenant spun around.

The patrol sergeant stood behind him, saluting smartly.

"Morning, sir," the sergeant said as the commander returned the salute. "Want a cup, Lieutenant?"

The sergeant was fully dressed, shaved, and ready to go, as were half the patrol, most of them eating morning chow, and a few already having cigarettes and coffee. One old corporal with horn-rimmed spectacles, a former Confederate officer, was on his second cup of coffee and smoking from a long-stemmed corncob pipe.

Lieutenant Wiggins was embarrassed. He wanted to be a good officer and set a proper example for his men, but Colt had made him feel foolish. Wiggins always awoke after the sergeant had already awakened, dressed, and saddled up. He couldn't understand it. No matter how early he told the sentries to wake him, the sergeant was always up and dressed first. He really respected the man—and Colt, too—but it certainly annoyed him. Little did the young commander know that the loyalty of the troops was almost always directed at the noncommissioned officers first. There were standing orders to awaken the sergeant one half hour before the lieutenant, no matter what. The young man pulled on his boots and waved off the coffee offered by a young buck private, telling the detachment to get ready to travel.

It was close to noon when Chris and Man Killer found the tracks due east of Music Pass. From the eastern side of the valley, the two scouts could look at the path through the tall mountain grass toward the big range. At first, the trail headed toward Medano Pass, but then it turned toward nearby Music Pass.

This was one significant way a tracker could catch up to a quarry. A scout not only had to read a track but also had to put a story to it. Using his powers of reason, he had to figure out where the person or animal was ultimately headed.

Man Killer said to Colt, "You saw the tracks where small horse left the ranch house back there?"

Colt said, "Yes, and I saw where the young lady dismounted, then got back on."

Man Killer said, "She stopped her horse to pick some pretty mountain flowers. How many girls do that?"

Colt said, "Some, I'm sure."

Man Killer said, "And the Utes started following her. Right here, she stopped and looked back and saw them coming and ran toward that pass."

Colt said, "Music Pass."

He added, "Man Killer, you know that I cannot come with you. I have committed to scout for Lieutenant Wiggins's patrol. I cannot just leave, or their point will be unprotected."

"I know this, Great Scout, but you know I must go and try to save her?"

"I know it. Take care, my friend. You'll do the right thing. I'll be taking the cavalry across Raton Pass. I told you how to get there."

Man Killer said, "I'll find you."

Colt smiled and nodded. He reached into his scabbard and pulled out his twelve-gauge Colt revolving shotgun. He tossed it to Man Killer, who smiled, wheeled his big horse, Hawk, and headed toward the unseen girl and the Ute warriors they had fought the day before.

Chris turned War Bonnet toward New Mexico and went on with his job. He was somewhat worried about Man Killer, but he viewed him as a man and a warrior, not a boy, which he might have done had Man Killer been white. He also noticed the concern on the Nez Perce's face when he read the story told by the tracks of the young ranch girl. Chris chuckled as he thought of Man Killer's impression of her stopping her horse just to pick some flowers. It had apparently really impressed him, and Colt didn't have the heart to tell him that many sensitive young ladies had done the same thing. The chief of scouts always yearned for action, especially coming to the aid of someone in need. He, however, had a patrol of cavalry troops following him who could be wiped out if he went off to save one person and missed a big war party that was setting up an ambush. He had to be loyal to his commitment, but he was glad Man Killer could go after her. The odds were tremendously against the young man—but he was a protégé of Chris Colt, and that put him far ahead of the game.

Chris Colt stayed in sight for a good while, as Man Killer pushed quickly across the narrow valley.

He could easily see his buckskin-clad hero as Colt rode south down the green valley, but soon Man Killer had to ride into the trees at the base of Music Pass. The girl had galloped, while the Utes kept their ponies to a steady trot. The whole time, Man Killer tried to think of what Chris Colt would do in this situation. He knew that the woman's horse would soon tire out, and the Utes would eventually catch up.

He kept on and admired her for pushing her horse into a stream running parallel to the trail. But the Utes had not been fooled. They continued on the trail going over Music Pass and Man Killer noticed that every so often, they would send one man to the stream to ensure that she was still climbing up the cold watercourse. Dudes and dime novels tried to indicate that one could lose a tracker by simply riding up the middle of a stream, but any good scout knew how to find rocks in the clear water which had been scarred by a scraping horseshoe or an overturned rock. With the young lady, the Utes were so close, they could tell she was still in the stream just by the mud flowing downhill through the fast, clear water.

Man Killer kept trying to figure out what Colt would do, and he finally concluded that the big scout would simply push on and deal with rescuing the woman when the time came. He was learning from the chief of scouts and his other hero, his former chief, Joseph, to be patient and take problems as they came.

He had no problem following the Utes, as he was fairly certain they would stay on the trail going over the pass. He wondered if she would at some point try to circle back and return to her ranch. He knew that the warriors hoped for that, and they would just let the natural features of the terrain funnel her right back to them. Man Killer also wondered if the girl or woman had been missed. For some reason, he felt that she was his age, and in his mind he also had developed a special bond with her already.

Man Killer rode higher and higher toward the clear blue sky above the Sangre de Cristos Range. Somewhere, not far beyond him, rode a frightened young woman, a young woman who liked to stop her horse just to pick some pretty flowers. Between the young Nez Perce man and the young woman was a war party of Utes with a thirst for blood. Man Killer knew that Chris Colt would be able to save the woman. No matter what happened, somehow, some way, the mighty Colt would win and the girl would be saved. How would he measure up to the test of his manhood? Man Killer wondered. Would he measure up as a mighty warrior?

Man Killer, alternating between a fast trot and a slow canter, knew that he was slowly catching up.

He looked down at his left index finger and held it up while he trotted down into the massive San Luis Valley. Around the end of it was wrapped a long golden hair. He had picked it up off some grass stems a few feet from the spot where the young woman had picked the flowers. She had long golden hair and tiny feet. The depth of her foot tracks and those of her horse, both when she was mounted and when it had no rider, showed the young tracker that she didn't weigh very much. He also estimated her height to be slightly over five feet, because of the length of her stride coupled with her boot size. These were all simple things that most any tracker would know just by reading sign, but Man Killer, like Colt, could see much more.

He swung over to the stream, as he knew she would try something else to throw the Utes off her trail. Less than fifteen minutes later, he found he was right. She had left the stream and headed due south, right across the face of the mountain. He followed the trail and knew he had to catch up because the Utes would notice it within minutes if they had not already. They were confident, he knew. They did not know about him. To them, she was just a lone white woman, just waiting to be violated and killed at their whim.

She was still rushing her horse and was jumping deadfalls instead of trotting around them. He started spotting scratch marks on a couple of logs; her horse was getting leg weary. Man Killer could even tell that the woman's horse loved her a lot, because it was working its heart out for her. He also realized that the Utes would pick up his tracks, too. Man

Killer knew that at least one of them would probably recognize the tracks of his big Appaloosa and know it was him, maybe thinking that Colt and the others were nearby. Horse tracks could be remembered by a good scout like a bank teller recognizing familiar signatures on bank drafts and documents.

Suddenly Man Killer caught a glimpse of the girl in front of him about a hundred paces. She was just beginning to traverse a wide avalanche chute, filled with trees knocked down by previous giant slides of snow and rock. Her horse was visibly stumbling and was lathered under his tail and between his legs. She hadn't seen Man Killer yet.

He kicked Hawk into a full lope, and the big Appy responded enthusiastically, unbothered by the numerous blowdowns in his path or the more than ten thousand feet elevation that robbed almost all living things of their breath. She turned her head, and even at that distance, Man Killer saw that she was indeed beautiful. He also could see the fear on her face. She quirted her worn-out liver chestnut gelding, hoping to get more speed out of it. The horse was game, but it was just too tired.

Man Killer was too far away to yell to her, but he admired her attitude. She didn't let out a scream like some white women would have done. She attended to the task at hand, trying to escape an Indian she had just spotted. The woman was headed south, probably hoping to make it to Medano Pass. Once at the worn trail there, she would turn left and try to get back home or turn west and head into the San Luis Valley. That trail would take her right out into the giant sand dunes, which Man Killer had heard about even as far away as his home, the Wallowa Valley in Oregon. Hundreds of feet high, the huge dunes, which had accumulated over the years from the blowing dust in the giant San Luis Valley, covered many square miles. Dust storms almost always blew the gritty sands up against the steep Sangre de Cristos at the southeast end of the valley and formed the giant dunes. In missionary school he had read about the Sahara Desert and seen etchings of its sand dunes, and they looked identical to the ones he had heard about from the Indians of his tribe and several others.

He had to overtake this frightened woman quickly before she killed her loyal horse. She turned, looking back, and Man Killer, at the height of the exciting and frightening chase, was almost entranced by her piercing powder-blue eyes. In his mind, it was as if the Great Mystery had torn two small pieces from the summer sky, rolled them up in two balls in His gentle fingers, and placed them where her eyes belonged.

Her horse tripped jumping a small blowdown, and only her skillful horsemanship kept her from going over the gelding's head. It skidded on the bottom of its chin, its knees making two furrows through the grassy turf, but she pulled up on the reins hard, and the horse quickly raised both feet, regaining its balance. It stumbled several steps and by this time Hawk was almost abreast of it.

Man Killer rode up next to her and saw a look of total fear and panic on her face, which quickly changed to total anger. He started to yell at her and let her know he was a friend, but she didn't give him a chance. Apparently thinking she was going to die anyway, she decided to take him with her. The woman dived sideways and struck Man Killer full in the body with her right shoulder, her slender arms wrapping around his waist. They flew through the air and hit the ground between two trees, rolling into a very thick mass of greenery about two feet high.

They slammed up against a tree, and Man Killer heard the drumming of hoofbeats approaching and a volley of shots. The momentum of the fall knocked the wind out of the woman and stunned her momentarily, but she soon started to struggle. Man Killer had landed on top of her when they rolled, and he drew his gun with his right hand, while covering her mouth with his left. Her bright-blue eyes were wide open, but she finally realized he was trying to help, and she stopped struggling.

He twisted, still lying atop her body, and watched as the entire war party ran by, less than twenty paces away. The Utes chased the two fleeing horses, not realizing that they were now riderless. As soon as the warriors had passed out of earshot, Man Killer stood and lifted the young woman. He held her at arm's length and stared into her hypnotic eyes. She was clearly full of fear, but a survivor nonetheless.

He said, "Hear me. I am Man Killer, and I am your friend. We are still in great danger. You must listen to me, and we might live. I cannot argue."

"I understand," she said softly. "My name is Jennifer Banta."

"Watch the ground," he said, taking her hand and running uphill toward the timberline.

They ran, and just when she felt as if she could not take another breath in the thin air, he stopped and hid her among some boulders. He had been carrying the Colt revolving shotgun, and he handed it, as well as his walnut-handled Colt .45 Peacemaker, to her. Her eyes widened with fear again, as he stood preparing to leave.

Man Killer said, "Stay here and hide. If they find you, shoot and shoot. Do not give up. That is a shotgun. Wait until they are close."

She said, "Please don't leave me. How can you? You gave me all your weapons."

He smiled softly and said, "You need them more than me. I will come back. Do not be frightened, pretty one."

He was away in a flash, and Jennifer watched him move very quickly and quietly down the mountainside. Man Killer ran quickly through the undergrowth to the spot where the two had landed when they fell off the horses.

Jennifer watched the handsome young Indian, admiring the breadth of his shoulders and his long, flowing black hair as he streaked down the moutain-side. She was amazed that he said he was a friend and that he gave her both his guns, leaving him with only a knife to protect himself. He may be an Indian, she thought, but he is the most handsome man I've ever seen. In fact, the sight of him now took her breath away again.

Man Killer pulled a knife out and suddenly slashed his arm. Blood started running down the arm, and he scraped some off and flicked it onto the path the Utes took. He then ran down the side of the mountain until he was out of sight.

She let out a whimper, but she stared at his actions with amazement. He had actually cut his arm so he could create a blood trail and lead them away from her. What courage, she thought, what incredible daring. And he had done it to save her life. Now she wondered where he had gone.

She waited. The dark woods got quiet. Then she started hearing birds and insects. Far off there was the sound of a red-headed woodpecker tapping on a hollow tree. Man Killer was gone, and an hour passed. Jennifer got more frightened with each passing minute. He was bleeding heavily from his large bicep, she thought, and she wondered if he might have fainted down the mountain somewhere. Her grandfather had been one of the early settlers in this area, homesteading along the Arkansas River. From the family she knew what would happen to a pretty young lady captured by the Utes. What had happened to the handsome young Indian? she wondered. If he was dead, she would never forgive herself, or forget him.

There was movement to her right. Without a sound the war party suddenly appeared. Three of them walked in front, studying the ground, leading their ponies. With their war paint and the looks on their faces, they frightened her a great deal. The last man in the war party led the handsome Indian's Appaloosa. Jennifer noticed that it was a large horse and not an Indian mustang. It was also saddled with a cavalryman's McClellan saddle and a blue and yellow-trimmed cavalry blanket.

The three warriors in front found the spots of blood and got excited, pointing it out to the chief. The entire war party followed the blood trail down the mountainside. She feared for Man Killer. She had a feeling that he and he alone could protect her. His coolness and quick thinking were remarkable. What had happened to him?

The war party disappeared down the mountain, slowly and carefully following his blood trail. Where was he?

Man Killer popped up out of the thick green carpet, not ten feet in front of her. She stifled a scream, and he grinned, making a shushing gesture. His wounded arm was bandaged with a strip of cloth, and she wondered where it had come from. As he ran up to her, she noticed tiny lace around the edges of the white bandage. She lifted the edge of her cotton dress and saw that a strip of her petticoat had been cut away with a razor-sharp knife. She looked into Man Killer's laughing brown eyes. He had cut it before without her knowing it; he was already planning then to cut himself and leave a blood trail.

The two stared into each other's eyes for several seconds. Volumes of love poetry and many stanzas of romantic ballads were sung with those looks.

Man Killer whispered, "I am a scout and work with Chris Colt, who bought the big ranch at the north end of the valley. He is my blood brother. I am from the Nez Perce."

Recognition came into her eyes, and she said, "I heard about you. You were the young Indian who was tortured and saved by Mr. Colt, then saved him after he was blinded by the grizzly bear. You both fought off many killers together."

Man Killer looked down at the ground and said modestly, "We have been close friends a long time now."

"You are becoming a legend yourself, Man Killer, just like Colt, and you're still a . . . you're still young yet." She then asked, "How did you happen to come upon me, Mr. uh, Killer?"

She giggled at her awkward question and corrected herself, "Mr. Man Killer?"

He smiled and said, "Man Killer."

She blushed.

Man Killer replied, "We have been hired to scout for the Ninth Cavalry in New Mexico Territory. We started our journey this morning, and I first found your tracks where you rode to the rise and picked mountain flowers. I saw on the ground where the Utes began to chase you."

She said, "You speak English very well. How did you learn?"

"Missionary school."

"Why did you come after me if you were scouting for the military? That is your job."

"I could not leave you to face the Utes."

"You did not know me, sir."

He replied, "Yes, I did, after I read your story upon the ground."

She blushed again and felt a great heat attack the flesh of her gentle ears.

He said, "We will talk later when it is safer, but now we must flee. You must stay with me."

"I will."

He grabbed her hand gently and, crouched over, led her off at a run along the same elevation in the direction of Medano Pass. She could hardly breathe because of their speed and the altitude, but she was from hardy stock, and she would not allow herself a whimper.

Actually Man Killer had learned the mile-eating trot of the Apache, which he was now employing, from Chris Colt. He hoped to put a long distance between himself and the Ute war party while they unraveled the fake trail he had laid upon the land. The Apache trot was the way to do it. Unlike the Nez Perce, Lakotah, Cheyenne, Crow, and other Plains and northern tribes he was used to, the Apache were not quite the same as horsemen. They could ride well indeed, but not like the other tribes that relied so heavily on their equine skills for war. An Apache would sometimes ride his horse into the ground, stop, butcher it, and eat it. Because of the arid, rocky, and often grassless terrain that they operated in, they learned to travel long miles on foot at a slow trot without stopping for water. In fact, one of the games Apache boys played was to run long distances in the heat carrying a mouthful of water without swallowing it. The winner was simply the one who could run the farthest and spit out the entire mouthful.

Man Killer had no idea what kind of trackers were in the war party, but they were red men, which meant that at least some of them were outstanding trackers. On the other hand, his skill in laying down a phony trail, or "ghost trail," was far beyond his years, thanks in part to the tutelage of Chris Colt.

When Man Killer finally stopped to let Jennifer breathe, her side ached as though she had appendicitis. Her breath came out in gasps, and she felt almost panicky, wanting to bring more air into her lungs. The beauty, however, fought back those feelings and kept herself calm. He gave her a blank look, and she wondered what he thought of her.

Man Killer wanted to lie down and raise his legs, close his eyes, and take a nap for the rest of the day. He was frightened, tired, and in pain from the cut on his arm, but he dared not let the beautiful young white woman see any of this in his face. She must surely be very frightened, he thought, and she needed him to be strong and brave for her. She must know she could count on him. He looked at her and kept her eyes from seeing his feelings inside, but he was in awe of her. The run they had just made would have worn out a good brave, yet she hadn't complained. He wondered how so much strength could be in a woman of such quiet natural beauty. She was perspiring heavily and the way her dress clung to her and the shape of her body and legs made his breathing harder than the running did.

He said, "Miss Banta, we have made it to the Medano Pass trail."

She interrupted, "Please don't call me that. Please call me Jennifer."

He continued, "Jennifer, the Utes will watch for us to try to return to your ranch. We will go west and try to lose them, maybe on the other side of the range."

"My father has taken us there before, several times," she said. "Do you know what is at the bottom of the pass on the other side?"

He smiled, "Yes, I have not been on this ground, but Colt has taught me about all of this land while talking and smoking over many cooking fires."

She said, "You smoke, but you are so young?"

He said, "I am not so young, and I am a warrior in my tribe. All warriors smoke. It is a good and sacred thing."

She blushed again, saying, "Yes, I didn't mean to intrude. Forgive me. Man Killer, I am amazed at the way you talk. Sometimes, your language is so, so poetic, yet most of the time you sound, so, so . . ."

He interjected, "White."

She again blushed.

He explained, "I studied hard in school and realized that I must learn the ways of the white man if I am to live a full life, but I am Nez Perce and proud of that and always will be."

She said, "You are a man of two worlds."

He smiled. "One world but two peoples. There is a difference."

"Do you think our two peoples will ever get along together?"

"Yes, some will. Many will not."

Jennifer said, "Why?"

"Because our cultures are different. Our skin is different. Our hair and eyes are different. Some people always fear that which is different, because they do not learn about it and understand it."

"It is a shame," she said.

"Yes. We must go."

He grabbed her hand and took off at a trot again. They had to make several stops, however, as they were now climbing toward the top of Medano Pass.

Before, they had been running at the same elevation, traversing the face of the mountain. Actually, they had been close to timberline to start with, so they didn't have to climb too much to reach the crest of the pass and start down the other side. The trail was wide and had two ruts from occasional wagons and lumber carts. It cut back gently from side to side.

Man Killer got very concerned as he heard Jennifer, slightly behind him, breathing very heavily now.

He said, "Just a little farther. We must keep on or die."

He knew that the Utes would not be too long in discovering that they had been tricked. Then they would be angrier than ever. He was weary and could not breathe himself. Jennifer stumbled and her hand jerked him back. He dived under her body as she fell headlong on the trail, and she landed safely atop his back. He helped her up, and she said weakly, "Thank you so much. Man Killer, I cannot go on."

Without a word, he swept her up in his arms and ran, forgetting the weaving trail. Dodging trees and logs, he just went straight downhill.

They rounded a bend and suddenly, there in front of them, were the Great Sand Dunes, some of them towering hundreds of feet in the air. He looked at her and smiled. She kept her arms wrapped tightly around his neck and stared deep into his dark-brown eyes.

Jennifer said, "Man Killer, if we get killed, I want you to know."

He interrupted, "We won't get killed. Now, you must listen and trust me. You must not argue. We have no time."

He set her down and she nodded meekly. If nothing else, she certainly trusted this incredible young man now.

He said, "If I am killed, you will wait until the Utes are gone and you will go to this stream down here. There will be several Ute ponies without riders. You will wait until they pass beyond here, and then you will return to this stream and hide. You must wipe out your tracks in the sand with a stick. Then catch a Ute pony and ride for home."

She got tears in her eyes and nodded meekly again, something which was unusual for her. She knew that this young man was planning to die now to save her life, but she had also agreed not to argue. He knew what he was doing, and she would already have been dead were it not for him. They drank from the stream, and he cautioned her not to get her feet or clothes wet because of the tracks.

Man Killer removed her boots and quickly put large sticks in them, wedging them into the boots with branches. Next, he led her just a short distance into the dunes and dug out a shallow grave with his hands. At his bidding, she lay down flat on her back. He had carried with him an old dry log, and he placed that below her feet to keep any horseman from riding over her hiding place. Then he pulled a reed that he had brought from the stream out of his waistband. He placed this in her mouth and cut it off so it would barely protrude from the surface of the sand.

He said, "Jennifer, do not move until you hear the shooting far off. Then it will be safe."

Suddenly, crying hard now, she pulled the reed from her soft lips and wrapped her arms around his neck, pulled him to her, and kissed him long and hard. It stirred his very soul, and he wanted to linger there and never leave. But suddenly he pulled back.

Man Killer said, "We are from two different worlds."

She said, "No, same world, two different peoples, but I do not care, Man Killer. I, I . . ."

He smiled. "Do not move until you hear distant shooting."

Working with his knife, he quickly cut patches from her petticoat and stuffed cloth in her ears and nostrils. He then put small patches atop her eyelids and replaced the reed in her mouth. Unable to see now, she felt his lips lightly kiss hers one last time; then he started covering her with sand.

She was soon under a light layer of sand, which had been made to blend in smoothly with the rest of the tall dune. Man Killer backtracked down the dune and swept the sand over their tracks.

Next, he retrieved her boots with the sticks inside and slung his shotgun over his back. He moved south fifty paces and started climbing up the middle of the dune at a dead run, digging in with the sticks with each hand, as he had seen white men do with two poles when wearing the wooden slats they called skis. These poles, however, would make an extra set of tracks in the loose sand. Unlike the rest of the terrain they had traveled over, he could make phony tracks for her in the sand, and no tracker could tell how old they were or how much weight was placed in each one. In the sand his tracks and her tracks would simply be indentations with no clearly defined edges or depth.

Man Killer made it to the top of the first dune and felt faint, but he went down the other side, still digging the boots into the sand. At the bottom, he felt he could not go another step, but he kept on. At the bottom of the third dune, a stream suddenly appeared, right in the middle of all that sand. Colt had told him about the underground stream that came in and out of the dunes at various places. Not far away, he buried the sticks and the boots, feeling that if he was killed, the Utes would suspect that Jennifer had kept going, following the water, which would have wiped out her tracks. He brushed the sand away from the burial spot and started down the small stream, but not out of sight of where he entered the watercourse.

He lay down against a dune and waited, catching his breath and steadying his nerves. After ten minutes, Man Killer climbed atop that dune, the highest around and rested again, lying down behind the crest of it. He soon saw the war party coming out of the trees, obviously following the tracks he and Jennifer had left.

They came forward, the lead men with eyes searching the ground, the ones behind scouring the terrain in front. They disappeared behind the first dune, and Man Killer prayed they would not decide to ride around the log he had placed there and step on the buried white woman. He checked his loads one more time as the Indians reached the top of that dune and started down the side toward him. They went up and down again and discovered the stream coming out of the sand and followed his tracks into it, starting up the dune he was on.

Man Killer ducked behind the crest of the hill and estimated their rate of travel. Earlier, he had watched them coming and counted how long it took them to work their way up that dune. Previously, it took a count of fifty-one, but the dune he was on now was taller. He counted at the same speed, and at forty he jumped to his feet and shot three Utes off their ponies with the first blast of the Colt revolving shotgun.

He turned his deadly sights toward the others and emptied saddles as quickly as he could fire. These warriors had pride, and this young Nez Perce had made fools of them all. They did not retreat and try to surround him, they charged up the sand dune and fired bows and guns at the enemy. He drew his

Colt Peacemaker and fired twice into the body of one large Ute, spinning the brave and sending him flying sideways from the saddle.

He was starting to fire at the war chief who was leading the charge armed with nothing more than a coup staff, when an arrow sliced through his right shoulder, stinging his whole arm and making him drop the gun instantly. He dived with a forward somersault, grabbing the gun with his left hand and firing up into the body of the war chief. A second shot ripped the leader's head half off.

A bullet slammed into Man Killer's thigh muscle, and he spun to the right, falling forward. He rolled to the left and fired, killing another warrior, and then rolled to the right, arrows and bullets missing him by inches. The few remaining warriors re-treated, or at least halted their charge and backed off a few feet.

The sky started spinning and Man Killer shook his head, seeing clearly again as the three remaining warriors charged at once. He fired at two while pass-ing out almost and drew his knife and plunged up-wards as one dived right at him while emitting a bloodcurdling war cry. Everything was dark, but Man Killer felt his knife strike something solid. Something slammed into his body, and Man Killer felt himself falling backward and hitting the sand with his head and body.

He fell through the sand and dropped into a deep cave. It was hot, blast-furnace hot, and he kept falling and falling. While falling into the deep, dark cave, Man Killer suddenly saw Chief Looking Glass, as he was about to open his tepee flap and walk outside. Man Killer tried to scream "No!" but the words wouldn't come out of his mouth. Looking Glass walked out of his door, and a cavalry trooper's stray bullet took him between the eyes, killing him instantly. Man Killer's heart was very sad.

Looking Glass actually was the last person killed in the Nez Perce war.

Man Killer saw his mother, father, and little brother, wearing white buckskins and broad smiles. His brother and father both held stout hunting bows and arrows with steel tips in their hands. His mother held a big, steaming pot of buffalo hump stew, and they all waved at him to join them. Suddenly he heard a noise behind him and turned to see Jennifer Banta. She was in a clear pond in a mountain meadow. Her hair in the bright sunlight looked like it had been dipped into a pail of honey, and the hot sun was melting it while it slowly dripped off her tresses. She was completely nude, her figure just the way he had imagined it would look. She was signaling him to join her in the pool. He turned his head and saw his parents and brother motioning for him, then turned back and saw her beckoning again. Man Killer faced his family and spoke to them in universal sign language.

He signaled, "Not-now-After-I-finish-my work."

He turned and walked toward the beauty in the

pool. He suddenly got dizzy and fell backward but landed on a bed.

Man Killer opened his eyes and looked at the tree branches passing above him. He was totally confused. He tried to sit up, but he was too weak and had too much pain in several parts of his body. The young Nez Perce saw that he was lying on a travois that was being pulled by Hawk, his Appaloosa. They were heading downhill, and trees were all around them. He saw the back of Jennifer and her long blond tresses shining in the fading sun. She was atop his McClellan saddle on the Appy's back.

He spoke weakly, "Jennifer."

She immediately stopped and came to him, smiling. She carried a canteen.

He passed out, but awakened feeling her supporting his head with her left arm. She was smiling broadly, and tears glistened in her eyes.

She said, "Man Killer, I knew you would live!"

He said, "What happened?"

She said, "You were willing to sacrifice your life to save mine. How can I ever thank you? I waited until I heard gunfire like you said, but I had to see if you were okay. I hid behind the crest of the first dune and watched. They tried very hard to kill you, but they couldn't do it, Man Killer. You killed every manjack of them, the rascals. The last one dived off his horse at you, and you were barely able to stand, but you didn't give in—not you. You drove your blade all the way into his innards, and he landed dead right on top of you. You just wouldn't quit. You were my hero. You saved my life, and I shall never forget."

He shook his head and tried to focus on what she said but had difficulty with it. She kissed him lightly, and Man Killer smiled, passing out again.

When he opened his eyes, he almost jumped with a start, but an ache in his side and leg kept him from rising. He was in a bed in a frame house. That much he could tell. He looked out the window and saw the nearby Sangre de Cristos, their snowy caps glistening in the moonlight. From this window he was looking almost directly across at Herman Peak and Horn Peak, so he must be in the large ranch house which he had earlier decided was Jennifer Banta's.

A man walked into the room, smiled at Man Killer, and turned his head, hollering, "Wal, Jenny, reckon ya outta git up here! Yer young hair-liftin' hero's up 'n about!"

The way the man said it and the smile in his eyes made Man Killer like him immediately. There was no judgment on his face about the young man's skin color. He could sense respect from the leathery old cowboy. Slight in frame, with graying hair and handlebar moustache, he appeared to be whipcord-tough and had the look of a man who knew cattle well. He was also one you would want on your side in a range war. He was bowlegged from way too many hours in a saddle, and a rolled-up cigarette dangled from his thin lips.

" 'Fore she gits here, youngster," the man said, "Want to thank ye. Jennifer's the most important thing in my sorry ol' life."

Mr. Banta turned away and Man Killer saw a tear rolling down his wrinkled brown cheek. Jennifer walked into the room, while her father bent over pretending to straighten a water pitcher on the floor. She wore a white cotton dress and a happy face.

"How are you feeling?" she asked.

Man Killer smiled and said, "Thank you for taking care of my wounds. Do I still have bullets in me?"

She said, "No, the doctor removed them. You'll be okay, but it will take a long time to heal."

He sat up suddenly and felt very lightheaded, but he refused to lie back down. She tried to gently push him, but she felt she may have just as well have been trying to push Marble Mountain. She also felt bad because he seemed friendly but a little more distant than before. He grabbed the headboard and hoisted himself to his feet.

Jennifer said, "Man Killer, you can't."

He said, "I must. How long have I been asleep?"

"We arrived here almost a week ago," she said.

"I have a job to do, and Chris Colt waits for me in New Mexico. Thank you very much for saving me and for the care your family has given me, but I must go right away. I must get dressed," he replied.

Jennifer quickly slipped out of the room, and Man

Killer stood up and started dressing. It was difficult, because he had no strength, but he knew that would return. He was impressed. She was smart enough to have placed his weapons within easy reach, and someone had carefully cleaned and reloaded them, even honing a new edge on his knife. He grabbed his war bag and slowly made his way downstairs. Jennifer and her father sat at a hand-carved table, and Man Killer noticed, out of the corner of his eye, her father gently grabbing her arm, as she tried to rise to help the Nez Perce down the stairway. He stumbled once, but he made it to the table and sat down.

Man Killer held his back straight, although he saw many little light-colored bugs flying around in his eyes.

He stuck out his hand to the father and said, "My name is Man Killer, sir, and I want to thank you for your help."

The man shook with him and said, "Name's Chancy Banta. Jennifer put ya up a bit of grub ta carry with ya, an' I can give you a horse ta pack supplies on, if'n ya want. Girl shore learnt how ta cook after her ma went under nigh on seven year ago now. Yer horse's in the barn. Far as thankin' me, I cain't never thank ye enough, Son. Long as I got me a roof, yer welcome to sleep unner it. Ye saved my little girl."

Man Killer said, "You are not bothered that I am red?"

Banta didn't answer, but instead took out the fixings and offered them to Man Killer. They both rolled cigarettes and lit them. Jennifer smiled and left the room.

Finally, Chancy took a long, slow drag, breathed the blue smoke toward the ceiling, and said, "One time this dude come out here from back east. He was a Banta, too, cousin or sumthin'. He asked me ef'n I could help him buy hisself a horse, so's I took him to the livery down to Bent's Fort, on account a they kept a good supply, bein' on the Santa Fe Trail and all. Wal, I reckon I picked him out the best old bay gelding ya ever did see. Straight cannons, straight back, good head, big bunchy muscles. I worked him on a couple calves, and the durn thing could stop on the head of a pin, do a roll-back, and cut left and right without fallin off'n the pin."

Man Killer grinned.

The man continued, "I tell him to lemme do the talkin' but he had to git hisself that hoss on account a he would have to search far and wide ta find a better one. Well, that ol' son of a buck tells me he's been lookin' at this ol' white mare thet seems real flashy, and his heart's set on it. I tole him ya never buy a horse for color, ya always buy 'em fer confirmation, stoutness, and sech. Wal, we argued, but his heart was set on thet white mare 'cause she looked so purty."

Banta took several puffs and Man Killer waited patiently, knowing this man enjoyed telling stories.

It reminded him of Ollikut, the giant brother of Chief Joseph, who also joked and told many stories.

Chancy went on, "Wal, my ol' cousin bought the durned horse, an' less'n two weeks later the blasted nag bucked on a mountain trail and started pitchin' a fit and sent him over her head flat on his back. Only problem was, jest beyond thet mare's head was a two-thousand-foot cliff. Yep, my cousin shore hit thet ground hard."

Jennifer walked into the room carrying two plates full of meat and potatoes, along with sliced tomatoes. She set them down in front of Man Killer, who nodded, and her father. Chancy took a big bite of steak and smiled while he chewed on it.

He swallowed and said, "Yes, sir, Sonny, don't never buy a horse fer color. Thet ain't what makes 'em a good or bad critter."

After four helpings of food, Man Killer felt a little better and made his way to his horse. He found out that Jennifer's horse had died from exhaustion, and her father was going to take her to buy a new one.

Man Killer sat his saddle proudly and looked down at the beautiful girl and her father.

He said, "Don't forget, don't look at the horse's color when you pick one out."

Chancy grinned, as did Man Killer, but then the warrior added, "Unless it's an Appaloosa."

Chancy tipped his hat and walked off to the house. Jennifer remained and appeared irritated.

The young scout said, "You are angry?"

She shuffled her feet and said, "You have been so, so distant. I thought you were concerned about me, before."

Her face reddened, and she was angry at herself for making such a stupid statement.

Man Killer smiled. "I simply must go. I have a job to do and must do it. Concerned? Someday I will marry you, Jennifer Banta, but for now, I must go do my work."

Openmouthed, she watched him while he wheeled his big horse and rode off toward the south. Jennifer was breathless and speechless, she was so shocked, but her heart skipped several beats and she wanted to leap for joy.

Then she wheeled, saying aloud to herself, "What conceit!"

Man Killer wanted to lie down under a tree and sleep for a month, but he had to find Colt. He would stop along the way and send a wire to Fort Union, telling Colt he would meet him there or get a message there from Colt about where to meet.

chapter 3

>>>>>>>>>>>>>>>>>>>>

Buffalo Soldiers

Lieutenant Wiggins looked at Chris Colt, studying tracks on the ground, and said, "We'll just charge across the valley and attack the scoundrels, Mr. Colt. Simple as that."

The scout chuckled and said, "Lieutenant, why don't you just send them a dispatch? Invite them to come over here for tea, and we'll talk about peace? Maybe we can talk them into escorting us to Fort Union. I remember the sutler's store even has a bowling alley and billiards. Maybe we could teach the Apaches how to play."

"Colt, I do not appreciate your sarcasm at all," the officer said.

Chris replied, "Well, Lieutenant, sorry about the sarcasm, but you are going to get a lot of men and me killed if you don't start listening. You seem to be a bright young man with some leadership ability, but if you act like a know-it-all your men will die. When you have people like me and your sergeants, with years of experience, use it to make yourself look better and accomplish your mission."

The officer was glad that Colt had at least made sure that their conversation was out of earshot of the others. He had trouble admitting to himself that the chief of scouts was right, but he knew that he was. What Colt said made perfect sense, and Wiggins wanted respect more than anything. Maybe, he thought, listening instead of always talking could win you respect.

"Very well, Mr. Colt," he said. "What do you suggest?"

Chris said, "The band of Apaches we've been following since Raton Pass is a small part of a much larger group. They have tried to lead us into a trap and want us to trail them."

"How do you know that there is a larger war party?"

Colt said, "It's my job to know. I'm a chief of scouts. Now, I suggest that we make cold camp here and wait on this ridge line."

Colt remembered when they reached the crest of Raton Pass, near the border of the Colorado and New Mexico territories. At the height of the pass, they were to the west of, and two hundred feet from, the peak of the summit. The patrol stopped to give their horses a blow and take a smoke break. Colt looked far out to the west and saw the snowcapped peaks of the Sangre de Cristos, which stretched all the way north just past his ranch. He thought of his beautiful wife there and his newly discovered brother. Above the southern range of the big mountains, he saw angry storm clouds, lightning flashes striking down on their peaks, gray shards of distant rain extending from the clouds to the ground.

The commander asked, "Why should we wait?"

Colt replied, "There's a monster storm, big enough to wake the dead, headed toward us from the northwest. The big bunch of Apaches is on that far ridge line across the valley. They will wait there to ambush us because they can see us crossing. Right now, we are in trees and rocks, and they can only guess where we are. If you'll look out there, we're over an hour behind the small party, and we can still see them crossing the valley. If you look carefully, you can even see the faint trail they made through the prairie grasses."

"And you recommend that we cross the valley along with the storm," the lieutenant said nervously. "But you said it's a monster storm. We'll be the tallest things out there in that valley. What if some of my men get hit by lightning?"

Colt pulled out a cigar and lit it, stared out at the prairie, then grinned at the officer, saying, "Shouldn't be in the cavalry if you can't take a joke."

Wiggins stared at Colt, then suddenly started laughing, shaking his head from side to side.

"You're crazy, Mr. Colt, but we'll do it. Are you sure the storm's coming?"

Colt nodded at the landscape down below the

wooded perch they were on and said, "See those birds flying around in circles way down there?"

The lieutenant strained his eyes and stared down at the valley floor. He finally pulled out his telescope from its leather case and looked.

He said, "Yes, I see them."

Colt said, "The birds are flying around close to the ground, because the moisture in the air makes the wings of bugs wet and heavy."

The words had no longer left the scout's mouth than the commanding officer jumped at the sound of a crash of thunder, which continued to rumble and reverberate around the mountains.

He gave Colt a grin and hollered for his patrol sergeant. "Sergeant, mount up the men and be ready to move out. We will be moving along with the storm when it crosses the valley."

The sergeant winked and saluted, "Yes, sir. That'll damned shore work, Lieutenant. We'll catch those 'Paches with their pants down."

The storm hit ten minutes later with winds strong enough to make the men give their hats a double pull to keep them on their heads. The troop moved out, grumbling and complaining all the way, as they trotted their nervous mounts across the valley. Lieutenant Wiggins simply followed right behind Chris Colt and trusted that he knew how to get them across the valley under that terrible storm.

Lightning crashed about them and hailstones stung their backs, but an hour and a half later Colt led the patrol into some trees heading uphill. He didn't go very far before stopping. Colt dismounted, and the officer called a halt and had his men dismount and form a tight perimeter. They all huddled under branches of trees and waited out the rest of the storm. Colt gave the commander a halting and shushing gesture and swung up on the back of War Bonnet. Then he disappeared into the storm.

Chris made his way through the trees, climbing higher and higher with the edge of the rainstorm. The higher he got, the larger the rocks were, until he reached a great outcropping of boulders which made a natural fort. Colt strained his eyes but could see very little. He rode around the rocks until he was downwind and he smelled wood smoke and meat, probably an exhausted horse being cooked. Colt walked War Bonnet away until they could not feel any vibrations in the ground. They cantered back to the cavalry patrol.

Colt said, "Lieutenant Wiggins, do you have any dynamite in your packs?"

Wiggins replied, "Yes, we do, to blow away any major deadfalls that hold up the column. Sergeant, have someone bring Mr. Colt some dynamite from the pack animals, also blasting caps, and time fuse."

"Yes, sir."

Colt prepared several sticks of dynamite and wrapped them together in groups of four sticks. With four of these explosive devices, with fuses and blasting caps attached, he mounted up again.

The scout said, "Lieutenant, give me ten minutes. They are holed up in the big rocks at the top of this hill. Just follow this ridge line up. Be careful, because they will put sentries out as soon as the storm has passed."

Without waiting for a reply, Chris took off back up the rocky finger. Ten minutes later, he left War Bonnet in the trees and crept forward, in the moccasins that he carried in his saddlebags. Colt found a small boulder, climbed atop it, and jumped up onto the next one. The dynamite was tied together and hung around his neck by a leather thong. He kept climbing from one boulder to another, until he was atop the tallest rocks in the outcropping. Crawling on his belly, he made it to the inside of the circle of big stones and looked down at the Apaches.

They were Jicarillas, not Mimbres or Mescaleros, which were the two groups following the renegade Victorio. There were about fifty of them, most of them preparing meals over four different cooking fires under rock overhangs. The rain was still coming down, but the lightning and thunder had passed on beyond this ridge line. Colt saw the leader speak to two men, who then took up rifles and climbed up onto the rocks as lookouts. Once the storm was totally past, he knew they would put out more sentries. On the other hand, the sentries would never dream that the cavalry was already on the same mountain.

Colt lay flat on the rock, and suddenly the rain

stopped as quickly as it started. He set the four bundles of dynamite on the rock and made sure the fuses and blasting caps were in good condition. Then he stood up and lit a cigar.

One sentry spotted him and started to raise his rifle, taking Colt's round from his right-hand Peacemaker in the right spot to send him on his journey along the spirit trail. Colt palmed his left-hand gun and felt the familiar buck as he sent a bullet into the midsection of the other sentry as he raised his old muzzle loader Springfield.

He looked at the assembled Apaches. Three of them had their rifles raised when Colt cut loose with a volley of lead from both guns. Three more Jicarilla lay dead. He spun both guns backward into his holsters and held up his hand. The chief raised his hand and stopped the others from firing. He was curious.

Colt spoke loudly, after picking up two bundles of dynamite, "I am Wamble Uncha, One Eagle, of the Lakotah nation. My white name is Chris Colt, and I will be chief of scouts with the U.S. Ninth Cavalry. I seek Victorio of the Mimbres, not the Jicarilla. You tried to trick us into a trap. You can leave quietly and peacefully, or we can finish this now, right here. I have spoken."

The war chief said, "I am Elizario of the Jicarilla band of the Apache nation. You stand there, one man, talking like you are a war party, but you are not so, Colt. The Sioux and the white eyes are my enemies, and you shall die like all the others have died on my blade!"

Colt grinned and said, "Well, you had your chance. There's a time for talking and a time for fighting."

Colt's right hand flashed down, grabbed the mother-of-pearl-handled Colt Peacemaker, and fired two quick shots into Elizario's chest. He lit the left-hand bundle of dynamite with his cigar and tossed it into the assembled warriors. Several jumped out of the way and several fired, missing Colt by inches, while he lit and tossed the second bundle. He quickly dropped down, with bullets and arrows now flying all about him, and lit the remaining two bundles, tossing them into the rock fortress. He heard numerous cavalry guns going off behind him while some of the Apaches escaped the circle of boulders.

Colt reloaded and stood again. The Apaches were gone, but many lay dead or wounded in the circle of rocks. He waved at the lieutenant and his men, who were now running around the hilltop trying to locate those Apaches who had escaped. Colt knew that would prove to be fruitless.

An hour later, he accepted a cup of coffee from the sergeant as he sat in the patrol bivouac spot in the circle of rocks. The burial detail was just finishing its duties and coming into the enclosure. Colt was pleased. The young officer had even asked Colt and his sergeant where he should locate his sentries. The chief of scouts decided that Wiggins would make a good Army officer, after all.

The officer said, "Mr. Colt, do you feel that this is a dangerous place for our night bivouac? After all, the Apaches know where we are and can see us if we leave in any direction."

Colt replied, "Well, Lieutenant, I believe we're real safe here tonight because they are always going to know where we are, but staying here, we can see them coming long before they arrive. Besides, you whipped those Jicarillas good. The word'll get around."

"We whipped them?" Wiggins exclaimed. "Mr. Colt, I have never witnessed or heard of such a sound military defeat of a superior force—by one man, no less. You whipped them, not us. It was incredible."

Colt laughed, "It was firepower. The dynamite made believers out of them."

The lieutenant nodded, then called out to his NCO. "Sergeant, have the men dig in night positions and set out a couple sentry posts down those two long finger ridge lines."

"Yes, sir," the sergeant replied, but then walked forward and spoke in a lower voice. "Uh, sir, can I speak with you privately a moment?"

The two walked off away from Colt, but the scout smiled. He figured the sergeant was probably relieved to now have a young officer who would listen to his advice, and Chris knew that the old trooper was advising his commander not to put out the sentries, as they would end up captured or killed during the night by the Apaches if they were separated from the main unit. The non-commissioned officer returned a few minutes later and set up night positions without putting sentries away from the unit.

Over chow, Colt spoke to the young commander. "Lieutenant, that was smart, not putting the sentries out on the ridge lines. The ridge lines you picked were likely avenues of enemy approach, as you West Pointers say, but the Apaches are notorious for cutting off isolated troopers like that. It was good that you changed your mind."

The commander tossed his shoulders back a little and checked his gig line on his tunic and trousers. He nodded at Colt and walked off to check the perimeter.

Many lieutenants on the frontier were in their thirties, forties, even fifties. There were a lot of "battlefield commissions" given out. On the other hand, there were privates and corporals who had been colonels, even generals, in the Civil War. Like Wiggins, though, there were also some second lieutenants who had gone to the prestigious military academy at West Point, so they were long on schooling and short on experience, at both life and actual battlefield conditions. The ones who lasted and became better commanders at some point learned, like Wiggins had, to listen to those around them with experience. It was one of those good traditions that would survive along with the military.

Two hours later, the lieutenant awakened in time to see Chris Colt in moccasins and his blue cavalry trousers, carrying his Cheyenne war bow and arrows. Colt stood by the command post campfire, took a charcoaled stick, and rubbed the black ash all over his chest, shoulders, face, arms, and back. He poured himself a cup of coffee. One of the sentries came over to the fire, and Colt handed the man a cup while downing the rest of his own. He then whispered to the sentry, and the officer watched him slip away into the darkness. The lieutenant was constantly amazed at this legendary scout.

The next day Wiggins was awakened by a trooper right after daybreak. He got up, stretched, walked to a nearby tree and relieved himself, then returned to his bedroll. He put on his uniform trousers and boots, and grabbed his straight razor and shaving cup. He walked over to the fire to heat up water for a shave. Seated on a log, drinking coffee and repairing a bridle was Christopher Columbus Colt. He was cleanshaven and had bathed and slicked back his hair. The dirty plate at his feet showed that he had already eaten his breakfast. Colt nodded at the officer and started building a smoke.

Wiggins sat down and accepted a cup of coffee from a corporal.

He said, "Mr. Colt, do you ever sleep?"

Chris said, "I'll get plenty of sleep after I'm dead. Right now, I've got work to do."

"Were you out scouting the Apaches last night?"

"Killed one, wounded another. But we lucked out, Lieutenant."

"How's that?"

The chief of scouts replied, "Big boar grizzly passed through here last night, down at the east end of the ridge line. The Jicarillas got the hell out of Dodge City."

Wiggins said, "But why? Why didn't they just kill it? If it was on this wooded ridge line, a mile away, we probably wouldn't have heard them shooting. Besides, I thought it was a big deal for Indians to kill bears. I hear some of them have even killed grizzlies with knives and lances."

Colt said, "Some tribes do, but not Apaches. Bad medicine. They do not kill bears, ever."

"Oh."

"Now, Lieutenant, I have to leave you. We got held up in Trinidad when you had to look for the deserters they wired you about, and those Jicarillas kept us really busy, as you know. Man Killer should have caught up with us long ago. I have to go back and look for him. If you follow that ridge line to the west and just keep heading south, you'll run into Fort Union by midday tomorrow."

Wiggins replied, "I understand your feelings, Mr. Colt, and certainly respect them. However, I was ordered to locate you and provide you with personal escort back to Fort Union."

Colt smiled, "Suit yourself. I am headed after Man Killer, and you are welcome to provide me with personal escort if you can keep up. I prefer just meeting you at Fort Union after I find out what happened to Man Killer. Make a decision, Lieutenant."

Wiggins smiled and said, "See you at Fort Union. Good luck, Mr. Colt."

"Good luck, Lieutenant Wiggins. Pleasure meeting you," Colt replied. "Owe you a game of billiards at the sutler's store when I get there."

The young commander said, "I'll win."

Colt said, "I bet you will." He paused briefly, winked, and added, "As long as you keep listening to people with experience."

Colt pushed War Bonnet hard. He wanted to make the Canadian River before nightfall and make camp in the trees where it spilled out onto the prairie south of Raton Pass. He would follow it west to the base of the Sangre de Cristos and look for sign of Man Killer.

Earlier in the afternoon, he had spotted a bright flash on a distant hill, so he figured that he had been spotted by Apaches. It probably wasn't the same group, because that first group had been headed south and probably still were. This new bunch might not be Apaches, too, but they most likely were because they used signal mirrors extensively.

Colt was going to go into the woods on the ridge line that ran north and south to his left, but he figured he'd make better time on the well-worn road. Besides that, the Apaches were good horsemen, but they were not Lakotah or Comanche, the finest cavalry in the world. If any war party attacked him, Colt knew that big War Bonnet would outrun them, in either a quick dash or a long mile-eating trot or canter.

They already knew he was headed north, and going into the trees would only slow him down and make him an easier target for ambush. The Apaches could fight in the rocks and trees like no other tribe, but then again, they were just as ferocious on the plains and in the desert.

Victorio, tall, handsome, with striking features, high cheekbones, and hawklike nose, was a part of the Mimbres. He was fed up with the white man's treatment of reservation Apaches and was no longer going to accept the arid, dusty locations the white man picked for his home. He would pick his own.

Unlike many Apache tribal leaders, Victorio had earned his way into leadership. Most ascended to the chieftainship of their tribe because their father had been chief. Victorio and Nana had broken away from the Warm Springs agency, and both started reigns of terror in the southwest, which could be equaled only by that of Geronimo and his followers. Besides Mimbres, many Mescaleros had also joined Victorio's fight. The Mescaleros traveled as far north as Colt's location, but the followers of Victorio were far to the south, wandering back and forth into Mexico and even up into Texas.

The Ninth and Tenth Cavalries both had been making it very hot for Victorio, and he had a plan. No one expected him to venture north, so he carefully made his way north in the Sangre de Cristos range. All the Apaches knew who Colt was. He had scouted against them before being sent for by Custer. Word had come through Apache scouts who were spies that Colt had been sent for and was on his way from Colorado, along with the young Nez Perce warrior, Man Killer, who was always at his side. In Victorio's mind, the deaths of Chris Colt, chief of scouts, and his sidekick, Man Killer, would indeed be a major blow against the U.S. military. He would take a respite from the constant pursuit by the cavalry and try to intercept the two on their way down to his country.

Victorio was pleased when his men found the tracks of Man Killer near La Veta Pass, not far from the Colorado–New Mexico border. That had been three days earlier, and two of those days had been spent trying to unravel the trail the young brave had made just in case he was being followed.

For the past day, they had been fighting him off and on in the rough Sangres not far south of the point where the Canadian cut into the mountains. He had holed up on a steep, rocky peak, and his big black and white Appaloosa made the warriors drool—the horse was so fast and surefooted in the rocks. Several of the warriors came face to face with the young man shortly after the fighting started.

The Apaches had chased him into a box canyon, not believing his horse could climb out of the steep rocky trap. Victorio, however, was a tactician and used his brains. He knew that Colt did so as well, and that this man would too, or Colt would not have had anything to do with him. He sent several pairs of warriors up above to make sure the young warrior could not escape the box canyon. Man Killer and Hawk had indeed climbed out; sometimes horse and master had to place one foot in front of the other with only half the foot or hoof on a rock lip and the other half hanging over five hundred feet of space. Coming out on top of the sheer-walled canyon through a thin crevice, Man Killer had run right into two of Victorio's warriors. His hand streaked down, and bullets tore into the flesh of both before they could even pull knives from their sheaths or draw back arrows on their bows.

Several other warriors witnessed this from a distance, and all were talking about the speed and accuracy of the young Nez Perce's barking iron. Victorio was not surprised at all; he assumed the great scout Colt had taught him to shoot so well.

On the third day after finding their tracks, the young man had been having a running gun battle with the Mimbres and Mescalero renegades. It was exceptionally difficult for him because he was still hurting so much from his wounds.

Finally, near dusk, they flushed him out of another hiding place and pursued him to a steep, but short, hill, where he holed up in some rocks with a natural water tank. It had rained more than usual, so he had a good supply of water for himself and Hawk. The Apaches encircled him completely and slowly started closing the circle. Man Killer knew they wouldn't enter the ring of rocks at night, so he slept lightly, while sitting up against a flat rock. He had done everything he could to fortify his position.

They would come sometime after daybreak. He sensed it. And he knew that when they came, it would be full out. He would die, but many of them were going to go with him, he decided. The Apaches would long tell stories about the brave Nez Perce warrior who died with many of their brothers in the Sangre de Cristos.

Chris Colt rode along the faint game trail and looked at the narrow, winding Canadian below him. Not much of a river at this point, he thought, more like a stream. The sun was just beginning to come up in the east, and the sky was painted with many colors.

Colt touched his heels to War Bonnet's flanks and pushed him up the side of the ridge line he had been paralleling. The big muscles on the pinto's rump bulged out as he easily charged up the hill. They reached the top, and Colt started riding uphill toward the distant peak, holding right along the top of the wooded ridge. He was looking for more sign, because the tracks he was following were too cold. He had to try to spot a signal mirror or maybe a smoke. The Apaches used both.

Victorio had about eighty of his warriors with him when he started after Man Killer, but now he had almost a half a dozen fewer. He had split the force into two groups and sent one group along the smaller ridge line along the east side of the valley and the larger, the one with him, along the Sangre de Cristos. Now that he had Man Killer trapped, he ordered two of his men to signal the other war party across the valley.

The men from Victorio's party did not know the exact location of the other group, so—fortunately for Colt—they decided to send smoke signals. Unfortunately for them, Colt could read smokes as well as tracks.

He kept climbing higher on the ridge line, and after another half hour of travel, he finally spotted what he had been looking for—a big puff of smoke from a mountain peak slightly northwest of his position. A few minutes later, this was followed by a steady stream of smoke rising in a thin vertical column. The initial puff meant that an enemy had been spotted. The steady stream meant that Victorio wanted the other Apaches to rendezvous with them, which meant to Chris that he had to ride almost directly to the smoke.

He was certain that they had Man Killer pinned down, as they would have sent up a series of puffs after the first one if they had encountered a force larger than one person. The single puff indicated the presence of an enemy, but more puffs after that would have indicated a number of people and weapons in the enemy force. Colt also figured that the Apaches would have split into two groups to locate the scout. It only made sense if they had known or suspected he was in the area: Have two forces covering the high ground, then watch the valleys on all sides and signal the other party once the enemy was spotted.

Colt set a course almost directly at the smoke and took off as fast as safety would allow, which meant that he would first put War Bonnet into a mile-eating fast trot, alternating with a canter, then slow down to a fast walk after that, finally dismounting, donning moccasins, and leading the spotted horse when he got close to the smoke-signal location.

An hour later, Colt spotted the backs of the two men who had sent the smoke up just before they rounded a bend in the trail along the eastern face of the Sangres. He had stopped on the ridge line earlier and put leather boots with drawstrings on each of War Bonnet's hooves. He knew the war party from his side of the valley would be following this trail also, and he didn't want any of them to look down and see the tracks of War Bonnet's iron shoes. The leather hoof covers would also cut down on the noise of his approach.

He stayed back just out of sight and followed the two men who had sent the smoke for a mile, before he heard the distant gunshots.

Colt slid the big horse to a stop and listened while his eyes scanned the terrain all about him. He wanted to know all possible avenues of both approach and escape.

The Apaches made fun of the white eyes, because most often they could set a trap for the cavalry of posses of white men by simply firing a gun. They knew that white men almost always rode to the sound of gunfire to investigate. Chris Colt was different, however. He had spent too much time and had too much respect for the ways of the American Indian. He would ride to a safe vantage point and investigate the sounds of gunfire and make battle plans from there.

From a rock overhang, Colt looked down and saw Apaches lying behind every rock and bush on a hillside, firing into a circle of boulders. He couldn't see Man Killer, but he sure could see Hawk. His young charge was pinned down by a superior force of Apaches, and they wouldn't waste much more time on one warrior. They would sacrifice a few braves and run over Man Killer's position. Colt knew that he had to act and act fast. He was watching a little longer to figure out how to handle this problem, when the other force showed up at the bottom of the hill. Then Chris spotted Victorio, as the tall war chief went down the hill to meet his other warriors. Colt and Victorio had run into each other before, and Chris had a respectful chat with him at the Warm Springs agency one time. They hated each other, but they also admired each other. As different as they were, they probably hated each other so much because they were so much alike in some ways.

Colt aimed down the barrel of his Winchester carbine and put the bead on Victorio's head. He started to squeeze, when Victorio suddenly dropped to a squatting position and zigzagged between the boulders, followed by some of the new arrivals. The others went to different places around the hill and crept up toward Man Killer's position.

The chief of scouts knew that there would probably be someone headed toward his own location, since it commanded such an overview of the battleground. He pulled his Cheyenne bow and quiver of arrows from his bedroll and strung the bow. He waited. Within fifteen minutes, two warriors showed up, working their way up the ridge toward Colt's position.

Chris Colt did not have much cover to hide behind or in. He didn't want to draw if he could avoid it, as gunshot would definitely be investigated. The ride coming out to his rock overhang was devoid of trees and brush and had a smattering of small boulders. The two Apaches were working their way up side by side and he had to kill them or disable them simultaneously, as both had guns and one would surely get off a warning.

In one desperation move, Colt nocked two steel-tipped arrows on the bowstring. He turned the bow sideways and ducked behind a small boulder. War Bonnet stood behind him, ground reined, as he had been expertly taught.

The Apaches came up over the rise and saw War Bonnet, partly visible. They gave each other mute signals and looked all around for some sign of Colt. Apparently they immediately figured he had gone on by foot, leaving his horse here for safekeeping. Their demeanor indicated this. Suddenly Colt stood up from behind the rock, arrows drawn. He held the bow straight out, parallel to the ground and released the string. The two arrows flew out and the one on the left caught that warrior in the throat. He dropped his rifle and clutched at his neck. The one on the right took that warrior through the left fore-arm, and he immediately dropped his Springfield rifle. The brave grabbed his large knife and faced Colt, his teeth bared. The rifle slid downhill behind him, and he turned his eyes to look at it. That was when Colt ran forward, pulling his own Bowie knife from its beaded sheath.

The brave faced him and grinned. No one had ever bested him with a knife, and no white eyes would now. He switched his knife from hand to hand to try to intimidate Colt.

Chris said quietly, "Sorry, pal, don't have time to play."

His right hand went up quickly and whipped forward, the blade slipping between his index finger and thumb heel. It spun over three times in the air and buried itself to the hilt in the man's chest, the blade hitting but driving between two ribs and slicing neatly into the left ventricle of the heart. The brave jumped convulsively straight up in the air, his eyes staring blankly into the sun. He came down in a heap, very dead. The other was strangling on his own blood, while much of his lifeblood was still spilling out on the ground.

Chris Colt picked up the dying Apache and raised him up over his head with both hands. He walked out to the end of the overhang and tossed him out into open space. The man didn't make a noise as he fell several hundred feet to the rocks below. Colt knew that several of the renegades would have seen him fall, though, and that would get the attention of some of the attacking Apaches. He went to the body of the other one and carried him to the edge of the precipice. After retrieving his Bowie, Colt, with his incredible strength, lifted the second brave's body and held it up high overhead. He saw the Apaches down below all staring up at him.

Holding the lifeless body high overhead, Colt let out a primal scream, "Victorio!"

With that, he tossed the brave over the cliff and saw Victorio pointing and barking out orders to the men down below. Colt ran to War Bonnet and vaulted into the saddle. They took off down the mountain, so they would not get trapped without an escape route.

Now I've opened a tin of worms, Colt thought, but he knew he had to give Man Killer some kind of chance to escape. He also knew that he would be a much bigger prize in Victorio's mind than the Nez Perce teenager. Most of Victorio's men would soon be after him with a vengeance.

Halfway down the ridge, Colt heard firing and knew that Man Killer was fighting his way through the waiting force that Victorio would have left behind. The firing kept up and started getting closer, so Chris smiled, figuring that Man Killer had broken through and was headed his way. He ran ahead, putting distance between himself and the Indians. Colt was scouting for an escape route. Dashing along a sandy-bottomed gulch, he saw that it spread out and climbed up on a sagebrush-covered low ridge. Man Killer topped out on the crest and slid to a stop at the edge of a sheer two-hundred-foot dropoff. Twenty paces to his front was the closest section of ground, the rest of the hill he was on, which had been split by an ancient earthquake.

Chris turned and trotted back toward the shooting. He knew that Man Killer would have found his tracks by now and would be following. He also knew that their two horses would outrun any horses that Victorio's men could come up with. The wily Apache war chief would, however, simply run all of his men's ponies to the death and then keep on after Colt and Man Killer on foot. The tenacious warriors would eventually run the two mighty horses down. Most any Apache brave could outlast a horse in a test of endurance, having trained extensively as a boy with such techniques as running for miles through the desert.

Chris knew that the men would have to take a chance and put a lot of time between themselves and the renegades. He saw Man Killer rounding a bend in the sandy wash and dashing for him. He grinned and wheeled War Bonnet around. Man Killer galloped up next to Colt, while the Apaches started around the bend.

Colt grinned and said, "You're supposed to be helping me as a scout. Why are you down here near the border playing with Victorio and his boys?"

Man Killer smiled. "Tired of playing with the Utes. They played too rough."

That single line told Colt all he needed to know. Man Killer had been hurt bad by the Utes while trying to save the white woman.

He said, "How're your horse's legs?"

Man Killer said, "Good. Good shape."

Colt said, "Follow me!"

He touched his heels to War Bonnet's sides again, and the big paint lurched ahead of Hawk. Once all the assembled warriors came into the straightaway and saw Colt leading Man Killer, a great cry rose up among them. Of all the white men on the frontier, Colt was the one whose scalp sported on any Apache's lance would be a trophy coveted as much as the great scout Kit Carson's would have been a generation earlier.

Man Killer followed the chief of scouts as the draw fanned out and disappeared, and they came with a rush over the sagebrush-covered hillock. The Nez Perce gulped as he saw the wide chasm suddenly in front of them, and he held his breath as he watched Colt place both hands up high on War Bonnet's neck. The big horse leapt up and over the giant slash in the earth. Man Killer wanted to do the same thing as his big Appaloosa executed the same jump, but he just rode the horse through the thin mountain air, buoyed over hundreds of feet of void by Hawk's athletic ability and pride. Both scouts hit the other side of the cliff running and slid to a stop on the short rise in front of the crack. They spun their horses and looked back at the approaching Apaches. The warriors all pulled up in a complete panic, but the lead warrior's mustang was bumped viciously and the pair went over the cliff and fell to their deaths on the rocks below.

Man Killer jumped down as Victorio came to the forefront of his war party. The young Nez Perce dropped his trousers and breechcloth and turned his buttocks toward the Apaches, bending over and swinging it from side to side. Victorio stared at them both with teeth clenched.

Colt stared at the Apache leader and waved his carbine at him. Victorio did the same with his Springfield. Man Killer remounted.

Victorio called, "We will soon meet again on the field of battle, Colt!"

Colt replied, "Yes, my red brother, and one of us will die!"

"Yes, so it shall be!" shouted Victorio.

He yelled, and his warriors followed him back down into the draw and out of sight.

Colt and Man Killer rode down the hill and south along the eastern edge of the Sangre de Cristos for another hour before stopping at a good spot that offered plenty of observation in most directions. They dismounted, and Man Killer kicked together some dry sticks for a smokeless fire. The thick tree cover on the mountainside would filter any smoke that should appear. Colt poured water into the coffeepot and placed it on the fire. He grabbed two cigars out of his saddlebag.

Chris and Man Killer waited until the coffee was ready and poured before they even spoke. Colt offered the young man a cigar and lit up for both of them. They each took several puffs, savoring the taste of the tobacco. Between puffs they sipped the hot coffee.

Colt spoke first, "Is she okay?"

Man Killer said, "Yes. She was beautiful. Her hair is made from the rays of the morning sun. Her eyes came from the ponds above timberline where the clouds shine down on them, and . . ."

Laughing, Colt interrupted. "No, Man Killer, I meant did you successfully save the young woman? Obviously, you did."

Man Killer said, "Yes. The Utes chased us out into the Great Sand Dunes, and I fought them there to the death. I received several bad wounds, and Jennifer got me to her ranch, where the white doctor saved me."

"How are your wounds?" asked Colt.

"There is pain, but that is much better than death. She was very brave and saved my life. She is intelligent, too. Her name is Jennifer Banta. Is that not a beautiful name, Great Scout?"

Colt chuckled and replied, "Yes, my friend, it is indeed. I am glad that you were not taken with Miss Banta, either."

Man Killer blushed and drank his coffee, looking out over the valley below.

Colt said, "Are any of your wounds bleeding?"

"No, they heal," Man Killer said. "I just am weak a little, I think, but I will be alright. I will now have some scars—like you have—that speak of battles I have fought. I just do not have as many scars."

Colt said, "You have not seen as many winters."

Man Killer teased, "Yes, and when I have, I am sure that my hair will be white and my skin will look like an old bullhide. My teeth will all be gone."

He laughed, and Colt joined in.

Chris said, "More jokes like that, youngster, and your teeth will surely be gone."

"Colt, do you think that Victorio will come after us again?"

"He will not be satisfied until I am dead or he is dead," replied Colt.

Man Killer asked, "Why would he want to kill you so?"

"Why did Colonel Potter want me dead? Why did Will Sawyer want me dead? Or Custer? Why did he also want me dead?"

"Because you threaten them, I think. I think I know another reason for Victorio to seek your death, Great One."

"What's that?"

Man Killer said, "You remind him of himself."

Colt stood up and kicked dirt over the fire, then poured out the rest of the coffee on it.

He said, "Come on. We have to get to Fort Union. Besides, Victorio won't give up. He wants us badly and will probably figure out a way to catch up and try for us again before we reach Fort Union."

Two thousand to three thousand freighter wagon-loads of supplies traveled from Fort Leavenworth, Kansas, down the Santa Fe Trail to Fort Union each year. The railroads springing up all over the frontier would soon end the practice, but at that time it was a very busy trail. There were also numerous wagon trains, stagecoaches, and travelers moving up and down the Santa Fe Trail. It became one of the primary routes of hostile Indian activity, with constant attacks on the whites using the main artery. The main tribes taking part in the attacks were the Apaches, the Kiowas, the Cheyenne, the Utes, and the Comanches. Because of the frequent trouble and the importance of the route, the cavalry heavily patrolled the Santa Fe Trail.

All of these factors made Victorio's decision even more amazing and brazen. He was now pushing his entire war party southeast along the Canadian with the intention of traveling as fast as possible down the north fork of the Santa Fe Trail and cutting off Colt and Man Killer before they could reach the post. He reasoned that his war party could travel much faster on the trail and that Colt would probably stick to the mountains for safety and cut over just north of Fort Union, which lay only a few minutes' ride from the foothills. Because of the size of the party, he figured to engage just about any entity encountered along the trail or escape into the nearby tree-covered foothills. If need be, he would simply avoid some travelers on the road.

The two scouts headed along the face of the big range with their rifles across their saddlebows. Chris figured that they would stick to the mountains and cut down just north of Fort Union. He assumed this would provide them with the best cover possible, but he would not assume that they would be safe from an attack from Victorio until they were safely rolling balls down the bowling alley of the sutler's store in Fort Union. Chris Colt would also see to it that Man Killer's wounds were healing properly, as there was a thirty-six bed hospital at the large post.

The two scouts could travel quickly and make it to Fort Union with some hard riding through the night, but Colt felt it was wiser and safer to make a dry camp overnight and then get into Fort Union the next afternoon. He also figured that Victorio would push his men to get in front of him and set up an ambush, so he would let Victorio cool his heels a while, and he and Man Killer could get some much-needed food and rest.

Man Killer asked, "Will we ride through or make camp tonight?"

"We'll fill our canteens and water bag and make camp up very high," Colt said. "I don't think Victorio will ever expect that. I am sure he'll be watching for us to try to sneak into Fort Union during the night."

"Why don't we?"

Colt said, "You're an Indian. You want to try to put the sneak on Victorio?"

Man Killer pointed at a nearby mountaintop and said, "That looks like a good place for our camp, Great Scout."

An hour later found them riding high through whistling pines and rattling aspen leaves. They were near timberline, and they found patches of snow here and there. Ten feet thick in some places, the piles of snow had dirt and stones stuck to their sides and little streams of water running off everywhere, seeking small courses downhill. All of these piles of ice were remnants of winter glaciers, and all were in the base of large avalanche chutes. The entire setting was a bowl surrounded by high slopes that went up to the rocky cliffs above timberline, which was just above the tops of the trees.

A thick carpet of green ferns, vines, and grasses covered the ground. Numerous large, dead trees lay everywhere, like so many broken matchsticks, all snapped off and thrown down by vicious avalanches in winters past.

Colt smiled and nodded at Man Killer, who stopped his horse and dismounted. He started preparing camp while Chris rode his horse all around the wooded bowl and looked for any possible danger signs and also potential escape routes. He was within sight of Man Killer the whole time, and when he returned, Man Killer already had coffee heating and was pulling out food for dinner. There was about an hour of daylight left. When Colt stopped his horse, he unloaded a small mule deer buck as Man Killer stared in amazement. The chief of scouts had been riding around checking things out for maybe fifteen or twenty minutes, and Man Killer never saw or heard him fire at anything.

Man Killer said, "How did you string your bow and shoot him so quickly and without me seeing it?"

Colt said, "I didn't kill him. A mountain lion did, not long ago."

Man Killer looked at the carcass and saw the bite

marks on the back of the deer's neck, right on the spine. He saw the claw marks where the big cat had grabbed the deer's sides. The buck's stomach and intestines were gone with just a big bloody hole remaining. Mountain lions always ate the intestinal portion of a deer first, usually eating just that at the first feeding, then returning later to feed on the rest of the carcass. Finicky eaters, they would eat only for as long as the meat was fresh, leaving it for other predators once it became the least bit tainted. The lions always bedded down on higher ground overlooking a fresh kill, so Colt and Man Killer both knew the big cat probably watched them for a while, then left in search of more prey. Contrary to popular belief among dudes, mountain lions seldom came around humans; they preferred to slink away quietly.

Chris cut off a hindquarter and butchered it. The two men chanced removing the saddles and bridles from their horses, letting them graze on the rich mountain grasses in the bowl. They wanted both horses to be well fed and well rested for the rest of the trip.

The dinner was filling, and an after-dinner smoke and conversation were relaxing. Both warriors needed this time to prepare for the trials they both sensed would come the next day. They also decided to chance sleeping without taking turns on watch. Colt felt very strongly that Victorio was much more likely to try to intercept them than to follow them.

They awakened right at daybreak, and this time

Colt made breakfast. Over coffee, the two men methodically and carefully cleaned each of their weapons.

It was so close to Fort Union when Victorio struck that a person listening closely could hear the distant gunfire, if the wind was still. Colt and Man Killer had come out of the trees, still riding with their rifles across their saddlebows. They both knew better than to let their guard down until they were actually within the confines of the red stone billets and buildings of the Fort Union grounds. The rear guard of Victorio had picked up their trail earlier in the day and signaled the sighting by mirror.

The Mimbres leader decided to employ the Apache method for killing a herd of antelope. He divided his force into two columns, each on a different ridge line. Man Killer and Colt were riding the ridge line in between.

Most of the trees they rode through were stunted piñons, but at one point they passed through an area abounding in taller evergreens and a few hardwoods. It was there that the two scouts heard the distant barking of red squirrels three different times, from different locations. Then the pair knew they were in trouble. Red squirrels were known as "tattletales of the forests," and their chattering was a surefire sign that the two were surrounded and being paralleled. Words were not shared between the two, just glances. That was all that was necessary. They pushed their big horses into steady trots, knowing that the steeds would have plenty left if they had to make an all-out run for it.

Colt used signs to suggest that they should head east and make the prairie and outrun the smaller Apache ponies in a dash for Fort Union. They had just started to move when Colt reined up at the sound of a whistle. It was not a marmot or a badger but a woodchuck, a groundhog. It was an animal not native to this area but to the east where Colt had grown up. He gave Man Killer a strange look, and they rode slowly, carefully, toward the sound.

Man Killer spotted the man first and held up. Colt followed suit and watched Man Killer's stare to determine the hiding place of the man. He was slightly ahead and to their right in a small jumble of rocks. The man held up a Winchester carbine in one hand and raised the other in friendship.

The two scouts rode forward while appraising him. Colt liked and respected the man immediately just by his appearance. Like Colt, the cowboy was tall, ruggedly handsome, and rawhide tough. His waist was narrow and sported a .44 that had been pulled out of the holster a number of times. He also wore a giant knife on his hip, somewhat similar to Colt's own Bowie but even bigger. He was dressed like a man who had ridden many a trail, and a few scars were visible here and there. He had honest eyes, and a twinkle appeared in their corners as he nodded at Colt and Man Killer.

The two men reined up in front of the man and he nodded toward a nearby rise.

He spoke, "Noticed something up on that rise. Seems you two are real popular with some Apaches. They're strung out and paralleling you. If you try a run in front or back, they'll close up on you."

Colt said, "Obliged, mister, but if you saw them, why didn't you get the hell out of here? Now, you're in the same fix as us."

The man took a cigarillo offered by Colt and lit it, saying, "Well, mister, I'm not a stranger to trouble, and I'll not stand by and watch any men get dry-gulched without at least giving them fair warning."

Colt nodded and puffed on his own cigar, giving the tall stranger a grin. Both men were accustomed to trouble in their pasts, gun trouble, and they each sensed it about the other.

Chris said, "Well, since you made it your fight, I owe you one. I will ask for one more favor. We'll set up in these rocks and make noise so Victorio will know we've stopped."

The man said, "And I run out the front between the two columns and hightail it for Fort Union and reinforcements."

Colt said, "Exactly. Just tell the cavalry there that Chris Colt and his scout, Man Killer, are pinned down and need a little help."

The man said, "Colt, huh? Heard of you, both of you. The plans sounds reasonable. Now, I have to help out a brother down here that needs help, but if I can't get you cavalry, I'll come back and we'll read to old Victorio from the Good Book. Never heard of him coming this far north."

Colt said, "Probably didn't like the heat down south and decided on a short vacation. The cavalry will come. You fetch them, then do you go on, please. You've been help enough, mister. Say, what's your handle anyhow?"

The man took another puff and wheeled his steel-dust gelding, saying, "Thanks for the cigarillo, amigo. Name's Sackett. Luck to you Colt, Man Killer, give those boys what for."

Colt said, "Heard of you and your kin, too, Sackett. All good. Much obliged. Keep the wind in your face."

Sackett touched his hat brim and touched his calves and heels to his horse's flanks, speeding off down the ridge line. Colt and Man Killer watched, then jumped down and starting making a parapet in the small jumble of rocks. Colt pointed at a knot in a far off piñon and said, "Draw!"

He and Man Killer both drew their six-guns and fired, Colt slightly ahead of the Nez Perce. The guns exploded one after the other, and the knot disappeared. The two grinning scouts ejected their empties and fed shells into their pistols.

They returned to their work building a little fortress.

Man Killer said, "I think they know where we are now, for sure."

Colt winked. "I'd say so. Let's get the horses better cover so they won't get hit by any stray shots."

The two horses were placed inside the jumble of rocks, and a few more boulders were piled on top of the larger ones to protect the animals from any bullets. Colt made sure that the two men had all their water, food, and ammunition in the rocks with them, where they also would not get hit by stray bullets. He set the flask of whiskey down in case of arrow or lance wounds, and Man Killer started a fire and shoved his knife blade into the flames. If either man got shot, the other would immediately cauterize the wound with the red-hot blade.

With everything prepared, Colt put a pot of coffee on and explained, "If we're going to get killed, partner, we might as well enjoy a good strong cup of coffee, so we are awake for the journey."

He offered Man Killer fixings, and the two men rolled cigarettes to enjoy with their coffee.

Victorio's band had good rifles, even repeaters, but many Apaches preferred using the bow and arrow, as they were such good marksmen. Unlike some tribes, who had to learn to sneak in close to their quarry to shoot them, the Apaches learned the sneaking skills but were also much better archers than most other tribal warriors. Many were deadly up to one hundred yards.

Colt was sipping a second cup of coffee when an arrow took his leather scout's hat off his head. He and Man Killer immediately fired a long and steady volley of shots into every bush and hiding place within sight. Both reloaded their rifles while taking an occasional shot at targets of opportunity with their pistols. Using an Army tactic, their reaction to getting fired upon was immediately to lay down a heavy volume of withering fire, then aim at actual targets. The idea was to get and maintain shooting superiority.

Colt looked around, watching for signs of Apaches. They were hard to spot—impossible to most people—but Colt knew where to look. He and Man Killer quickly determined that they were surrounded, which was no surprise. A yell was heard and a heavy fusillade of arrows and bullets rained in on the two scouts. Instead of ducking and cowering, they fired back quickly, aiming at every exposed piece of Apache they could spot.

After a few minutes, there was suddenly a lull in the fighting, and Chris hollered out, "Victorio!"

Victorio answered back, "Speak, Colt!"

The chief of scouts hollered, "The mighty Victorio brings the entire Mimbres nation and maybe the Mescaleros, too, to fight against two warriors!"

Victorio yelled, "Maybe he who is the keen eyes for the Long Knives thinks that Victorio has the mind of a child!"

Colt cried out, "My name is Colt, and my guns are from the thunder. My knife is a lightning bolt, and my spirit came from the mighty bear, which brings bad luck to your people. Just you and me,

Victorio! I will fight you here and now! You pick the weapon!"

"Colt!" he answered. "That is not the Apache way! You know that! We pick when and where we fight and when we choose to leave! Walk out here, and you shall die quickly!"

There was no answer.

Victorio yelled out, "What is your answer?"

He flew off his horse as a blinding flash burned his cheek. He reached up and felt blood running from a crease along his left cheek. He saw Colt standing on a boulder, firing both pistols rapidly at many targets. Man Killer jumped up on another boulder and fired at more targets. The Nez Perce held a cup of steaming coffee in his other hand and drank while he shot. The word of this foolhardy but extremely courageous deed quickly spread among the warriors surrounding the hillside. The Apaches, like most tribes, greatly respected acts of bravado and courage in battle, even from an enemy. As usual, the Apache warriors did not cry out, but many were hit and wounded. Several were already dead from the accurate fire. The two scouts dropped out of sight.

Chris chuckled while the pair reloaded and said, "Son, what in blazes was that stunt?"

Man Killer said, "They will now know they face not one man but two."

Chris said, "Good point, but I think they already knew that they face two men."

Man Killer straightened his shoulders a little more and jumped up, firing more shots at the hidden attackers.

The firing slowed down again, and Victorio yelled out, "Colt!"

Chris replied, "I hear you!"

The Apache chief said, "I have gone to Colorado! Your wife liked it under my blankets!"

"She probably was able to get lots of sleep! That's why, Victorio!" Colt yelled back. "I tried to catch your wife in your village last week, but she was busy chasing a bone around your wickiup!"

The scouts ducked as the heaviest barrage of fire yet poured upon their position and bullets and arrows whistled over their heads. Leaning against their respective boulders, Colt and Man Killer looked over at each other and started chuckling, softly at first, but then it grew into tension-relieving, sidesplitting laughter.

Man Killer said, "Maybe you have made Victorio angry with your words."

Colt laughed even harder, tears spilling down his cheeks. He jumped up, barked loudly like a dog, and fired wildly at the Apaches, then dropped back down again.

Both men figured that they were going to be dead before help could arrive anyway, so they each had subconsciously made a decision to go out grinning at death in its face. They also covered up the great fear they were feeling with humor.

Getting serious, Colt said, "This is good anyway. We've made him angry."

Man Killer asked, "Why is that good?"

"Angry man fights like a fool. Maybe Victorio will make a mistake. We need any help we can get."

Several Apache warriors talked about the raw courage of Man Killer, standing on a rock firing his pistol while nonchalantly drinking coffee. Victorio crept by and heard the conversation. At his icy stares they quickly shut their mouths and looked at him blankly. Victorio went on, and one looked at the other and made a quiet barking noise. Both Apache warriors started giggling together. One of the other warriors, Nah-Kah-Yen, understood English and had translated Colt and Victorio's words for the others. Like Colt and Man Killer, the Apache braves also relieved their own tension and fear with humor during battle. This would amaze those reporters who wrote accounts about the Indians for the eastern newspapers. Portrayed primarily as bloodthirsty, screaming savages by those writers with their smooth hands and creamy skin, the Apaches would be the last group they would expect to have or exhibit a sense of humor, especially during battle.

Although the warriors were laughing behind Victorio's back, they all respected him, to a man. Like many other tribes, each Apache warrior was a very independent, hardheaded individual. Tribal leaders were a necessity for organization and unity, but ultimately each individual had the final word over his own destiny. Chiefs had to be respected, and Victorio had earned his way as chief, instead of gaining it by birthright, like many had.

He also was a good tactician, and he was troubled by the smoke he was now seeing from the direction of Fort Union. It indicated that a lot of enemy, or very well-armed enemy, were on their way. It was the Apache way to vanish if a superior force entered the battlefield. It had nothing to do with courage or honor, just common sense. Many tribes followed this practice, for they had so few men available for war that they could ill afford to lose warriors over ego-oriented challenges.

Victorio had a decision to make. Should he try to swarm over Colt's position and possibly lose many men to the accurate firing of the two scouts, or should he disappear? Should he head back toward southern New Mexico, where he was familiar with the terrain and the possible hiding places and ambush sites, or stick around this area, where he was out of his element strategically?

He yelled, "Colt, we will meet again, in battle, and I will cut out your heart and eat it!"

"You better bring a lot more braves than you have now, Victorio!" Colt responded. "It's going to be a long, hard task to cut out my heart, and you might give thought to retirement in Mexico instead!"

Chris and Man Killer smiled at each other and poured coffee as they listened to the far-off melody of a cavalry bugler sounding, "Charge!" Chris and the teenager made cigarettes and lit up. Both were drenched with sweat and grime, weary and drained. They risked standing and no shots were fired at them, nor did they hear any shots coming from the cavalry.

They heard the military unit entering the trees and heading toward them. Then they finally saw a military detachment as it poured in all about them. The patrol looked to be wearing gray uniforms and was led by a sergeant who had big yellow stripes showing on only one sleeve.

The sergeant threw up a gloved hand, and his big bay slid to a stop in front of Colt and Man Killer. Several of his troopers stopped, one on either side of him. They all removed their hats and started slapping at their clothes, as great clouds of white and gray dust flew into the breeze. Soon it was clear that the uniforms were standard blue, not gray as they had appeared. The soldiers' skin was also dark brown; no man among them had white skin. Brushing off the dust, the sergeant now had stripes showing on both sleeves.

He saluted smartly and said, "Sergeant John Denny, Company C, Ninth Cavalry, at your service, Mr. Colt."

Chris said, "Little dusty, huh? Coffee, Sergeant?"

The man had a straight back and a distinctly military bearing.

"Thank you, sir, for the offer of coffee," he replied, "but I could not participate with my men gagging on alkali dust."

Colt said, "We got plenty. Let them dismount and have some. You boys spot Victorio or his people coming in?"

"Victorio!" the sergeant said. "I thought that Sackett gentleman was playing the fool when he said it was Victorio."

"You sure don't talk like a . . ." Colt started to say.

Denny angrily interrupted him, however: "Nigger, sir?"

It was now Colt's turn to be angered. He replied, "No, Sergeant, I was trying to say you don't talk like a sergeant."

John Denny was now embarrassed, and his reddening face clearly showed it.

He said humbly, "My deepest apologies, sir. I try so hard, Mr. Colt, to not represent myself as a former slave, but rather as a man of learning."

Colt grinned and looked over at Man Killer, saying, "Man Killer, here's Sergeant John Denny, of the all-Negro Ninth Cavalry, the buffalo soldiers. Last September 16, near the head of the Las Animas River, he distinguished himself with so much heroism and courage in a major skirmish against Victorio that he was awarded the Congressional Medal of Honor. He is also noted for numerous other courageous acts—and the man is worried about how he comes across to others."

John Denny said, "I'm flattered, sir, but that's how it is when your skin is this color. It is a constant struggle for acceptance and approval."

Colt said, "Well, Sergeant Denny, you just saved our bacon and it's a real pleasure meeting you. I want to tell you something right now, too. You don't have to carry water for any man. The only acceptance and approval you need is from yourself."

Denny grinned and said, "Mr. Colt, I sincerely appreciate your remarks, but you have never had brown skin in the United States of America."

Chris poured the coffee on the fire while Man Killer fetched the horses and said, "Nope. You're right about that."

Changing the subject, the hero said, "When that Sackett gentleman approached us, we were just beyond a large alkali bed not far from the fort. That is why we were so covered in dust."

Colt relieved his bladder on the smoking coals and kicked dirt over them. "I assume you don't want to track out Victorio?"

"Mr. Colt," replied Sergeant Denny, "as mentioned, I am a sergeant and a veteran of the Apache wars. I do not want to waste our time or yours. They disappeared among the rocks before we showed and will reappear at some rendezvous point miles from here. Besides that, my mission was to take a patrol out to provide assistance and escort to you, sir. It was happenstance that we ran into Sackett when we did."

"Whatever it was, Sergeant," Chris said, "we sure loved the sound of your bugler."

"I am certainly glad that we were able to make it to your location in time, Mr. Colt," Denny said. "Are you prepared to complete your journey to the fort, sir?"

Colt mounted up on War Bonnet as Man Killer walked up and handed him the reins.

He winked at the medal of honor winner and replied, "Yep, but please, Sergeant Denny, call me Chris or call me Colt. Please don't call me Mr. Colt or sir. Makes me feel like I'm my father."

"At your command, si . . . ah, Colt," said Denny. "Corporal, let's move them out, column of twos, and the same size point elements, and rear and side guards."

A slight man with a pair of rockers on each arm nodded and spurred his horse, saying, "Yassuh, Co'poral Denny, suh."

Colt grinned to himself as he compared the differences in the speech patterns and actions of the two men.

The patrol moved out and arrived at Fort Union in less than an hour. Colt learned on the way there that Victorio had become extremely bold in his attacks. For example, he found out that Victorio attacked and killed fifteen Mexican civilians near Carrizal on November 7, 1879. Thirty-five rescuers rode out from the town to save them, and Victorio and his men ambushed the rescuers, killing eleven more. At another New Mexico town in 1879, Victorio attacked some people less than a mile from their town, killed several, then fled into the nearby mountains.

Man Killer hadn't seen a fort the size of Fort Union—or as busy. Being the key supply depot for virtually all the forts in the West, it bustled with activity. Colt had a meeting with the commander, so the young Nez Perce scout was free to roam the fort. It had first been established in 1851, when Lieutenant Colonel Edwin V. Summers, commander of the First Dragoons, decided to establish a fort away from "that sink of vice and extravagance, Santa Fe," where Fort Marcy had been located.

Man Killer could see the almost-twenty-year-old remains of the "star fort," with earthen parapets jutting out two hundred feet in star points. It had been built during the Civil War to block Confederate advances from the south. Very few people knew that some Confederate troops had actually moved this far west under Brigadier General Henry H. Sibley and invaded New Mexico Territory in 1862. The territory was successfully defended, including a pitched battle at Fort Union, by troops under Colonel E. R. S. Canby.

The fort was later moved, rebuilt, and refurbished. Man Killer walked along the rows of officers' houses, wood-frame buildings in a neat row with native-stone fireplaces and chimneys. The hospital was also a large wood-frame whitewashed building near the post corral, and the Santa Fe Trail actually passed between them. Next to the corrals, toward officers' row, were the laundresses, a series of small buildings where clothing and uniforms were cleaned daily. Between there and officers' row were the enlisted men's barracks and the fort parade ground. On the other side of the post corral was the large transportation corral, which was also bounded by the mechanics buildings and corral, the yard filled with numerous freight wagons in various stages of repair and disrepair. Next to that were many long warehouse buildings. Out behind the officers' row and headquarters building directly across from the old star fort, was the sutler's store, where much of the post activity by those who were off duty took place.

Man Killer observed one troop of soldiers being marched around the parade field, and it was obvious these men were brand-new raw recruits. The teenaged scout wondered why they spent so much time learning how to march and not more time learning how to shoot, clean weapons, and devise tactics.

Walking by one barracks building, Man Killer observed a troop of black soldiers sitting on the ground, smoking pipes and cigarettes and vigorously rubbing bootblack on their tall cavalry footgear. Several of the men were singing an old Negro spiritual, and Man Killer stood for several minutes enthralled by the melodic chorus of voices in the sad lament.

Finally he headed to the sutler's store, where he was to meet Colt. Man Killer was thrilled with the bowling alley inside and the fancy billiard tables. He knew that this would become his favorite place whenever they were at Fort Union. He bought a bottle of sarsaparilla and was pleased to learn it had been kept in ice. The rest of his wait for Colt would keep him happily occupied watching troopers bowling and poking little colored balls with a stick and knocking them into holes in the felt-topped table.

In the commandant's office, Chris Colt accepted another cup of coffee from an orderly while he continued to listen to the briefing about Victorio. The Apache leader had been very busy since fleeing Fort Stanton the previous August.

On September 4, Victorio and his followers got into a pitched battle with the buffalo soldiers of the Ninth Cavalry's Company E, near Ojo Caliente in southern New Mexico. On modern-day maps, Ojo Caliente is a small community in the north central part of the state, above Santa Fe and west of Taos, but in the 1800's Ojo Caliente was located not far from Silver City in southwestern New Mexico. On that day, Victorio, under indictment for murdering a judge and prosecutor who poached deer on reservation land, and sixty of his followers hit the horse herd of Captain Hooker's command and killed eight troopers while stealing forty-six cavalry mounts. Hooker himself was knocked off his horse and had to unceremoniously watch his unit's defeat from the ground. Nine citizens were killed by Victorio over the next week, and the Ninth Cavalry regimental commander, Colonel Edward Hatch, immediately ordered troops into the field to run him down. Their orders were simple: locate Victorio, press him, corner him, and take him down. They were also told unofficially that Victorio was not to be returned to the reservation. He was just too dangerous. He was angry, determined, and had tremendous leadership abilities.

Colt got a better insight into Victorio's abilities as a tactician when he heard of the Apaches' next contact with the buffalo soldiers. Scouts for Lieutenant Colonel Dudley's column found Victorio's trail on September 16. His column consisted of Captain Hooker and E Company and Captain Dawson with B Company. Victorio fled, keeping a short distance in front of the column, and the cavalry pursued him and his followers for two days, to the rocky canyons at the headwaters of the Las Animas River. It had all been a ruse. Victorio had numerous Apaches hidden in holes with small rockpile parapets around each of them. They were all dug in along both sides of one of the steep-walled canyons, and Victorio and the rest with him took their places, which had been already prepared. The cavalry was pinned down, and only the providence of Companies C and G hearing the battle saved him and his command. They rushed to the scene but, even with reinforcements, the cavalry were not able to rout Victorio's deeply entrenched and fortified band, and the buffalo soldiers had to retreat under cover of night, leaving behind five dead troopers, three scouts, and thirty-two dead cavalry mounts.

Killing the horses of the cavalry was one of Victorio's tactics early on. He taught his followers to aim at the horses, as they were bigger targets and a man on foot would be easier to kill or capture. On top of that, if the soldiers' mounts were killed, some would have to ride double or walk, either way slowing down the rest of the command. The final bonus was that the dead horses provided fresh meat for the renegade band.

Shortly thereafter, Lieutenant Colonel Dudley was transferred and replaced by Major Albert P. Morrow, whose idea was to find Victorio and pursue him into the ground, using command after command, if necessary. This tactic was employed by Morrow immediately, and he pursued Victorio for eleven days in a row, not allowing him to rest and finally bringing him to bay on the Cuchillo Negro. Morrow was faced with an entrenched Victorio, as Dudley had been, but he first deliberated on what tactics to employ, then attacked in the afternoon. The fighting raged until well after dark.

Knowing that Victorio wouldn't fight at night or go anywhere, Morrow called off his men and let them rest during the night. He was a good commander and thought things out thoroughly before making a decision. He also kept his men in mind, as well as the damage he could inflict on his enemy.

Victorio had realized that this was a different and

better commander than the others. He had also learned about Morrow from Apache scouts who were spies for their people. As soon as full daybreak arrived, Victorio had his men mounted on horses— except for his best rifle shot. As one of Major Morrow's black sentries took a sip of his first cup of coffee, the Apache sharpshooter put a bullet between the soldier's eyes. The sniper then jumped on his mount, and Victorio led his braves in an all-out charge through the weakest part of Morrow's line. The cavalry was already saddled and packed, ready to continue the battle, so the buffalo soldiers pursued and fought the warriors for two hours before finally having to give up because of exhausted horses. Morrow had lost two soldiers, but Victorio lost three and had a number wounded. He would not take the new commander lightly.

The next day, when the scouts located Victorio's camp, they told Morrow that it seemed that the wily Apache chief had again previously prepared fortified positions. He moved his troops up and decided to attack at midnight, a time when Apaches did not like to fight. Earlier, at dusk, one of Victorio's men had spotted one of the Navajo scouts as they crept out on a rock overhang to check the Apaches' position. Waiting until full dark, Victorio employed the same trick sometimes used by Chris Colt. He had all of his men tie rawhide covers over the hooves of their ponies. They then carefully crept away from their fortified positions. Morrow decided not to attack until daybreak because of the darkness of the night sky and the difficulty in seeing in the rocks. When they moved in close, they had no idea that the clever red leader and his men were quietly sneaking away into the darkness.

At dawn, Morrow's men, in position and ready to launch an all-out assault, moved forward on line and were greeted by numerous dug-in holes, with rock walls around each one. Victorio was miles away.

While Victorio made his way into the Mogollon Mountains, Major Morrow hurried to Ojo Caliente for more horses and supplies. He also called for reinforcements out of Fort Bayard. The next day he moved out and was joined by reinforcements from Companies H and C, along with troopers from the Sixth Cavalry, and twenty-four extra scouts, most of them Apaches. Morrow was one of the first southwestern commanders who learned to use Apaches to catch Apaches.

Colt looked at the back of the colonel's head as the briefing went on. Chris heard that he would be under Morrow's command, and he was pleased. It would be a pleasure to get to work under a commanding officer who was good and solid and probably listened to those around him who offered expertise and experience. He also liked Colonel Hatch, so far. Colt had been treated with respect and dignity by the commander and was asked his opinion as the briefing went on. This was a far cry from the way he had been treated by Custer or Howard in his two previous campaigns, and it was a relief. It was a way, he thought, to get the job done.

Man Killer was drinking his second sarsaparilla when a gravelly voice behind him said, "Didn't know they let any a Chief Joseph's red niggers in this here drinkin' 'stablishment."

Man Killer knew he had just heard trouble and he turned around slowly, wishing Colt was here to help him out with trouble in a white man's world. He looked at the giant barrel chest of a behemoth of a man with a gray-streaked bright-red long beard and long, unkempt salt-and-red pepper hair. Beer suds were sitting on his beard, and he had a giant grin on his scarred and windburned face. He pointed at the lad and laughed loudly, guffaws rumbling out of a chest that looked to Man Killer to be bigger around than Hawk's. A Sharps buffalo gun rested against the man's side, and he wore across his rib cage a large beaded sheath and Bowie knife, not unlike Colt's.

He said, "Got ya, didn't I, youngster? Yep, yer a salty one, ain't ya? No wunner old Chris Colt taken ya in under his wing. Reckon you'll do to ride the mountain passes with. Here's to ya."

With that, the big bear gulped down the rest of his mug of iced beer, slammed the big thick glass down on the bar, and nodded for a refill.

"Barkeep," he roared, "give my young friend here a refill of his sasparilly, will ya? Man Killer's yer name, ain't it?"

Man Killer nodded at the jolly big man.

He accepted the sweet drink and started downing it.

Finally he spoke. "You know my name."

"Shore have, I'm a man a the mountains, son, but up there we hear the news, too, time to time. You and Colt been the talk a the West past coupla year. Heard 'bout him rescuin' his woman from the Sioux, grinnin' down Crazy Hoss an' becomin' friends with him, and rumor has it that he was with Chief Joseph on his famous retreat crosst the mountains. That ol' Colt's shinin', boy. He'd be one fer ya ta stick with if'n things was different."

"What do you mean, different?"

"No matter. Drink up," he said. "I'll buy ya nuther."

"Why?" Man Killer said out of honest curiosity.

The man said, "Yer famous and yer still a lad. I like the cut of ya. I'm an ol' white nigger come down outta the mountains smelling a wood smoke, beaver guts, and bar grease. I don't never git to see other folk hardly, much less someone famous."

Man Killer was suspicious. "You know my name. I don't know yours."

The man grinned and stuck out a giant ham-sized palm which engulfed the Nez Perce's hand, as they shook.

He said, "Name's Thadeous Webster Sawyer, but folks call me Barrel on account a one time I picked up a big barrel a nails with my arms wrapped roun' it and carried it crosst a room. Won me a couple a double eagles, too, I did."

Man Killer said, "Sawyer. You said your family name is Sawyer. Chris Colt killed the Sawyer brothers."

"My cousins," the brute said. "Will an' me was jest 'bout brothers growin' up."

Man Killer felt his heart pounding in his ears and neck.

"So you are here to kill Colt?" he said.

"He's a hell of a man," Barrel said, "but it's a blood thing. Yer Injun. You understand."

Man Killer said, "How long have you been after him?"

"Coupla year. Went to his ranch up in the Wet Mountain Valley, but he wasn't there. I ast aroun' and found out he was headed down here."

Man Killer was very concerned now about Shirley and said, "What happened at his ranch?"

Barrel said, "Aw, some uppity nigger run me off with a scattergun. Claimt he was Colt's brother. Imagine that? I figgered he was some stable nigger what was teched in the head, so I paid him no never mind."

Man Killer said, "You left the ranch, didn't you?"

Barrel's watermelon-size head got beet-red, and he said, "Careful, young un. I jest bought ya a drink. Learn respect."

Man Killer replied, "I didn't ask for a drink. You

have wasted much time. Outshooting Chris Colt would be like trying to lasso a windstorm."

"Hell," Barrel laughed, "I don't even own me a short gun. I'm a gonna kill him with my blade."

With that, he pulled his Bowie out in one easy move and admired it like it was a family pet. He replaced it in the sheath.

Man Killer said, "Will Sawyer tried that already, and he is sleeping now at the bottom of a burning mud bowl in the Yellowstone."

The big man roared with laughter again. "Nobody seen it but Crazy Horse supposedly, an' he's conveniently livin' in the happy huntin' grounds. Naw, I knew Will and the only way Colt coulda kilt him was ta backshoot him."

Man Killer's gun came out in a flash and was cocked with the barrel literally stuck up the right nostril of Barrel Sawyer. He surprised himself with his anger and speed, but this man had just accused Chris Colt of a cowardly act. Colt was Man Killer's hero, and he would not stand for that kind of talk. He was seething inside.

"You have called my brother a coward," Man Killer said. "Before killing him, you will first have to kill me."

Barrel stared down at the barrel of the gun and said, "Easy fer even a young pup like you ta say with'n a gun barrel shoved up my nose."

Man Killer had had enough. All eyes in the place

were staring. He stepped back and expertly spun the gun back into his holster.

He said, "You will still have to kill me. You have insulted and threatened my friend and put his woman in danger by going to his ranch."

The bartender, who hadn't even seemed to notice the young scout earlier, said, "Kid, don't be crazy. If you're with Colt, I don't want to see you murdered. This man has killed at least ten men with that knife and two with his hands and feet."

Man Killer kept his eyes on Barrel but spoke to the bartender: "If I do not kill him now, he will shoot Colt in the back with that Sharps when he rides out to look at the sky."

Man Killer remembered that Colt told him to make a man angry in a fight because a mad man fights like a fool. Barrel let out a roar like a grizzly and charged forward, his teeth bared. Man Killer didn't have time to think, only react. He dropped to the floor, and scissored his legs around the big man's as he passed. Sawyer crashed headfirst into four chairs and a table, breaking several chair legs with his head.

He came off the floor with blood streaking from his nose. He stood straight up and shook his head to clear the cobwebs. While taking that time, he set himself up for Man Killer's next maneuver as the lad ran and jumped up feet first, kicking both feet into the big man's face. Man Killer landed on his hands and feet and sprang up immediately, knowing that he was dead if Sawyer got his hands on him.

Just then, Chris Colt walked in the door, escorted by Colonel Hatch.

One of the troopers yelled, "At ease!"

And Hatch immediately hollered, "Carry on!"

This yelling threw Barrel off, though, and he paused to stare at the men. Man Killer took advantage of it by swinging his right foot up as hard as he could into the man's groin. The air left Barrel Sawyer with a rush, and he doubled over in pain, holding himself with both hands. Man Killer reached up and grabbed the man's big head in a front headlock and he kicked his feet out behind him, holding Barrel's head, as he drove the big man's face into the plank floor.

Colt chuckled but was concerned for the young teen against this giant, muscular foe. He became more than concerned when the bartender ran over and explained what had happened to the three men. Colt started forward, but Man Killer's glance stopped him. The young man had saddled this horse and was going to ride it.

Getting up slowly and weaving slightly, Sawyer pulled the big Bowie, blood streaming from various facial wounds.

He said, "Now, young un, you've made me mad, and when I git mad, someone dies."

Colt's voice stopped him in mid-tracks: "Too bad

that someone is you, Sawyer. Your family just doesn't possess much in the way of brains, does it?"

Barrel said, "You're next after I skin this red nigger boy."

Man Killer said, "When you are in hell, tell Satan that a red nigger boy killed you."

He swung the sarsaparilla bottle at the knife hand, but Sawyer's arm dropped and the bottle passed harmlessly by him, throwing the teen off balance. Sawyer rushed in and viciously kicked Man Killer in the thigh, causing a deep bruise. The force of the kick literally sent the youngster flying, and he landed against the bar and bruised a rib. Sawyer ran at him, but Man Killer kicked backward like a mule into the big man's solar plexus and the wind rushed out of Barrel. He slashed left and right at Man Killer next, as the youth backed around the bar, his mind working as fast as it could.

The Nez Perce scout tripped over one of the broken chairs and jumped up as Barrel laughed loudly and rushed forward with the knife raised high overhead, bringing it down in a vicious and powerful arc. Man Killer sidestepped, but the blade caught his shoulder muscle and made a slash through it. The young warrior's adrenaline was pumping now, and all he could feel was the need for victory. Sawyer slashed down again: this time Man Killer sidestepped and the blade missed him cleanly. The brave's left hand caught Barrel behind the left elbow, and his right hand trapped Sawyer's hand on the handle. He used the momentum to swing the knife all the way down and force Barrel to stick it well into his own left thigh. He let out a roar of pain and backhanded Man Killer with a blow that knocked the scout's teeth together and sent shock waves through his brain. He felt himself fly through the air and crash on his back on the floor. He couldn't breathe and fought back the panicky feelings inside. He shook his head and saw Sawyer bearing down on him, the blood gushing out of his leg.

Barrel was now holding the Bowie underhanded straight out with the blade up, hoping to thrust it into Man Killer's stomach and rip the intestines out. Man Killer's own knife suddenly appeared in his hand from the sheath hidden inside the back of his war shirt, and he rolled to the side while thrusting the blade into Barrel's chest. The momentum from the big man's rush helped bury the blade almost all the way to the hilt in the left side of his chest.

Man Killer rolled three times and grabbed a bowling pin that had been set on the bar for patrons to inspect close up. Sawyer, his face white with shock, came forward, hands outstretched, but the young Colt protégé never stopped his action. As he grabbed the heavy wooden pin, he swung around and swung it backward, striking the end of the handle of his knife and driving it all the way into Barrel's chest. The big man let out a death scream and fell face first, his body convulsing for a full half minute before it stilled forever.

All Sawyer could see was darkness and the image of himself with a trident and horns. Mentally he said to the image, "I was killed by a red nigger kid."

The image laughed, and Barrel Sawyer heard a voice in the darkness say, "Damn, that kid killed that big monster."

He screamed inside his brain, but his blank eyes just stared at the bright-red pool of blood all around them. He felt hands touch his body and roll him over, but he could not see or hear or move anymore. He panicked, then everything in his brain stopped.

Man Killer stood, and one of Colonel Hatch's orderlies started forward to help him but was stopped by Colt's touch. The Nez Perce stood, straightening his shoulders and sticking out his chest. He walked to Sawyer's body and stepped on the giant's chest and grabbed the handle of his knife. He yanked hard and pulled the blade free with a sucking sound. He then wiped it on the dead man's wool undershirt. Man Killer replaced it in his sheath and took a big swallow of sarsaparilla. He walked over to Colt, the room spinning. Chris was grinning.

Colt said, "I got to go meet with the brass here and you decide to have fun without me around. You always pick on people with red hair?"

Man Killer looked at Colonel Hatch and Chris and said, "We will find Victorio for you, sir."

He fainted and fell forward into Colt's arms.

"Orderly," Hatch commanded, "an ambulance quickly. Get this young man to the hospital." He added, "Tell the doctor to put him in the commandant's private room."

"Yas, suh!" the corporal snapped to attention, heels clicking together. He quickly exited the sutler's store, while Colt easily lifted the limp scout and set him on a billiard table. The bartender rushed over with some clean towels and applied them to the young man's knife wound.

"Mr. Colt," Hatch said, "if you trained this young Indian, I would like for you to teach some of the same behavior to our scouts."

Hatch's aide laughed and added, "Scouts, hell, sir. Our troopers, too."

Hatch chuckled and said, "And our officers."

He paused for humorous effect and added, "Present company excepted, Lieutenant."

The young officer laughed. "Of course, sir. Of course."

chapter 4

>>>>>>>>>>>>>>>>>>

Victorio

Man Killer was out of the hospital the next day, despite the protestations of the regimental surgeon. He learned from Colt about all the activities of Victorio which had been going on for months. Listening to Colt's briefing, he then sat against the side of a red adobe laundress building with all the other scouts, most of whom were Navajo, and the rest of which were Jicarilla, Chiricajua, and Mescalero Apaches.

Chris stood tall in front of the cross-legged scouts and spoke, pausing occasionally while two translators repeated his words in Apache and Navajo. "Some of you will wonder if I will know what I am doing scouting against the Apache. I have been here before in campaigns against the Apache, the Ute, and the Comanche. I wear articles from the Lakotah and Cheyenne, and even a necklace from the Nez Perce, but my heart is with all my red brothers. I know Victorio from before, and he knows me, and we have declared ourselves as enemies, but I respect him as a warrior and a leader. You will all do the same. The white eyes do not understand that you of the Apache nation can scout against your people, because our ways are different, but I understand. You who are of the great Navajo nation will not think of Victorio as a chief of an inferior tribe, for that will get your scalp on his belt. He is smart and tough, and we will always respect his knowledge in warfare and his determination. We will be moving a lot through much desert, as you have all done, so you will each carry saddlebags with extra food for your horses or ponies. You will also carry extra canteens.

"I am your boss, and you will speak and hear only from me when we are on the same patrol. If any officer or NCO tries to order you or speak down to you, tell me. If you have a question, ask me.

"Some of you are spies for Victorio or Geronimo. You are here as their eyes and ears among the white eyes. If I catch you, I will kill you. You will all keep your jobs as they are now, including those who are leaders among the scouts.

"This is Man Killer, my second in command. He is young, but would be chosen chief in any of your tribes. If I die, listen to him. Now, does any man have a problem with this?"

One stocky Apache rose, a Chiricajua who knew the great Cochise as a boy. He spit on the ground.

He spoke, "I do not listen to council from a boy

who has no hair between his legs even. Too-Ah-Yay-Say has spoken."

Colt said, "Okay. Draw your pay from the paymaster and fork your pony. Return to your reservation."

Man Killer stood and raised his hand. All the scouts had heard about his fight, loyalty, and courage, and most were already in awe of the young man, who seemed destined for greatness. They also admired him for walking toward Too-Ah-Yay-Say with a fresh white bandage over his left shoulder. His left arm slipped out of the sling, and he tossed it aside on the ground. Colt smiled imperceptibly as he saw Too-Ah-Yay-Say's Adam's apple bob slightly with nervousness. The assistant chief of scouts walked directly up to the Apache and stuck out his hand, smiling. The southwestern scout spit on the lad's hand.

Moving within just inches of Too-Ah-Yay-Say's face, Man Killer reached out and yanked the man's war club from his belt. He handed it to the shocked Apache scout.

Man Killer said, "If you think I am a boy, strike me with your war club. Strike me anywhere, as hard as you wish, just one time. Then you will hand it to me, and I will strike you one time, anywhere I want."

Chiricajua boys grew up standing at rock piles throwing stones at each other and making cuts and bruises all over each other's bodies, simply to learn to accept pain.

The gauntlet had been thrown down, but these two were not boys. They were both men and could kill each other with one blow. And what if his blow did not kill the Nez Perce, Too-Ah-Yay-Say thought. Then he would surely make the spirit journey. He also wondered why he was now thinking of the Nez Perce as a man. Too-Ah-Yay-Say was angry at himself, for he was not ready yet to make the spirit journey. He had not even taken a wife. Well, he had one briefly, but she committed adultery with his cousin and the tip of her nose was cut off for such violation of tribal law.

Sensing that the man was now having second thoughts and Man Killer had just made a true believer out of him, Colt knew that the Apache could not back down now, because he would lose face with his compatriots.

Chris said, "I am the boss and Man Killer is my second. Do you, Too-Ah-Yay-Say, want to argue all day like children or do you like the money the Army pays you?"

The Apache looked at Colt, sensing a way out.

Colt then gave him a big grin and said, "Maybe this is the time in each moon when Too-Ah-Yay-Say bleeds much."

All the scouts laughed heartily, especially after the translation. Too-Ah-Yay-Say started to glare at the chief of scouts, but then he laughed at himself, too.

In seconds, he was releasing the tension with heavy laughter. He stuck out his hand and gripped forearms with Man Killer, and they shook in Indian fashion.

Man Killer was relieved, but he knew he had to impress all these men immediately after Colt's declaration about him. He was also very thankful for Chris's incredible leadership ability and quick thinking.

Morrow was in the middle of a vigorous campaign against Victorio far to the south and Hatch, Colt, and more scouts were being sent down to him as quickly as possible. Sergeant Denny would accompany them along with his unit.

Hatch had told Colt that his knowledge and expertise would be invaluable to him, and he would be sent wherever necessary to get the troops to close in on Victorio and conquer him. Colt's first suggestion had been to guard water holes all over the area of operations, and Hatch said that he would carefully ponder that strategy. It was basically desert land where the Apache was operating, and water was very scarce, but Hatch at first had trouble agreeing that the answer could be as simple as guarding water holes.

Hatch told Colt that the Tenth Cavalry, also buffalo soldiers from Texas, were being brought into the campaign. Colonel Benjamin Grierson, commanding officer of the Tenth, felt that such a move was going to open up west Texas to attack, because he felt that Victorio was headed there next.

Hatch also told Colt that they had been ordered by Sheridan to head to the Mescalero Reservation and dismount and disarm the Mescaleros, because they had been supplying men, food, and supplies to Victorio. Hatch wanted Colt's opinion on this. Colt explained that it could be a two-edged sword. The Mescaleros would be angry for the mistreatment and would be more firmly aligned with Victorio. On the other hand, they were going to be totally sympathetic and loyal to Victorio no matter what the United States did. Second, tactically Colt felt that the Army had no choice but to disarm and dismount the Mescaleros if they were supplying Victorio. Any good commander, he stated, knew that an army, any kind of army, could not function without logistical supplies.

They headed south the next day, and Chris remembered the country where he was headed. It was harsh and hot and dry. Around Fort Union and north to the border and beyond, the prairie was green at this time of year, most of it turning somewhat brown in late summer. There were many areas with lush grazing grass. Fort Union was in a small fold of prairie surrounded by small rocky cedar and piñon-covered ridges. These foothills gave way to much taller mountains directly to the west and running north and south for miles. Out to the east, the prairie stretched out for hundreds of miles. Some of the mountains after crossing into New Mexico at Raton Pass were actually more flat-topped mesas, but the Sangre de Cristos, as in Colorado, were tall, snowcapped, and steep. As the patrol moved south, trees became more scarce and so did graze and water for the animals. Water holes took on a much greater importance, and that is exactly why Colt had suggested that they just guard all water holes and wait. Colt knew that Victorio and all his followers could live for months by using little tricks that Colt and the Apaches knew, such as cutting the top off of a barrel cactus and drinking the water stored in the hollow core. It tasted bad, but it was water. The problem, however, was that the Apaches needed cows for meat and horses for mobility, and they could not water them by cutting barrel cacti in half. There were no tricks that could provide that much water in arid desert country. Thus they were dependent on water holes. That was the key to victory in this campaign, Colt knew, and he was glad that he had an open-minded commander working with him who might come to realize it.

Pushing Victorio and not letting him rest was also good strategy, because the cavalry was much better equipped logistically and could take advantage of that. Although the Apaches could go for days without water and trot many miles without rest, food, or drink, it didn't mean that they could keep doing it on a sustained basis. Nor did it mean that they wanted to survive that way. It just meant that they were very tough.

It was mid-April when Colonel Hatch, Colt, and the rest of the available command rendezvoused with Colonel Grierson at the Indian Bureau Agency at the Mescalero Reservation. Colt was introduced to Grierson, and noted that he, too, seemed to be an effective commander. Again, Colt explained his idea about guarding all the water holes and Grierson seemed interested in the strategy but not ready to commit to it either.

The combined forces from the Tenth and Ninth cavalries prepared to disarm and dismount the Mescalero Apaches, after several delays because of rain and bickering among the commanders. As Colt predicted, they met with some very angry and resentful people, but they did have around four hundred Apaches assembled to disarm and dismount.

The next day, April 16, Hatch moved to the west of the Indian agency to prepare for the next drive against Victorio. It was agreed that Grierson would handle the disarming, along with Company G of the Fifteenth Infantry, commanded by Captain Steelhammer. The new Indian agent, S. A. Russell, was also with the Tenth Commander waiting for more Apaches to come in for disarming. The plan was to then move them close to Fort Stanton for better control.

Many of the Apaches had been resisting, though, and were camped across the Tularosa. Hatch and

Grierson had been having a little disagreement on how to handle the situation. Hatch had wanted to spend a little time and exhibit a little more patience, while Grierson more or less wanted to charge the stragglers and force all the Apaches under the government control. Colonel Hatch felt it was Russell's job to take care of the Apaches properly, and he wanted to afford the man that opportunity without suppressing the Mescaleros so much. The main thing was that he had been given orders by Sheridan, and he was a good soldier, if nothing else—as was Grierson.

A problem developed around mid-morning, though, when Grierson quickly mounted his troopers and charged out south of the headquarters in response to a heavy volume of rifle fire, not far away. Russell, with a security patrol, followed a short distance behind. Navajo scouts, who had not been with or met Colt but had come with Grierson from Texas, ran into some Mescalero warriors driving a small herd of cattle and horses. They opened fire on the Apaches, killing two and recapturing the herd.

When Grierson rode up, they proudly displayed the herd they had gotten back from the Apaches and were congratulated by the commander for their quick thinking and courage. Agent Russell, on the other hand, was furious.

"You stupid niggers!" he fumed. "Those two Apaches you killed and those you caused to take flight were ordered to round up that livestock and drive it to the agency compound!"

Grierson interrupted the tirade. "Mr. Russell, in the future, if you have a complaint you wish to express to any of my charges, you will file a formal complaint to me through my office. You will not engage in recriminations, slanderous remarks and slurs, and any other forms of badgering any of the troopers of my command. Have I made myself sufficiently clear, sir?"

"Ah, yes, sir," Russell stuttered nervously. "It's just that, ah . . . nothing, sir. It shan't happen again, Colonel. My sincerest apologies."

"Accepted. Carry on," Grierson said, and spun his horse around, trotting away.

Hatch came over and met with Russell to formulate an expedient plan. Captain Steelhammer and one company would disarm and dismount the Apaches, while Grierson and Hatch would stand by with their troops for help. Chris Colt would take a detachment of scouts and check around the outskirts of the assembly area to ensure that no warriors assembled for attack or escaped undetected. If Steelhammer had any problems, he would immediately fire three rapid shots and Hatch and Grierson would bring or send troops. Colt and the scouts would remain to pick up the trail of any fleeing warriors.

An hour later, Grierson, watching through his field glass, noticed movement on the mountain behind the camp. At first he thought it was Colt and his scouts, but then he dismounted, rested his eyepiece against a tree trunk and realized that it was a number of Apaches, on foot and on horseback. He immediately sent a courier to Hatch and asked if he had seen them and if he knew the location of Colt and his scouts.

Before he got the reply from Hatch, both commanders heard three rapid shots ring out from Steelhammer. The two colonels charged with parts of their units, leaving the rest for reinforcements and security, and a gun battle began between the unit and the Apaches on the mountainside. The two commanders faced a rough challenge, as the fleeing Apaches (or at least most of them) found good shooting positions among the rocks. Some were still moving higher, so the cavalry troops poured more fire in on them.

The two commanders sent couriers to each other as they took up parallel positions near the base of the mountain. Hatch, the ranking officer, would be in charge. Neither one knew the whereabouts of Colt and his scouts, but both were concerned about their getting attacked without warning by the large fleeing force.

Hatch had Courier's men lay down a heavy volume of fire from prone positions, with each trooper stacking a few rocks in front of himself for protection. While that kept the Apaches' heads down, his men would try to move forward, closer to the base of the mountain. They would then lay down another heavy volume of covering fire while Grierson's troopers charged forward. This leapfrogging tactic, called fire and maneuver, was an effective strategy at times, against an entrenched enemy. In this case, however, Grierson and Hatch's men were sitting ducks, basically out in the open and exposed to rifle and arrow fire from the rocks above. Because of the stretched-out line of entrenched Apaches and the rocks, a flanking movement would be impossible.

The two officers rode behind their line and met together to discuss strategy.

"Do have any idea where Mr. Colt and his scouts ventured?" Hatch asked.

Grierson replied, "No, sir, I just know that when he left out of here this morning, he had that tough Nez Perce buck with him and about ten Navajo scouts. My field first inquired if he had enough manpower, and Mr. Colt just laughed as they pulled out."

Hatch said, "Well, I hope we don't have to end up rescuing the group from trouble, too."

As if a command were given from the mountainside, bullets started pouring down at the two commanders from all over the Apache positions. Both men ducked as they withdrew at a gallop to try to outdistance the range of the renegade guns.

When they halted, Grierson grinned and said, "Guess someone up there said, 'Hey, two chiefs. We kill.' "

Little did he know that that was exactly what had happened; in fact, he was guessing almost the exact words. The heavy fire continued, keeping the men of both commands essentially pinned down behind their little piles of rock.

"I'll send a courier back for our artillery," said Hatch. "We'll blast the buggers out. My lands! Look."

Grierson looked at the mountainside and saw the unmistakable splashy horses of Colt and Man Killer as they rode side by side down the mountain toward the hidden Apache positions. The ten Navajo scouts were spread out in file alongside them. The Apaches had not seen them yet.

Down below the military crest of the ridge, the area below the mountaintop, where one could maneuver without being sky-lined against the blue by observers from below, the scouts stopped. The two commanders watched in amazement as Colt and Man Killer fanned apart and both raised Winchesters, along with the scouts and opened fire simultaneously. They yelled with loud war cries as they rode back and forth across the incline and poured deadly fire into the Apache positions.

Within a minute, Apaches started jumping out of rockpiles and running toward the cavalry units, none firing their rifles. The terrain was so rough and rocky and steep, it was incredible that the horses of Colt and Man Killer could maneuver so. The Navajo mounts were cavalry issue and lagged behind somewhat.

Grierson said, "I do not think, Colonel, that I will ever worry again about Christopher Columbus Colt. It appears he lives up to his reputation."

Hatch said, "How would you like to have a whole troop on a pair of mountains like that?"

Looking at the coup stripes and other war paint on Hawk and War Bonnet, Grierson said, "The decorations and markings of their mounts are not what I would term very uniform in appearance, but that is indeed a pair of mountain horses."

Some of the Ninth and Tenth Cavalry troopers cheered as they saw the Apaches coming toward them, some with their hands up in surrender. Commanders among their ranks got the soldiers up to start assembling the runaway warriors. A group of thirty started to run up the mountain to Man Killer's left and the two field grade officers watched as the young Nez Perce was grabbed off his horse by a pair of stocky Mescaleros who had been hiding in the rocks. Colt charged to his left to save his downed comrade. They saw his right-hand pistol come up and fire as he charged across the hillside, then they saw the big man dive into a group of Apaches who had Man Killer on the ground.

The Navajos kept pushing the remaining Apaches down the hill to the waiting cavalry. However, the thirty who pushed to the side were making their escape, heading for the top of the ridge line.

Hatch and Grierson both watched through their telescopes where Colt and Man Killer had engaged in hand-to-hand combat, but it was a partially obscured mass of hands, arms, and bodies, mainly Apache. At one point, they saw an Apache fly over a boulder, blood clearly streaming from his neck. They at least knew that either Colt or Man Killer was still alive at that point.

After fifteen minutes, the fighting stopped, and the two men watched intently as both Hawk and War Bonnet were summoned, apparently by some command or whistle. The horses trotted over to the bouldered area, and the two scouts leapt into their McClellan saddles. They rode down the long hill amidst the cheers of the black soldiers below.

Colt gave Man Killer some direction, and the younger scout rode over to the group of surrendering Apaches and supervised the Navajo scouts as they helped organize the prisoners, who were being disarmed. Colt cantered his big pinto up to the two field grade officers, nodding at both, a suppressed grin on his rugged face. They both noted that his gold-striped trousers were covered with blood, and Colt was sporting a badly swelling left eye. It was, in fact, almost swollen shut.

Hatch said, "Mr. Colt, are you okay? Your leg is bleeding badly and your eye."

Colt said, "Apache blood, Colonel. Just need to change my drawers."

He touched his swollen eye gingerly and went on,

"The eye'll be black, but it's not the first one. I need to learn to block knees with my arms instead of my face."

Grierson laughed, "I would say so, sir."

Colt went on, "Counted a total of fourteen Apache dead, gentlemen. Don't know how many wounded. About thirty more made good their escape. I can take some scouts and pick up their trail."

Hatch said, "No, Mr. Colt. You and your scouts did a wonderful job, a lot more than you're being paid to do. You stopped most of them from leaving and joining Victorio. That's enough."

Colt said, "Well, the thirty that got away may decide to come back. Hard to say. They also might join Geronimo."

Hatch said, "Yes, there was a bit of discussion about using you against Geronimo, but we insisted that we have you head our scouts against Victorio. Colt, we have to catch this scoundrel. He has killed well over a hundred so far, and he attacks Americans almost daily."

Chris said, "I agree with you, Colonel, but we have to do more than catch Victorio."

Grierson said, "Damned right, Mr. Colt. Damned right."

Hatch said, "Let's march the rest of these Mescaleros to the agency corral and place them under guard there. It will be easier to keep an eye on them."

"Colonel," said Grierson, "why don't I head off in

the direction that thirty took and see if I can round up them or any others?"

Hatch said, "Good idea. The Guadalupe and Sacramento mountains are still full of Mescaleros, I would wager."

"Mr. Colt," said Grierson, "I know that Colonel Hatch will order you to see the regimental surgeon, and you'll refuse. You're the type. Will you lead my command while we search for hostiles?"

Hatch interrupted, "No, Colonel, he cannot. Mr. Colt is going to stay with the main column. I need him more here for now."

Colt said, "You said I'm the type, Colonel Grierson. Now what type is that?"

Grierson said, "Hero."

Chris blushed and started making himself a smoke. He lit up and looked off at the mountains.

Grierson said, "How about that outstanding young man of yours? May I use Man Killer?"

Chris said, "Sure can. He'll do a good job for you."

Grierson said, "I know, and he can't be more than seventeen, eighteen years. Amazing young red man."

Colt was amused, as Man Killer wasn't even that old. He was, however, mature and tough well beyond his years. Part of that was because of his companionship with Colt and Chief Joseph, and part of it was simply because he took the bull by the horns growing up.

Chris rode to the agency corral with the colonels and summoned Man Killer.

The two smoked while they watched the proud Apaches under guard.

"Sad, isn't it?" Chris said.

Man Killer said, "You can put an eagle in a cage, and it is still an eagle."

"True. Besides, they'll only be in the corral for a few hours."

Man Killer added, "It is a constant thing, what has happened to all Indian Nations. I do not get used to it, and there is always one part of my heart that is sad and heavy."

Chris teased, "Even when you're around pretty blond girls named Jennifer."

Man Killer blushed and looked away, grinning.

Colt said, "Lieutenant Colonel Grierson requested that you be his chief of scouts while he goes out and looks for more Mescaleros in the Guadalupe and Sacramento mountains. Interested?"

Man Killer's shoulders went back perceptibly.

He said, "Of course."

Colt said, "Then get out of here, Young Brother, and report to him."

Chris proudly watched his young colleague ride away and speak to the Tenth Cavalry commander. Colt wondered how Shirley was doing at the ranch, and how she was getting along with his newly discovered half brother.

*   *   *

Joshua Colt had handled the Sawyer fellow very firmly and quickly, but he wondered if he would have any other challenges.

The group of men riding up the road toward the ranch house looked rough, but this was a very rough country.

Shirley was inside the house making pies. They were delivered to the restaurants and sold in Westcliffe every day, as many as she could make. People in Wet Mountain Valley had really come to love her cooking. The Westcliffe banker had even offered to back her in a restaurant, but he obviously hadn't seen her account at Fremont County Bank down in Canon City. Along with Chris's money, the Colts were actually fortunate enough to be able to do simply the work that they enjoyed.

The auburn-haired beauty had a tear running down her cheek as she reread the latest telegram sent to her by Chris. She missed him very much, but she didn't really worry about his getting killed. He was the best there was, and Shirley knew that Chris could find and probably kill Victorio, if anyone could. He had told her by wire that he was not being used for Geronimo; he had heard that Tom Horn was being brought in as chief of scouts in that campaign.

Tom Horn had been cattle detective, rodeo champion, gunslinger, lawman, scout, and chief of scouts. He was a tough man. He had even been brought in nearby to help arrest and catch train robbers and cattle rustlers Tom and Streeter McCoy, who had a ranch north of nearby Cotopaxi down on the Arkansas River. Cotopaxi, named for a mountain in South America, was located on the river just a little over ten miles from Coyote Run, the Colts' ranch. In fact, Joshua had gone there twice to fish for trout when he had a little free time.

Joshua watched the approaching group of men. They rode only about a hundred yards down the road, however, and suddenly halted. Joshua made a mental note that one of the horses looked like a very prancy black Spanish Barb, another was a tall chestnut thoroughbred, two were solid buckskins, one a standard honey-colored dun buckskin, while the other was bleached out by the sun and looked almost like a white horse with black stockings, mane, and tail. At this distance, Joshua couldn't make out the faces of the men involved, but he was a cattleman and could definitely identify horses at a distance.

He wished Chris was there, but he wasn't, so Joshua would handle whatever was going to happen. He had been handling problems most of his life, including plenty of life and death situations, and he had never turned tail yet. Somehow, some way, he decided, he would protect Shirley Colt and Coyote Run. It was part his, just about the first substantial thing he'd ever been a part of. He had just met his half brother some weeks earlier, but it was as if they had always been there. They were different colors and from different worlds, but Chris had said the same blood ran in their veins, and that meant something. It meant that the large group of men, maybe twenty of them, were up to no good, and it meant that they were not going to run roughshod over that ranch, unless it was over Joshua Colt's body.

Little did Joshua know that that was exactly the way those twenty men wanted it to be—over his dead body. They withdrew and galloped back the way they came, but hitting the main road, they continued east into the trees.

Joshua ran into the main house and went straightaway to the gun cabinet that Shirley had purchased to surprise Chris upon his return.

"I saw them, Josh," she said very calmly. "What do you want me to do?"

"I want you to hide in the fruit cellar," Joshua said, getting more weapons and bullets from the well-stocked hand-carved cabinet.

Shirley said, "Absolutely not. This is also part my ranch, and it is part my responsibility to protect it. That is non-negotiable, Joshua."

He had learned enough about his tough-minded sister-in-law over the past few weeks to know that what she had just said was a blood oath.

"Very well, Shirl," he said. "I want you to stay in the house with a rifle when they come. Just protect yourself and stay in here. I cannot worry about you coming out and getting where you shouldn't be. I do not know who they are or what they want, but I have a bad feeling."

"Where are Tex and Muley?" she asked.

"Rounding up some of our strays that wandered all the way down to Long Gulch and have been watering in the Arkansas. They could get back tonight—or it might be another day or two."

"Can I ride for the sheriff?"

Joshua said, "Nope. They are watching and will see anyone leaving or coming. It's twenty miles round trip anyway. You'd never make it there and back. Especially in your condition."

Shirley tossed her shoulders back and walked to the gun cabinet, extracting a Winchester .45-caliber carbine. She cocked it, jacking a round into the chamber, then lightly squeezed the trigger while easing the hammer forward.

She said, "Very well, Josh. It is just you and me. It might not be the way we like it, but it will have to do. You'll handle whatever happens, and I will be here to back you all the way."

Shirley went to the cupboard and got down a bottle of whiskey and strips of clean white cloth. She laid them out on the dining table.

Joshua said, "What's that for?"

She said matter-of-factly, "Tending to bullet wounds quickly."

Josh grinned. "You know what? I would darned sure rather have you here with me in a shooting situation than plenty of men I know."

She smiled and walked to the stove, getting two cups off the table and pouring coffee for herself and Joshua.

He said, "Thanks, Shirl. I could use a cup, but then I have to get back out to my chores. We have a lot of work that needs to be done, and I wanted to finish repairing our calf-branding chute today."

"What about all those men?" she said.

"They can sit out there and rot, or do what they're going to do. We'll have to deal with whatever they throw at us. I have a ranch to run and the hell with them."

"Sounds like something Chris would say," she said.

He sipped his coffee and thought again how comforting it would be to have Chris there. He had become a legend stacking himself up against odds like twenty men against one.

During the rest of the afternoon, Joshua kept a rifle and a greener close by. He had his .45 Peacemaker in the worn holster, along with a .44 Russian belly gun, and he had shoved a pair of .36 Navys in the top of his boots.

Joshua had been a man not a stranger to gun trouble from time to time, and he just sensed that these men were not on a hunting expedition. Shirley had been around, too, and she sensed the same thing.

She made Joshua an early supper and made sure it was thick steak, baked potatoes with butter, home-made bread, corn and peas, and hot apple pie. If it was going to be their last meal, she decided, it would be a darned good one. Shirley also felt better having him in the house, instead of wandering around the ranch grounds, where she wasn't sure he was maintaining a close vigilance. He certainly had, however, all afternoon.

After dinner, Joshua rose and walked over to a humidor where Colt's cigars were kept. He pulled one out, bit the end off and spit it in the fireplace, and lit it with a hot ember. He sat back down at the table and enjoyed the cigar and accepted another cup of coffee from Shirley.

"I sure want to thank you," he said. "It was a wonderful meal."

Shirley grinned. "I figured if we were going to eat our last meal, it better be a good one."

Joshua walked to the door and turned, his hand on the knob. "Don't you worry. We will eat plenty more meals, and so will my little nephew or niece. I'll be outside, close by. I can do more good there. With that many, I have to be able to move around. Stay inside, no matter what happens. I'm sure that they'll be coming after dark."

Joshua walked back to the humidor and grabbed another cigar, winking at his sister-in-law on his way back out the door.

It was close to midnight when he heard the horses' hooves coming down the road at a gallop. Next he saw the lights; they were actually torches.

And next he saw the men. Joshua's worst fears had come true. They all wore white robes, with large white cone-shaped, pointed-top caps with eyeholes. Each man had a torch, a rifle in his scabbard, and one or two short guns on his hips. Several had crosses sewn on their white robes.

They pulled up in front of the ranch house.

One rode forward and yelled, "Mrs. Colt! We know you're in there with that nigger boy! We won't harm you! Just send him out!"

Joshua watched from the shadows by the barn and moaned when the door of the house opened and Shirley walked outside, her teeth clenched and her hands wrapped around a Colt revolving twelve-gauge shotgun.

Joshua whispered to himself, "Womenfolk!"

Shirley said, "I wonder how many of those saddles I can empty with this shotgun, before it's totally empty. I've fired at men before, and I used to take plenty of pheasants, grouse, and quail back in Dakota Territory! You cowardly masked felons are on my land. Get off now!"

One man rode forward with a noose and a coiled lasso in his hand. Shirley pointed the shotgun and squeezed the trigger. The man flew backward off his horse and landed on a bush behind the horse. The white robe was covered with red, except for the large double-aught buckshot pattern of holes through it and the chest.

"Lady, you just bought yerself a heap a trouble," the first hooded man said.

Joshua stepped out of the shadows, a Winchester leveled at the man's stomach.

"There ya are, boy," the man said. "She kick ya outta the big house?"

Boom!

The bullet from Joshua's Winchester took the man full in the breastbone, and he somersaulted backward over his horse's rump. The horse, which was the bleached-out buckskin, bolted, and his right hind hoof caught the dead man in the middle of the face before he hit the ground. This unnerved the other Klansmen even more, especially the snapping sound when the dead man's neck broke.

Joshua quickly cocked the rifle and swung from one man to the next.

Joshua said, "Shirley, get inside, now!"

Another masked man spoke, "Nigger, Canon City is the headquarters for the Klan in the whole Colorado/New Mexico territory. You came to the wrong place to try and act uppity."

Shirley heard this as she closed the door, and she ran to the gun rack, grabbing a rifle. It would be more effective from that distance. The tone in Joshua's voice had told her not to argue, and she felt guilty. By not listening, she had probably endangered him even more, as he had jumped out to protect him.

She yelled through the gun slit in the window,

"This is my ranch and Joshua's, my husband's brother. My husband is Chris Colt, and when he finds out what you cowards are up to, they will use your sheets to cover your dead bodies instead of your cowardly faces!"

"How can you be Colt's brother?" one Klansman asked.

Joshua said, "Different mothers, but that's none of your damned business anyway. I am not the gunman my brother is, but I can shoot. I am also not afraid to die to protect this land, and I wonder how many bullets it'll take to put me down, and how many saddles I can empty before I die. Now, boys, I can't see your faces, but I already got your horses memorized, so when I see you around and recognize each horse, we'll have a one-to-one discussion. Now, whenever you bushwhackers see me, you can call me Joshua, Josh, or Mr. Colt, but don't ever call me nigger again. Now, I said I'm willing to die to protect this land. The question is, Are you willing to die to try and run me off it? You forked this horse. Who's willing to ride it?"

The riders slowly moved closer. A very large shape came out of the trees and up to the sorrel horse of the lead man. The figure suddenly swung a powerful roundhouse hook punch that struck the red horse below the right ear. The animal's knees wobbled and he fell unconscious, spilling his rider on the ground. The giant man was Muley Hawkins, and he punched the horse's rider and knocked him out, too, then drew his six-shooter.

Tex Westchester stepped out from the shadows and lit a cigarette he had rolled. He had a six-shooter in his hand, too, and he drew a belly gun after he lit the cigarette.

The wrinkled old puncher said, "Now, I recollect one time down past the Llano Estacado, the Staked Plains, I seen this old Comanche who took twelve bullet holes in him, and still waded into a mess of cowpunchers. One of 'em finally drilled him twixt his portholes, but, man, he was a fighter. Still git me an itch when it's fixin to rain, from one a his arrows. He figgered we was invadin his land, he did. That's how come he fought so durned hard, died hard, too. Me and Muley ride for the brand, fellers. Ya know what thet means. Means we'll go down shootin fer it, too. Now, Joshua Colt here is our boss, and we respect the man, and you will, too. You'll also respect Mrs. Colt on account a she's a high-class lady and his kin. You probably figgered ya was gonna run off some runaway slave or somethin, so we'll chalk this one time off to stupidity. Next time, though, come a gunnin, cause we'll shoot ya on sight, and my boss don't like seein no burning crosses or white robes with hoods. We won't see 'em no more, will we, boys?"

Nobody moved. They just looked at each other.

Tex fired both guns and another man fell from the saddle. The hood flew off another.

Tex said, "Shootin business is serious business. Let's git to it or ride."

Joshua said, "In fact, ride before I get to three—or die. One, two—"

The Klansmen, following the lead of several in the back, spurred their horses and dropped the torches, fleeing into the night.

Shirley ran out of the house and up to the three men.

She asked, "Will they be back?"

Joshua said, "Not a chance. They learned, and the word will get around. Took you two long enough."

Tex, still smoking, said, "We wasn't comin. We was down there dippin our feet in the Arkansas, and old Muley takes out his fryin pan. He heats up some grease, then tells me we ain't got no vittles. Well, says I, yer big enough, Muley. Tell them durn trout to jump in the pan. He does, and the next thing ya know it was rainin fish on us. We decided ta jest build us a cabin there and spend the rest a our days there. Then, we heerd you was havin a party and dint give us no invite. Muley finally reckoned it might be a necktie party, so we come a-runnin to see ya git yer comeuppance, Boss."

Muley said, "Aw, Tex, quit funnin all the time. Glad yer okay, Boss."

"Thanks," Joshua said.

"Thank you very much," Shirley added. "Let's go in and have some pie."

She wondered how Chris would have handled that if he were home.

Over pie and coffee, Muley said, "Do ya think they'll come back?"

Tex said, "Heck, no, they won't. They learnt who was they messin with and what was a-waitin them if they wanted to come here and start trouble."

Joshua said, "This is Chris and Shirley's home, and it's mine. It is also your home, Muley, Tex. There will always be others who will try to take it away, because that is the nature of man. We will always protect it, though. No matter where you live, if you have a good place and are a good person, there will be those who want to take it from you."

Tex started chuckling, little pieces of crust dropping out of the corners of his mouth.

Shirley said, "Whatever are you laughing at, Tex?"

He wiped his mouth on his right sleeve. "I was jest thinkin what woulda happened if yer ol' man was here tonight. Hee, hee. Them sheets those boys was wearin coulda been used to set over all our cattle as a pattern ta paint pokey dots on em."

Muley laughed with a deep rumble and said, "Yeah, and those hoods could have been turned upside down, and you could use them to sift flour."

Everyone started laughing and laughed even harder, because it was unusual for a joke to come out of Muley.

Shirley said, "In one sense, I'm glad Chris wasn't

here tonight. I'm sure he has his hands full right now."

Chris Colt said, "Hold the torch closer, Corporal."

He held the Apache baby's rear end in his hands and attempted to turn it around in the mother's womb. She had been in tremendous pain in breech labor when the cavalry came upon her and captured her and her daughter, where they had been abandoned by Victorio's band. The woman had not let out so much as a whimper, though.

Chris got the baby turned and felt to make sure the umbilical cord was not wrapped around its neck. Several soldiers stood guard and watched with interest, as the delicate medical procedure was being performed at the base of a small hill in New Mexican desert at about ten o'clock in the evening. Chris Colt felt very good about the buffalo soldiers he was with. Because of their life as Negroes in America, they seemed more sensitive to the poor woman's plight than other cavalry troops he had worked with. Colt thought about white soldiers and the comments they would have been making. Some would even have insisted on killing the woman and children.

Victorio had moved into the Mogollon Mountains in the southwestern part of New Mexico and was still on a killing spree. He and his band killed miners, sheepherders, and settlers with reckless abandon. No white person that crossed Victorio's path was released from a death sentence.

Captain Cooney, commander of Company A, Ninth Cavalry, had been hot on Victorio's trail. He sat his bay gelding while several troopers went on a scout down below at the hand-dug mine. The horse pranced nervously while the company dismounted and the commander watched their activities. The patrol down below dismounted and crouched over something behind a creosote brush. One of the privates turned and gave a hand signal to the company commander.

The captain hollered, "Sergeant Kelly, mount up and move them down."

A large tan-skinned sergeant stood and hollered at the other soldiers, "Prepare to mount! Mount! Column of twos! Company ho-o-o!"

The company rode along the cliffside and headed down the ridge running off to the west. Within thirty minutes, they were down below. They trotted over to the mine and dismounted. Captain Cooney rode over to the patrol behind the mesquite brush. There he saw a scalped miner lying face down in a coagulated pool of blood, three arrows in his back.

One of the privates in the patrol said, "Po' miner, got hisself kilt, suh."

He rolled the dead man over with his foot and Captain Cooney stared at him, a blank look on his face. He dismounted, walked slowly to his first sergeant's horse, and took a small shovel from the side of the saddle. He walked back to the miner and started digging a grave next to him. It looked to the men like their commander had tears running down his cheeks.

The trooper said, "Wondah what da po' man's name was, suh?"

Captain Cooney kept digging and didn't look up, saying sadly, "He is James C. Cooney, my older brother, Trooper."

Colt smiled and passed out cigars as the little Apache boy cried. He lit them for everyone, and even Colonel Hatch enjoyed one, patting Colt on the back.

The commanding officer said, "Congratulations, Doctor Colt. Now that the baby's delivered, the regimental surgeon has arrived with the train. He can take care of her now, and we'll send them back to Ojo Caliente."

Back in Colorado, Shirley finished washing the coffee cups and pie dishes and started to get ready for bed, wondering about Chris. She felt a stirring in her lower abdomen, and she placed her left hand on it, a warm smile on her face.

Shirley said to herself, "Don't worry, baby. Your daddy will be home someday, and won't he be surprised when he learns about you?"

Chris lifted the Apache baby up and held him to the sky. A cigar stuck out of his mouth, and he clamped down on it with his teeth. He purposely puffed and blew smoke as he turned around facing each of the four points of the compass. Completing his expedient and made-up birthing ceremony, the chief of scouts gently handed the baby back to his proud mother. She looked up at Colt with a look of genuine warmth and sincerity. Indians did not say "thank you." Her look was enough for Colt anyway, and he thought of his wife whom he missed so much. He could not wait until they had their first baby.

Major Albert Morrow had killed some of Victorio's people in skirmishes in Alamo Canon and Dog Canon. He then pursued the Mimbres leader through White Sands and by San Nicolas Spring and into the San Andres Mountains. They finally spotted Victorio near San Augustin Spring, and Morrow started chasing the Apache band. By this time, all the horses of the battalion were beyond exhaustion and many died in the extreme heat. Morrow had to give up the chase and head back toward Ojo Caliente.

It was after that when Chris Colt found the trail of Victorio, and he led Hatch, with the battalion led by Captain Ambrose Hooker. Victorio headed due west and they followed him into Arizona. That was where they captured—or found—the Mescalero woman in labor. Chris Colt always tried to think one step ahead of whatever quarry he was following, but he admired Victorio because the leader mixed up his tactics. It was almost impossible to second-guess him.

They followed his trail well into eastern Arizona, until Colt noticed that suddenly a lot fewer Apaches were headed toward the Warm Springs agency. He also noticed that the hoofprints of the Apache ponies were not as deep in the soil. Victorio had sent women and children on toward the Warm Springs area, and he himself had apparently doubled back. Chris Colt had been telling Hatch for some time that he felt that Victorio was working his way toward Texas, and Grierson had expressed the same feeling. It just didn't make sense for Victorio to head into Arizona, where he would not be able to use the international border to stop the American troops and where he would have less cover with the terrain. Colt explained about the tracks and convinced Hatch that they had to head back into New Mexico.

They turned back immediately, and Colt sent his scouts out in several patrols in front of the column. They worked far ahead of the command, tracking back and forth in giant fan patterns, trying to pick up Victorio's trail. Staying near the Mogollons, which the Spaniards named the Sierra de Mimbres, named for his own tribe, Victorio headed toward old Fort Tularosa, which was located two days' ride northwest of Ojo Caliente.

Chris Colt and Captain H. K. Parker, who was military officer-in-charge of the scouts, were summoned by Hatch, and they reported to the commander. Chris admired the old man, because he could tell that the hard, forced marching and lack of water were taking their toll. Hatch was not a young man, and even the hardiest of the young troopers were suffering mightily.

The colonel said, "Gentlemen, our horses are just about used up in this godforsaken country with little water and no graze. I'm surprised that the mounts have not taken up eating sand and rocks. The scouts and your animals seem to be faring better and have a better chance at it. Leave the column and find Victorio. Once you discover him, Captain, use your brains as to what to do next. Listen to Mr. Colt. He is the one man in this country who has the knowledge to corner Victorio, that sly devil, and he has not steered me wrong so far."

Colt interrupted, "Colonel Hatch, I appreciate the vote of confidence, but if you do believe what you just said about me, please heed my advice about simply manning the water holes and mountain passes with troops?"

Hatch replied, "Colt, I have, and I believe we are going to take your advice, but for now, find and contain that red son of a . . . well, just find Victorio. I am sending patrols to several areas where you thought he might head, Mr. Colt. Someone will find him. I will take most of the command to Ojo Caliente to resupply and remount the troops. Good luck, gentlemen."

Parker, Colt, and the scout patrol were ready to go within ten minutes. They set off at once.

Sergeant George Jordan looked at the pocket watch he proudly carried that was given him by his previous company commander. Even those white officers serving with the buffalo soldiers who were prejudiced came to respect the courage, discipline, and daring of the black cavalry troopers. That was the case with the captain who had given the sergeant the timepiece. He had dreaded his assignment with the Ninth at first. He was like Custer, who had been told that he would command the Ninth and he abhorred the idea and talked Sheridan into letting him go to the Seventh Cavalry instead. But the captain, after serving with the black soldiers for a while and observing their courage and professionalism, came to love them and respect them.

It was almost ten o'clock at night, and Sergeant Jordan wondered where Victorio was. He wanted to know if the man was close or maybe down in Mexico. Like all the other frustrated soldiers in the Ninth and Tenth, he wanted a shot at that elusive Apache, just one. It was May 13.

One of the privates in Jordan's patrol hollered, "Hey, Sarge, rider comin' in! His horse is really used up, too!"

The man was a little taken aback as he jumped off his horse and saw an entire patrol of U.S. soldiers who were all black. Sergeant Jordan stood out, however, among the twenty-five soldiers from K

Company and the personnel manning the Barlow and Sanders stagecoach station. He looked like someone in charge, so the short white man ran up to him.

"You a sergeant?" the man said.

Jordan grinned and looked down at the three very large V-shaped stripes on each sleeve of his blue tunic. Then, realizing his military obligation to protect civilians, Jordan said, "Yes, sir. You okay?"

The breathless, exhausted man said, "Sergeant, you've got to come quickly! Victorio and a bunch of Apaches was getting ready to attack Old Fort Tularosa when I left. I'll bet everyone is dead by now."

"Detachment, K Company! Mount up! We move out in five minutes!" Jordan yelled without hesitation. "We've found that son of a buck, and we'll give him the what for!"

Within three minutes, the twenty-five troopers were mounted and headed toward Old Fort Tularosa, normally a two-day ride away. Jordan headed them out in a column of two's at a fast trot, alternating with what the cavalry called a "hand lope," which was simply a gallop, or fast canter. Most of the time, however, Jordan held them at a trot and the tough Army remounts held up, arriving at Old Fort Tularosa by morning.

The sergeant figured he should get there to save the people at the settlement. The horses could rest up while he and his patrol defended the town. He rode around at a rapid pace, being told by one person after another about sightings or incidents involving the Apaches. Jordan had his troopers round up every wagon, buggy, buckboard, water trough, and feed bag they could find. They started constructing an expedient fortress around the settlement. He then stationed his men and several civilian volunteers at every point he could think of where Victorio's men might breach their security. Jordan never rested, never ate—he was so dedicated to the task of saving all the white and Mexican citizens in Old Fort Tularosa.

Several times smokes were seen, and twice Apache signal mirrors were also spotted by people in the town. They continued to prepare for the inevitable attack.

At dusk it came. Victorio led a large group of Apache warriors directly at the barriers constructed on the main road into the settlement. In the meantime, two groups of Apaches attacked two other points. Dodging bullets and arrows, Sergeant Jordan dashed back and forth to the three points of attack and directed fire against the Apaches. His display of courage steeled the defenders so much to their task that they all fought courageously and viciously.

Jordan ran his horse to the main point of attack and spotted Victorio himself leading his fighters.

"Boys," he hollered, "there's the old man himself! I'm gonna shoot that son of a bitch, so I can rest!"

Sergeant Jordan ran his lathered horse at the Apaches, and jumped it over a buggy, followed by several troopers firing at the Apaches, and more specifically Victorio. Unnerved by this bravado and Jordan's bloodcurdling war cries, the Mimbres and Mescaleros retreated into the rocks.

In the meantime, Colt had picked up the trail of Victorio and was leading his men toward the town, spurred on by the smoke signals seen earlier.

Half an hour later, Victorio attacked again, this time an all-out frontal attack on the main road. Again Jordan rode back and forth, braving the withering hostile fire, and yelled encouragement to the vastly outnumbered buffalo soldiers and civilian volunteers. Their volume of fire was heavy, and Jordan got them to yell at the Apaches just to unnerve them even more. The Apaches started withdrawing, and the buffalo soldiers—with Jordan again in the lead—left their secure positions and pursued the renegades into the darkness.

The Apaches met at a prearranged rendezvous point outside the town. Victorio addressed them in their native tongue. "We will leave. These buffalo soldiers want to protect these wooden wickiups more than we want to take them. The one with the stripes on his arms, their leader, is a great one. That black man could have been Apache. He has saved his village. We go."

That was it. The Apaches, and many other Indian nations, did not consider it cowardice to give up on an objective in the midst of a battle. It was common sense. They were not like the *wasicun*, the white man. Each nation or tribe within each nation had only a limited number of men. Although there were thousands of red men, each belonged to a certain nation and, with few exceptions, once the men from that nation were gone, that was it. Some close nations, such as the Lakotah, Cheyenne, and Arapaho, might do some cross-over courting and marrying, but most Indians married only within their own nation, or even tribe within the nation, or band within the tribe. In short, the band of Victorio, or any other group of Indians, could not afford to commit the lives of vast numbers of warriors just to take an objective or win a battle. If they were losing or overwhelmed in battle, they would simply retreat and look for a simpler target. Ego did not get involved.

Jordan and the few men with him wearily rode back into the settlement amid the cheers of his own men and the townspeople. One of Colt's scouts came into the town during the night and got the news of the attack and the heroism of the soldiers from two of the sentries, while the rest of the exhausted soldiers slept. He carried the news straightaway to Colt and Parker.

"What do you think, Mr. Colt?" Captain Parker asked.

"I think, Captain, since you're not some old field grade officer, that I'd rather have you call me Chris or Colt."

The captain offered Colt some coffee to drink with his jerky.

Chris sipped the brew, which wasn't strong enough to satisfy him, and added, "I think we ought to keep after Victorio. Hound him and try to keep him from water. At least we might keep him from attacking any more settlements, ranches, or mines that way."

Parker had already deferred to Chris and just simply rode along with him. The scouts were all loyal to Colt anyway and would listen only to the legendary chief of scouts. And Parker realized he was working with the best there was. If he let Colt lead and simply went along for the ride, he would learn something, and it would make him look good in the reports.

Colt and the scouts pushed on through the night, hot on Victorio's heels. They wouldn't let the weary Apaches rest. They finally decided to take a break in the heat of midday in a rock outcropping, and most of the scouts were asleep as soon as their eyes closed.

Chris Colt unsaddled to give War Bonnet a break, too. Using the saddle as a pillow, he, too, fell immediately asleep. Chris, however, like many warrior leaders, had a sixth sense when something was wrong. His eyes opened as mere slits, then opened wider. Right away he saw a puff of smoke going up into the sky. It was coming from the edge of his camp.

Colt took his moccasins out of his saddlebags and slipped off his boots and spurs. Tapping Parker with the end of his Cheyenne bow as he crawled by, he crept toward the boulder that blocked the signal fire. Holding his rifle and having the sense to stay put, Parker sat up and waited to back Colt if need be. He could not believe how quietly the tall, muscular scout moved. There was not a noise at all. He couldn't even hear clothing rustle. Several of the Apache and Navajo scouts sensed something and awakened, too, watching Chris with interest. Each man held his rifle at the ready.

Colt crept up over the boulder on his belly and slipped headfirst off the other side. Captain Parker saw only his moccasined feet as he dropped over to the unseen far side of the rock. There was the sound of a scuffle, and a minute later one of the Apache scouts walked around the boulder with Chris following, arrow nocked on the bowstring. The traitor scout held his hands high. Colt nodded, and another scout rushed around the boulder and extinguished the signal fire.

The treasonous scout turned and faced Chris with the others watching.

Colt said, "You speak the tongue of the white man?"

The scout nodded.

Colt said, "You are of Victorio's band."

The scout confirmed this observation with another nod.

Parker said, "Oh, no, we'll have to send two men back with him so he can be court-martialed."

Colt said, "Captain, you said you had no problem with me being in charge, and these men know that we have to use their own laws out here to govern us."

The traitor suddenly said, "Me Christian. Learn at mission school."

Colt said, "You can pray."

The scout grinned and said, "This is good."

He bowed his head and folded his hands, praying, then stood and threw his shoulders back, sticking his chin out, proudly.

Captain Parker just wisely kept his mouth shut and watched.

Colt said, "You know the law?"

The scout nodded, raised his arms and face skyward, looking toward heaven, and chanted something the captain couldn't understand.

Colt raised his bow, and a knife flew forward from one of the older scouts. The man knew that Colt had to kill the traitor, but he also knew that white justice might deal with this differently than the Apaches would. His knife flipped over and buried itself into the chest of the man who had committed treason. The guilty brave looked down at the blade sticking into the left side of his chest and grabbed the handle, but he again raised his face skyward and yelled something triumphantly. He fell onto both knees, but still faced up. As the blood drained from his chest and mouth, he slowly folded forward and died with his head bowed, as if in prayer, sitting on his folded legs. He didn't even fall over. The brave that threw the knife got a "Thank you" nod from Colt, then walked over and yanked his knife from the dead Apache's chest, wiping the blood on the corpse's copper-colored shoulder.

"Glad I didn't have to do that," Chris said to the captain.

Parker said, "But you would have?"

Colt said, "No choice."

"You're a very hard man, Colt."

"This is a very hard country, Captain."

"I've heard that," the officer responded.

Colt replied, "Many times—and you'll keep hearing it until this land is tamed."

When Hatch came into Old Fort Tularosa, one and all told him about the extraordinary courage and leadership of Sergeant George Jordan. The commander took a number of reports on the incident and set out a message by courier to the Department of the Missouri, recommending the Negro noncommissioned officer for the Congressional Medal of Honor, the nation's highest award for bravery. Jordan would end up receiving the medal.

Morrow and Hatch both made Ojo Caliente within twenty-four hours of each other, and both columns were in rough shape, very rough shape. In fact, in the pursuit of the Apache chief and his people the cavalry lost a lot of horses from exhaustion and thirst.

Two days later, Colt located Victorio's camp at

the head of the Palomas River. None of Victorio's outriders had picked up sight of Colt's scouts, so Parker sent one volunteer to carry the message to Hatch that they would sneak in on Victorio's camp and try to engage and hold him at daybreak.

They made cold camp with no fire, and Chris said to the captain, "I'm going to try something tonight that might get me killed, but if it works, it is something that will make Victorio think about us until he is killed. I may get close enough to kill him, but I'm not going to unless I have to. I want to send a message to all his followers, too. It may help convince them to think about returning to their reservations."

"What the hell you going to try, Colt?" Parker said.

"I'll let you know if I don't get killed."

Chris took off his buckskin war shirt and trousers. He stripped down until he was totally naked, in fact, then donned a Cheyenne breechcloth, and his big Bowie knife, along with his soft-soled Lakotah moccasins. He smiled at the assembled scouts, winked at the cavalry officer, then disappeared into the darkness of the night.

Victorio's camp was on the western side of the river. Colt went up the eastern bank, slowly making his way through the darkness. The Apaches had camped in a grove of cottonwoods by the river and had made several small fires, hidden by piles of rocks around them. Colt, however, could find them because of the glow they made on the leaves of the cottonwoods. One hundred yards from the encampment, he slipped into the river and started swimming upstream. He swam underwater and enjoyed the coolness of the liquid. The current wasn't too bad here, so Colt wasn't very tired when he came parallel with the camp.

Barely sticking his head out of the water, he located each guard and took his time identifying which ones were sleeping, dozing, and alert. The only alert one was actually the farthest away from the center of the camp. He was guarding the tethered horses.

Colt was grateful for the recent gully washers in those area, for they had left the water level in this river much higher than normal. He stayed in the water until he had identified all the sleeping figures and guessed the likely location of Victorio.

One sentry sat facing the small campfire with his back to the river, not really expecting the enemy to come from that direction. Colt slipped out of the water on his belly and crawled forward toward the unsuspecting guard. His right leg was cocked forward, and his right hand was reaching out. Colt moved two small twigs and a pebble with his left hand. He carefully inspected the ground in front of and around him to ensure there was nothing that could make any noise. He pulled with his right hand and pushed with the ball of his right foot and moved forward again, slowly, ever so slowly, resembling a large lizard in the moonlight.

This continued for a half an hour as he covered the twenty yards between the river's edge and the lookout. It took another five minutes for Colt to carefully maneuver into a crouching position with his Bowie knife out. Then he moved forward like a flash, his left hand wrapping across the mouth of the guard. His right hand plunged the big knife into the guard's right kidney from the rear.

The brave felt the excruciating pain in his kidney, and it literally paralyzed him. He couldn't cry out, he couldn't even breathe, it was so bad. Any slight movement he tried to make brought even more pain. He was a young warrior, still in his teens, but he had a number of kills to his credit. His name was Janamata, or Red Buffalo. The brave flashed in his mind to his childhood, then back to the present. He wanted to squirm away from the horrible pain in his back, but he couldn't move at all. Finally, relief, the blade came out of his back, and he took a deep breath. He saw the blade and the hand of Colt out in front of his chest now, but it was too late to react. It was like slow motion as he saw the knife go out in an arc and drive forward at his heart. He saw the blade enter his chest and felt it tear through his flesh. A hand was clamped over his mouth, but it didn't matter. He had been conditioned since childhood never to cry out because of pain. It would only alert the enemy. It felt like a mighty horse was prancing on the center of his chest. His jaw quivered involuntarily, and he felt a very sharp pain running up and down his left arm. His eyes went out of focus, and he felt suddenly very weak. His eyes closed, and he tried to cry out "Usen," the Apache word for God, but nothing worked. His mind went blank. Janamata heard and saw no more.

Colt carefully stood erect and gingerly lifted the 180-pound corpse up and carried it across his shoulders. He walked Indian-style, toe first then heel, among the sleeping warriors. Chris checked each man's face carefully until he found the sleeping figure of Victorio. He was careful not to move too quickly now. Slowly, quietly, the chief of scouts slipped the dead body of the Apache off his back and laid it down next to the sleeping Apache chief. Colt lay down next to the body, just in case someone arose and looked around.

Grinning to himself in the darkness, he carefully drew Victorio's knife from its sheath. He pulled his own Bowie from Janamata's breast and stuck Victorio's knife into it. He then dipped his finger into the blood on the dead brave's chest and wrote the name "Colt" on Victorio's breechcloth.

Chris started to move away from the sleeping chief then, picturing what would go through the famous man's mind when he awakened in the morning. Colt made it about ten feet, and then an Apache woman stood up, not more than seven feet away from him. She looked around in the darkness and yawned, scratching her thighs with both hands.

Colt didn't breathe as she looked in his direction and apparently didn't notice him in the darkness. He could reach out with each hand and each foot and touch Apache braves.

The woman walked to the edge of the river and Colt watched as she pulled her garments out of the way and squatted by the running water. She relieved her bladder, then took a sip of cool water from the river and made her way back to her sleeping spot. Colt watched her as she lay down and closed her eyes. He waited until the rise and fall of her chest became a slow, steady rhythm, and he continued crawling back to the relative safety of the Palomas River.

Colt took one last look around at the other sentries before sliding headfirst into the water. It was easier swimming downstream underwater, and he got out of the water in the same spot.

It was two hours before daybreak when Colt sat by a small fire, hidden in a jumble of rocks, and sipped hot coffee, a blanket wrapped around his shoulders. He briefed Parker and the other scouts about the layout of Victorio's campsite and the rocky hillside that overlooked it. Colt figured that the wily Apache had already prepared sites there in case his camp was attacked.

"We can get within fifty yards of the camp before daybreak," Colt said, drawing a map on the ground, "if we set up on line right here. I can take one man and get their horse herd here and drive them to our line of attack and see if they'll want them bad enough to attack us. That'll also help slow them down so maybe Colonel Hatch can get here in time."

Parker said, "Sounds good to me. Which man you want to help you with the herd?"

Colt pointed at a young Navajo who was very gung ho, always looking for action. The lad had a perpetual smile. The rest mounted horses after striking camp, and Colt led them single file to the camp of Victorio. Leaving one man with their own horses, they moved forward with one Chiricajua scout getting Parker to remove his boots and carry them until they each got into position.

Colt crept up and down the line and warned the scout to take care when they opened fire, as there were women and children in the camp, too. He knew that it wouldn't matter with most of them. An enemy was an enemy. But it did matter with him, so he warned everyone anyway. With that completed, Colt led the young Navajo to a spot where they could stampede the horse herd. They both knelt behind a bush and patiently waited for the sun to rise.

When the sun came up, some of the Apaches in Victorio's camp started to stir. Parker gave the command to open fire, and the scouts opened up with repeating rifles. About ten of Victorio's men fell in the first volley, and more started dropping as the scouts kept up a continuous barrage of heavy fire. Colt and the Navajo ran forward toward the pony herd, yelling and waving the blankets they had carried. The herd started toward the cavalry captain and scouts, and Colt grabbed one pony by the mane and swung up on his back. The young scout followed suit, but an Apache, apparently a sleeping herd guard, previously unseen, came off the ground and yanked the Navajo scout off his pony. Colt's left hand went down and came up in one smooth motion, bucking as he fired once, twice. The first bullet caught the Apache in the rib cage, and the second hit him in the side of the neck. He crashed into a saguaro cactus and fell on the ground.

The Navajo jumped up, smiled at Colt and nodded. Chris dashed his pony over to him and extended his arm down, and the young scout grabbed Colt's forearm with boy hands and swung up behind as the chief of scouts rode by. They took off after the other ponies and pulled alongside a small paint, and the Navajo leapt onto his back, grabbing the rawhide reins from the war bridle.

The two rode quickly toward their compatriots, both men bent low over their mounts with bullets and arrows whistling about their heads. The other scouts and the captain fired over and over again, and Colt saw the band of Victorio's men running toward the rocks as he had predicted, some warriors setting up a covering fire for them. Chris saw many women and children lying dead and bloody on the ground at the campsite. He was sad.

The herd rushed past the scouts and was stopped by a natural rock wall barrier at the cavalry scouts' own picketed horses. The animals ran in a circle and slowly calmed down after much sniffing, snorting, and pawing. Soon the assembled herd was milling around. In all, Colt had made off with seventy-five of Victorio's ponies.

The Navajo waved at his smiling buddies as they made it back to their positions, but Colt slid his little red dun mustang to a stop. He turned, hearing the cries of a young child, and he spotted a young Apache girl crying over the body of her dead mother. She was at the leading edge of the Apache camp and had apparently been deserted inadvertently by the camp defenders.

Parker jumped and hollered, "Colt! No!"

At the same time, Chris Colt kicked the pony hard in the ribs and sent it flying back at the camp of Victorio. Seeing him bearing down on the young girl, all the Apaches figured he was going to strike down such an easy victim, so they directed all their fire at him. Colt lay across the horse's neck and held the reins down along the bottom of the neck. As he approached closer, the fire at him picked up. One bullet grazed the neck of the pony, and it screamed out in pain, but Colt kicked him hard and kept him going.

Reaching the little girl, the chief of scouts was

able to sit up, because the Apaches could not fire at him then for fear of hitting her. He leaned down and scooped her up in his right arm and lifted her onto the horse's withers in front of him. He held the reins in one hand and her in the other and rode straight at the Apache defenders.

Victorio was so amazed by this action that he stood straight up in the rocks and stared. Much fire from the scouts made him duck back down, though.

Colt rode up to the base of the rocks and set the girl down behind a large boulder so she would not be exposed to fire from his own men. Then he wheeled his pony and dashed back toward his line. Halfway there, a few gunshots were fired at him, but they whistled harmlessly by. After he jumped off the pony and dived behind a rock, Winchester in hand, the firing by the Apaches started up again. By that time, about thirty of Victorio's people were dead.

Captain Parker worked his way over to Colt and said, "Too bad we don't give medals to civilians."

Colt replied, "Yes, the next time I get into battle I could just hold it up and all the Indians would raise their hands and surrender."

Parker laughed.

The legendary Chris Colt had pulled off another one of his amazing exploits and lived. He didn't do it for glory. He simply did it because a little girl was in danger and needed to be saved.

The firing kept up for another two hours. Then

Parker again returned to Colt's position and said, "Colt, we have to withdraw."

Chris lit a cigar and handed one to the captain, lighting it, and saying, "Captain, I notice whenever you officers talk about the enemy moving backward you say they're retreating, but when your troops move backward you say you are withdrawing—or a new one I heard is 'disengaging.'"

The officer's face turned bright red.

Colt chuckled loudly and continued, "Why do we have to withdraw?"

"All our men are out of ammunition—or will be in a few minutes."

Colt took a puff and blew the smoke skyward, then said, "You know what? I think we need to disengage and attack while moving backward at a rapid pace."

The captain laughed heartily and slapped his leg, forgetting the bullets flying all around them both. They withdrew.

Major Morrow was well on the way with reinforcements. He met Colt and Parker an hour later, got briefed by them, resupplied them, and set out rapidly after Victorio, who was now hightailing it for the Mexican border.

Colt and Parker returned to Hatch along with the horse herd. They had lost no men in the fight against Victorio.

Morrow kept on at a killing pace for his horses and men, but it paid off. He caught Victorio before the Apaches made it to the border. It was May 30, and Morrow's point engaged Victorio's rear guard. Morrow and the rest of the column came forward and had a running gun battle with the rear elements of the renegades, killing three and wounding many more. The fight continued until the band finally made it to the Rio Grande and splashed across, leaving the frustrated cavalry troopers watching helplessly on the American side.

Morrow was angry, but he made camp nearby and waited. Five days passed and nothing happened. Morrow decided to go back and rejoin Hatch. The next morning, as the troop struck camp and moved out shortly after breakfast a scout rode up to the commander with the report that a small party of Apaches was headed south.

They were at the mouth of a small rocky canyon that opened out into a wider gentle canyon. Morrow quickly spread his men out in two directions in an L-shaped ambush, a common and practical military tactic. The two lines of troopers could catch the enemy in fire from two directions without worrying about hitting each other with crossfire.

There were only ten warriors in the group, but each was leading pack animals loaded with fresh supplies from one of the Indian agencies. The ten rode into the apex of the ambush, and Morrow gave the signal to fire. The troopers opened up, and three of the Apaches were hit simultaneously, falling off their mounts. Two were wounded and took off at a run. One of the three fell from the pony's back, jumped up, his arm bleeding, vaulted back onto his horse's back, and galloped off after the others. The other two on the ground were unmoving.

The Apaches and Navajo scouts went first to the bodies of the two dead warriors, and Morrow was puzzled by their actions. As he approached, he noticed that all the scouts had left the one body and assembled around the body of the other, a younger warrior. Blood had spilled out of several wounds. A great cry rang up among the scouts and Morrow saw that they were elated.

He rode straightaway to the crowd, his adjutant, guidon bearer, and bugler trying to keep up with the determined field grade.

Looking at the scout with the best command of the English language, Morrow said, "Now, see here. What goes on with you boys?"

The Navajo pointed at the dead young warrior and said, "Ma-Jer. Apache brave here. He son of Victorio."

Morrow grinned broadly, saying, "That's Victorio's son?"

The scouts all smiled and shook their heads positively. Several laughed, as did the major.

"Good Lord Almighty!" Morrow enthused. "May the saints be praised. That'll fix that red nigger devil. Pardon the expression, boys."

The last remark was directed at the two black soldiers standing by him.

Very excited, Morrow went on, "I'll just lay a wager that this action will bring the son of a buck running back to American soil, and the old serpent will be hopping mad."

He walked over to the corpse and gave it a kick, saying, "I sincerely wish this was the body of your nearest ancestor. Indeed I do, but you could be the bait, young man. You did it for us maybe. You certainly lacked your father's military prowess, didn't you, boy?"

The scouts watching wondered why this crazy whites-eyes chief was speaking to a corpse, but they had long since decided that white men were all a little daffy anyway.

Lieutenant Colonel Grierson looked at Man Killer studying the rocks and tried to figure out how the Nez Perce scout could possibly ascertain anything about the Apaches from the rocks. Man Killer walked over to the colonel and threw himself up into his McClellan saddle without the aid of a saddle horn. He just leapt onto the tall Appaloosa's back. He was holding something in his left hand and kept looking closely at it.

Grierson said, "Did you learn anything from the rocks, Man Killer?"

The scout said, "Yes. A small group of Apaches came this way not long ago."

"What are you looking at?" Grierson asked.

"Manure," Man Killer said. "The droppings of the Apaches can tell me a story about them."

"Like what?"

Man Killer said, "They can tell me what type of land this band of Apaches likes to stay in. The droppings may have cactus pulp, and I know what type of ground that cactus grows in, or it may have mountain grasses that only grow so high in the mountains, or there may be grain, which tells me that they are getting supplies from a reservation. Do you understand, Colonel?"

Grierson nodded and watched the scout ride ahead, his eyes scouring the ground and horizon.

After they had ridden for another half hour, Man Killer rode back to Grierson.

"Come with me, please?" he said.

The commander rode up ahead of the column, a small detail accompanying him. A half mile ahead of the column, Man Killer raised his hand and quickly dismounted. The colonel could see a fresh pile of horse droppings on the trail. He dismounted and joined the scout kneeling down.

Man Killer said, "We were talking about droppings, Colonel, and I want to show you. See these tracks?"

The commanding officer said, "Yes, I do. They're wearing shoes."

Man Killer said, "Yes, they are military shoes."

The colonel said, "There's no other cavalry unit in this area."

Man Killer said, "These are Mexican cavalry horses."

Grierson was certainly astounded, and his face showed it.

"How in tarnation do you know, young man?"

Man Killer held up one of the fresh droppings. He pointed at whole corn kernels in the manure.

"See the maize and hay in the horses, Colonel Grierson?"

Grierson replied, "Yes?"

Man Killer said, "Most times, a scout can tell Mexican cavalry shoes from American, but around here, they are much the same. The Mexican cavalry feeds its horses maize and hay, though. Your army feeds its horses barley and hay. That is how we can tell which is Mexican and which is American."

Grierson said, "Amazing. I didn't know that the Nez Perce were such incredible trackers."

"We are not," Man Killer said. "Most Indians of most nations are good but about the same."

"How did you get to be so knowledgeable?" Grierson asked.

"Chris Colt," he replied, "the mightiest scout of all."

Man Killer led him several feet farther and showed him a number of boot tracks.

The scout said, "You see, they stopped here, because this horse had a stone in the frog of his hoof. Here is the stone. See where the knife marked it when it was pried out?"

Grierson said, "You not only speak as well as any white man, I have never seen a tracker like you,

Man Killer. I wonder why Mexican troops have crossed the border?"

"They haven't, Colonel," the Nez Perce warrior said. "These are Apaches. They killed Mexican soldiers and stole their boots and horses to try to fool us."

Lieutenant Colonel Grierson stared at the young man and cocked his head in wonder and curiosity.

Man Killer explained further. "In two places, there and there, I found drops of blood from the boots. The main reason is that all these soldiers dismounted and mounted their horses on the right-hand side. That is the Indian way. White men and Mexicans always mount and dismount on the left side of their horses. Also, all these men wearing boots walk with the toes pointed out. That is how the Apaches hold their feet, and only some Mexicans and some white men do so."

Man Killer stood up and lit one of the cigars given him by Colt. Grierson looked at his adjutant and guidon bearer and shook his head.

Speaking to the adjutant, he said, "Have you ever seen such a tracker?"

The lieutenant shook his head negatively, saying with a thick Irish accent, "Never, Colonel Darling. Never have I seen the likes a the young red lad here. I'd bet a pretty copper or two that the lad could trail a trout upstream and give the fish a one-day head start."

"How far ahead are they and how many?" Grierson asked.

Man Killer said, "There are seven of them, and they are two hours ahead."

"How do you know how far ahead?"

"How fresh the droppings are."

They tried to catch up, but the group turned and headed back toward the Rio Grande, which they crossed before Grierson could close and engage.

Grierson had been in New Mexico for more than twenty-four hours now, having been ordered there, over his protests, by General Phil Sheridan.

A few weeks earlier, on May 12, eight Mescaleros killed a Mr. James Grant and Mrs. Margaret Graham, wounding Harry Graham and another man, and stole their supplies. H Company of the Tenth chased them, but the braves, on their way to join Victorio, fled and also crossed into Mexico. The ambush and attack had taken place in Bass Canon, due west of Fort Davis, Texas.

It was mid-June. Simon Olguin and a party of his Pueblo scouts had been out on patrol in the Chinati Mountains. They were on their way back to Fort Davis when they were ambushed by Victorio in Viejo Canon. Simon Olguin had been Grierson's chief of scouts for the Tenth but was out with other units when Man Killer went to Texas. He was killed, along with all the horses and several more scouts.

chapter 5

》》》》》》》》》》》》》》》

The Tenth

When Grierson got the news about Simon, he sent a dispatch to Hatch, asking if Colt could be attached to the Tenth for a while, since Victorio was now shifting his activities to west Texas and southwestern New Mexico, as well as making border crossings into Mexico. Chris and War Bonnet were sent on the next train.

Colt met with Grierson and was reunited with Man Killer at Fort Concho.

The first order of business was Grierson's declaration. "Mr. Colt, we are at last going to try your advice. I have sent out dispatches to secure all water holes along and near the border, and we will also try to man mountain passes as well. I would like you to remain with my command to run the scouting operations."

Colt said, "Well, Colonel, I believe that the next order of business would be for our government to convince Mexico's government to let us make cross-border excursions after Victorio. He is starting to see that dotted line as a military strategy, and it's working, so he'll keep on."

As they spoke, Chris learned that Grierson had given his commanders orders not to leave any water holes unguarded if they engaged Victorio and his men. In the case of a battle, a rear element was always to be left at the water hole, while the rest of the patrol gave pursuit or engaged in running battle.

He would still try to wear Victorio down by continuing to pursue him when possible, but he also wanted to make it as difficult as possible for Victorio to get to water. In this area of the country, water was more important than gold.

Colt and Man Killer sat at a table in the mess hall talking over glasses of milk.

"What have you heard from the ranch?" Man Killer asked.

Colt said, "They apparently had some trouble with a gang of desperadoes or rustlers or something, but they handled it quite well. That's according to a short telegram. I haven't received Shirley's letter on it yet. Your horse herd was brought in by some Nez Perce boys and a couple of Montana cowboys, I guess. They all look good for Appaloosas, Joshua said."

Man Killer laughed, "For Appaloosas, huh? They are the finest mountain horses anywhere."

Colt said, "Yeah, I suppose, if you can teach them how to put one leg in front of the other. I figured the Nez Perce raised them, because you can run out to the pony herd in the morning and just pick out the one you want and chase him down and jump up on his back, they're so slow."

"Slow," Man Killer said. "Do you want to race that black and white animal you ride? I have heard you call it a horse, but I think it is a cow with the horns gone. I think Crazy Horse gave him to you as a joke, because you are a white man."

"I am afraid to race against you," Colt replied, "because War Bonnet might kick Hawk in the face when they start the race and hurt him very much. Of course, maybe getting kicked in the face will make Hawk look better."

He pulled out two cigars and gave Man Killer one. Then Chris, getting serious, said, "Little Brother, we must find Victorio. He has killed many and will not stop."

Man Killer said, "I know. He does not give anyone a chance. He just kills anybody he sees who is not Apache."

"He has much anger," Colt said, "but he has killed over three hundred people now. I feel that I will kill him."

"If anybody can kill Victorio," the young scout said, "it is you, Great Scout."

"If anyone is going to find him," Chris came back, "it must be us."

"At ease!"

"Carry on!" Grierson said, entering the mess hall.

The smiling lieutenant colonel walked directly over to Chris and Man Killer. He was followed by two troopers and a pleasant-looking young man, who was obviously a civilian and was noted by both men to be from the East, by his clothing and untanned, non-windburned skin.

Grierson said, "Chief Colt, Man Killer, I would like to introduce you gentlemen to my son Robert. He is visiting from back east. I'm going to let him accompany us on a few patrols."

Both scouts shook hands with the young man and found him to have an honest look and a firm handshake. He wore a well-tailored brown broadcloth suit. Colt put his arm around his shoulder and walked toward the door. Man Killer walked next to them.

Turning at the mess hall door, Colt said, "Have your son back to you shortly, Colonel Grierson."

The Tenth Cav commander gave the legendary scout a troubled look but shook his head and simply grinned. He did not know what to make of it.

Fifteen minutes later, Colonel Grierson's orderly knocked on his office door.

"Suh," the snappy young black private said. "Ya have visituhs, suh!"

"Who is it, young man?"

"I believe it's yo son, Suh, along wif Mr. Colt and dat tough redskin."

"Send them in. Send them in."

"Yas, suh!" the orderly stated.

Colt and Man Killer walked into the CO's office, followed by Robert Grierson. His father took one long appraising look at his boy and beamed with pride.

He handed Colt a glass of brandy and started to hand one to Man Killer, who was about to accept it, but Colt interfered. Man Killer gave Chris an angry look.

Colt explained, "If you recall, Colonel, liquor has proven to have a very adverse affect on Indians, but, more important, Man Killer is a man but not a full-grown one yet. He can drink after that if he wants."

Man Killer got a little perturbed by Chris's remark, but he also knew that Colt was his boss and he was always to act loyal to him. He would complain when they were alone, but he wouldn't consider embarrassing Colt in front of the commander—or anyone else, for that matter. It was unthinkable to him to question Colt in front of anybody, too.

"Well, in any event," Grierson said, "I just want to thank you both for outfitting my son here. He looks quite the outdoorsman."

He gave his offspring a long look of approval, broad smiles beaming across the faces of both father and son.

Robert Grierson wore a pair of high-topped teamsters' boots, pulled up over a pair of dark-brown, tight-fitting elk-hide trousers with fringe running down the outside seams. Atop that was a sun-bleached red bib shirt and a fancy red scarf around the neck. On his head, he wore a floppy-brimmed leather scout's hat, not unlike Chris Colt's. On his hips was a well-used rough-out leather belt and a quick-draw holster, containing a cleaned and oiled Smith and Wesson Schofield .45 revolver, the gun of choice of the famous shootist and bandit Jesse James. Man Killer had taken this fairly new and well-cared-for firearm off the body of an Apache he had killed while scouting for Grierson.

"Well, son," Grierson beamed, "it looks to me like you are well equipped and ready to take to the field, thanks to our outstanding frontiersmen here."

"Yes, Father," Robert said, "I am ready to go, and I hope you will let me accompany Mr. Colt and Man Killer on one of their scouting excursions."

"That will be entirely up to Mr. Colt. He is the chief of scouts."

"We'll take you out once or twice, as long as you listen to what you're told," Chris said.

"Yes, sir," Robert said. "I'll do whatever either of you says. I certainly appreciate all of this."

Chris Colt was tickled that this young man was enthusiastically offering respect and obedience, not only to himself but also to Man Killer, even though the Indian scout was several years younger than Robert Grierson. His young Nez Perce friend, who had started as a boy several years before, was really growing into a man.

Man Killer looked at Colt as he walked over to a

map of the frontier and started talking tactics with the commander. The Nez Perce realized that the chief of scouts had actually been watching out for him, and instead of being angry, he realized how much he appreciated him for it. Every once in a while, Man Killer would look at the broad back of the big white man and it would strike him that Colt was actually the closest person to him in his life, yet he was also one of the biggest legends in the West. It made him wonder if he had been blessed by God, and he felt that he had.

Man Killer had been a Christian as long as he could remember, having been taught by a white missionary.

On July 10, Colt, Man Killer, Robert Grierson, his father, and a detachment of soldiers left out of Fort Concho, headed on patrol for Fort Davis. A dispatch came in to Grierson a week later at Fort Davis that Victorio was being chased below the border by Mexican colonel Valle and four hundred soldiers. Victorio seemed to be headed towards Eagle Springs, Texas, so Grierson saddled up his detachment and set out immediately. With Chris and Man Killer acting as point guard to lead the way and keep the troop from riding into an ambush, they made it to Eagle Springs on July 23.

Once they arrived, they found out through dispatches that Victorio was actually fifty miles southwest, near Ojo del Pino and had gotten into a battle with the Indio scouts for the Mexican cavalry. The next dispatch told Grierson that Victorio had broken off the engagement and was headed for the Rio Grande. Unlike Grierson's own standard operating procedure, the Mexican colonel left the border unguarded by chasing after the Apache renegades with all available troops instead of leaving blocking forces at the likely border crossings.

Grierson marched for Fort Quitman immediately and, arriving there, discovered that Colonel Valle was directly across the river with his troops. A courier had mentioned that Valle's troops were worn out and badly in need of resupply.

Chris Colt walked into the colonel's temporary headquarters office at Quitman and immediately poured himself a cup of tea. He made another for Grierson and handed it to him.

"You sent for me, Colonel?"

Grierson said, "Mr. Colt, Colonel Valle is supposed to be just across the Rio Grande—not far, due south. I would like you and a few scouts to go and find him, take some supplies, and try to win him over. Even if the governments cannot get together on this Victorio issue, maybe we can find someone like him who will look the other way sometimes, if we chase Victorio across the border."

"We're on our way, Colonel. Want your son to go?"

"No. Too dangerous this time. Take whoever you want and get whatever you need."

Less than two and a half hours later, Valle's sentries alerted the Mexican colonel that some Indios and black gringos were approaching. Colt halted the small detail in front of the commander.

"Buenos dias, Jefe," Colt said, holding his hand up, palm outward.

"Buenos dias," Valle replied.

Colt said, "Colonel Valle, I come to you on behalf of Colonel Benjamin Grierson, commanding officer of the Tenth Cavalry. He has sent you supplies, sir, hearing that you were running low and far from your headquarters. I am Chris Colt, chief of scouts for the Ninth and Tenth Cavalry."

"Muchas gracias, amigo. Please come sit weeth me. Cigarito?"

Colt accepted the offered little cigar after being introduced to the Mexican comandante. The two smoked and compared notes about Victorio.

Valle said, "You know, amigo, eet ees not necessary for your soldiers to try to chase Veectoreeo. He was most fortunato to escape my grasp. We keeled many of hees people in thees latest battle, an' he was very lucky to geet away."

Colt said, "But, Colonel, don't you think that you might be giving him the opportunity to cross the border again by concentrating your force here now and bivouacking?"

"Señor," the colonel replied testily, "I have been fighting savages for many years now and know very well how to deal weeth thees Veectoreeo. I don't need a greengo scout trying to tell me how to plan strategy."

Colt put up his hands. "Oh, Colonel, you misunderstood me. I wouldn't try to tell a fine officer like you how to fight. I was just asking out of curiosity. Why, sir, your reputation for being a fine commander and an outstanding officer extends far into the United States. Many soldiers speak of your exploits."

Valle wondered what exploits he was being credited with, but he would not question it. Instead, he chose to bask in the glory. His shoulders went back a little further and his chest stuck out a little more.

"Oh, I suppose, Meester Colt, I meesunnerstood your comments, Señor. Yes, I weel handle Veectoreeo. No problem. You may go home now."

Colt said, "One question, Colonel?"

"Sí, ask eet."

Colt said, "If we should get into another running battle with Victorio, and he crosses the Rio Grande into your area of operations, can we pursue him across if we are still in active contact with him?"

"No, you cannot, Meester Colt," Valle replied. "Unless our governments decide and order me, you are not to pursue Victorio into Mexico."

Colt said, "Okay, Colonel, just wondered. Well, we have to get going. You take care, sir, and please think about letting us cross if we must. If we work together we might be able to corner Victorio."

Valle said, "I weel theenk about eet, Señor Colt.

That ees all I weel promise. Ees that the horse given you by Crazy Horse?"

Chris was shocked to hear that question from a Mexican army officer.

"Sí, Colonel, it is," he replied without further comment.

"Eet ees a magneefeeco aneemal."

Colt said, "Gracias."

Chris put his heels to the stallion's flanks, and they cantered north, the other scouts following. At the same time, Grierson left Fort Quitman heading for Eagle Springs. He knew Colt would easily pick up his trail and follow.

Colt, half an hour later, saw three different smoke signals. He smiled to himself, because he knew these were from Man Killer and were their own that they had devised. He led the patrol toward Eagle Springs.

The first smoke, whether three, two, or one puff, let Colt know if he was dealing with a regiment or a battalion-size unit, company, or troop. The second let him know whether it was friendly or enemy. The third would show Colt which direction the unit was heading.

Colt went up on a high bluff on the American side of the river and pulled a telescope from a leather tube in his saddlebags. He saw Man Killer and two scouts half a mile out in front of Grierson's small detachment. Then he saw further movement off to his left front. There was a point element of three Apaches, riding ponies and spread wide apart approaching Man Killer's position. Far to the south was a cloud of dust, but it was too far for him to make out. He assumed it was a large war party of Apaches, probably Victorio.

He was too far away to warn or signal Man Killer, so he just watched. Man Killer's group kept getting closer, while the three Apaches moved forward cautiously. The large group was still on the south side of the Rio Grande. Colt was concerned, and then his biggest worry came true. He saw the lead Apache staring in Man Killer's direction and taking cover behind two large boulders. He pushed a rifle out in front of his position, apparently waiting for Man Killer to get within range. Colt had to do something—fast.

He jumped off War Bonnet and signaled his scouts forward, his eyes quickly scouring their rifle scabbards for a Sharps buffalo gun. There was none. He started grabbing mesquite brush and dry sticks together. Tossing the telescope to someone else, Colt lit the fire. He ran to his horse and pulled his powerful Cheyenne bow. The other scout, seeing the prepared ambush for Man Killer, spoke to the scouts, and they started adding brush to the fire. Colt was not going to try a smoke signal, though, because it would be too vague and would not stop Man Killer from walking into an ambush.

He got some of the cloth strips that he used for bandaging from his saddlebags. He also got the flask of whiskey he carried for treating wounds. Chris quickly wrapped the strips around the arrows, just behind the heads, and tied them off. Next, he soaked them in the whiskey. He placed the first one on the bow and nocked it on the string. Carefully, clutching the powerful bow in his left hand, he wrapped the first joints of his first three fingers around the bowstring, the sides of his index and middle fingers pressed against the nock point of the arrows, just behind the carefully trimmed turkey feathers. Colt stuck the arrowhead in the flames and pulled it out.

Pointing the flaming arrow in the direction of the hiding Apache, he aimed it in a high arc, drew the string, and released the arrow.

It was no use. Man Killer and the other scouts missed it as it dropped onto the dry rocky land several hundred yards out. Even with the flames from the arrow, the distance was too far for it to be very noticeable. He tried another arrow, and it flew out in a magnificent flaming arch, but it wasn't noticed.

Colt grabbed his last arrow, but he didn't light it. Instead he ran to War Bonnet, bow and arrow in hand, and leaped onto the pinto's back. He untied the leather thong holding his lasso and slipped the bow over his neck and let it lay diagonally across his back and chest. He held the arrow in his teeth.

Colt quickly swung the lasso around and ran to the big brush fire. He tossed the large loop out and it encircled the flaming mesquite and sagebrush.

"Easy, War Bonnet, easy, boy," he said, trying to calm his big horse as he took off dragging the flaming pile.

Although the colored horse was well trained and very intelligent, dragging flaming brush with any horse would require tremendous trust on the horse's part. War Bonnet stayed calm and galloped where he was reined, which was directly to a very large cedar tree. Sliding to a stop at the tree, Colt unwrapped the rope from his saddle horn and tossed it over the lowest large branch. He took another wrap around the horn and hoisted the flaming mass up into the cedar branches. The partially dry tree took hold, and soon flames were leaping skyward, sixty or seventy feet in the air. That was going to get someone's attention.

Colt rode War Bonnet back and forth in front of the tree and watched through the telescope. Man Killer looked at him, and so did the Apache hiding in the rocks. At this distance, War Bonnet would just be a small black and white spot moving back and forth, but he was a colorful horse. Then Colt stopped and looked more carefully, seeing that Man Killer now had stopped, barely within the Apache's rifle range. Man Killer was looking with his own spyglass. Colt quickly rode to the tree and lit the third flaming arrow, firing it in the direction of the hidden Apache. Man Killer immediately got behind some rocks, rifle in hand.

Colt breathed a sigh of relief. He saw the Nez

Perce scout drop down out of sight and pop up again behind a boulder thirty yards closer to the Apache. The Mimbres couldn't see the flaming arrow with his naked eye, but he did see the tree and horse and rider and hadn't yet figured out what was happening. His immediate thought was that the horseman was an Apache because cavalrymen did not ride painted horses—or light-colored horses, for that matter. It made them too easy to spot. He wondered if somehow some brave in his party had gotten to that spot and was trying to warn him about something.

He watched for Man Killer and couldn't see him. Colt looked back at his sidekick, and he was gone. Chris waited and watched a full ten minutes, but Man Killer was still nowhere to be found. The young scout suddenly popped up fifty feet in front of the startled Apache. Colt saw a puff of smoke come out of the end of Man Killer's rifle and the Apache dropped down into the rocks. A few minutes later, Colt saw the man, leaning over the back of a blood bay mustang, blood streaming from his side. He rode rapidly toward the Rio Grande and was joined by the other two, who had been out of the action.

Colt signaled the other scouts, while he unstrung his bow and put it away in his bedroll. He swung up into the saddle again, and they trotted off toward Man Killer and the scouts who now had ridden up to him.

It took another half hour for Colt and his scouts to catch up with Man Killer. Man Killer, seeing Colt coming, kept heading toward Eagle Springs while the chief of scouts rode parallel, angling toward him.

"Was he heading toward me or waiting to dry-gulch me?" Man Killer asked.

Colt said, "You were in his sights, boy. See anything else?"

Man Killer said, "No. You made it easy for me to see. I read about the burning bush in the Holy Bible. You have done it again."

"I'm just glad that I didn't have to read over you with the Holy Word."

"Were there others?"

"Yep, a large party miles to the south and two others were near him. You wounded him bad."

"The bullet tore the flesh along his rib cage," Man Killer replied. "I think he will live. We must report to Colonel Grierson."

The other scouts stayed ahead, while Colt and Man Killer rode back to the commanding officer. Grierson was pleased to see Chris riding up. This time he offered the two men cigars. All three lit up and smoked while they talked.

Colt said, "Colonel Valle wants all the glory himself, or he doesn't want us to make him have to fight Victorio, Colonel. He won't cooperate but says he'll think on it."

Man Killer interjected, "I just wounded an Apache, and he was with two others. They might have been the front scouts for Victorio."

"I watched from a bluff and saw the dust cloud

from a large party just a little across the Rio Grande," Colt added. "They were headed north."

"I'd wager a month's pay that it's that mangy cur dog Victorio," Colonel Grierson said.

Colt said, "It could also be one of his band, Colonel. He does sometimes split them into smaller groups. But one thing is sure. They are definitely Apaches, and they were trying to cross the Rio Grande."

Grierson said, "Well, we better get going to Eagle Springs and see if we can intercept that devil."

He yelled, "Sergeant, move them out!"

"Yes, sir."

The small column started to move, and Robert Grierson came forward.

He said, "Father, may I escort Mr. Colt and Man Killer now?"

Colt nodded and smiled at the colonel.

The CO nodded, and the smiling Robert Grierson followed Colt back to the point of the column.

That night Colt picked a spot for them to bivouac which held a natural-rock water tank still holding water from the recent gully washer. The night was uneventful, and they proceeded on the next day, until midday, when Man Killer first spotted an approaching rider. He rushed out to meet the man and held up a red scarf, which was an idea Colt had in case soldiers from other units ran into his scouts. Each time they went on an operation, other units were wired and told what color scarf would be carried by the scouts as an identifying device.

Man Killer greeted the rider and escorted him, at a full gallop, back to the main detachment, which was really quite small for a colonel.

The exhausted soldier saluted the colonel and handed him the dispatch, then fell off his horse in a faint. Two others grabbed him and set him gently on the ground. Another brought him water, and they started fanning him with a branch from a large bush.

Colt had been far out in front of the cavalry, but he spotted Man Killer and the courier from a distance. He rode in right after the courier came around.

"Wounded?" Colt asked.

"No, suh, Mr. Colt, jes' exhaustasized," a short private replied.

Grierson read the dispatch and said, "Corporal, tell the men roll 'em and smoke 'em. Fill up on water. Be ready for a forced march."

"Wal, suh," a large corporal, with an even larger smile, said, "I reckon I kin do somethin' like that. S'pose, Colonel, it might git me promoted to sergeant?"

"Always a joke, Corporal Riggins," the commander said, smiling. "Suppose I could find a private that would love corporal stripes?"

Corporal Riggins laughed and cleared his throat, turned and suddenly yelled, "Smoke 'em if ya got 'em, boys. Drink up! Don't need nobody fallin' down from the heat, heah! Keep yer mounts riddy though, boys, and stand to. We're the cavalry and we need ta be riddy to go when the colonel gives us the git-go!"

Grierson, always tickled by Riggins's joking, turned and winked at Colt.

He said, "The scoundrel's crossed over, by golly, Colt. We might have him if we run the course with our corsets. Captain Gilmore's sent dispatches from Eagle Springs telling us he's crossed the blue line, Buster. Gilmore got the news from Captain Nolan, who I have at Quitman. His folks spotted the red devil. Good old Flipper. What a boy!"

Grierson was totally elated.

Colt said, "Flipper?"

Grierson explained, "Lieutenant Henry Flipper, the only Negro officer in the Tenth Cav. That brown sweetheart, I could kiss him. His men carried these dispatches, and according to the time on it, the couriers went ninety-eight miles in twenty-two hours. I tell you, Colt, a lot of people will have no truck with these colored boys, but the buffalo soldiers have the lowest desertion rate in the U.S. Army and the highest rate of medals for heroism per battle-ready soldier. What's funny, Colt?"

"Oh," Chris explained, "I'm not laughing at you. Just society. Just one of the expressions you just used."

"What's that?"

Colt said, "Colored boys. I guess if they were boys and not men, you wouldn't have such a good unit, would you, Colonel?"

Grierson was embarrassed, but Colt was also one of the few people who had the man's respect. His comment didn't fall on deaf ears.

The CO said, "Something to think about, Mr. Colt. Well, we must get moving. Do you think Eagle Springs is where we should be headed?"

"Headed, yes, but I don't think we should end up there."

"Where, then?"

Colt said, "Colonel, Victorio isn't going to try to water at Eagle Springs. He knows you have men there. He'll try for Tinaja de los Palmos. It's fifteen miles west of Eagle Springs and just about the only place around where he can water besides Eagle Springs."

Grierson thought a minute and finally said, "I'll tell you what, Mr. Colt, if you're willing to do it. I'll send most of these men to Eagle Springs, and I'll take a few volunteers to Tinaja de los Palmos myself. Would you be willing to go?"

Colt said, "That's the only place I want to be. Man Killer, too."

"Why's that, Chief Colt?"

"Because that's where Victorio is headed, and he and I are headed for a showdown."

"How do you know he's going there?"

"It's my job to know."

"Well, then," Grierson added, "how do you know you two are headed for a showdown?"

Colt mounted up and said, "It's my job to know."

Grierson mounted also and hollered, "Men! I need six volunteers for a potentially dangerous mission."

Every single one of Grierson's men stepped forward, either on horseback or leading their mounts.

He cleared his throat and said, "I appreciate it, men. I'll have to pick six. Corporal Riggins, pick five men."

"Wal, sir," Riggins drawled, "if ya know fer sure they was gonna git kilt, I know which six I'd pick, but I don't reckon ya want all officers."

Grierson laughed, and Riggins picked six men from his squad immediately. The colonel met with his ranking sergeant and sent the rest of the detachment ahead to Eagle Springs. He wrote out a quick note to J. C. Gilmore and sent them on their way. Colt sent all the scouts with them except for himself and Man Killer.

He and the Nez Perce took off at a trot heading out as point patrol for the small detachment. Robert Grierson was summoned back to the patrol by his father, and Colt turned looking for the young college man. The chief of scouts rode back to the main patrol.

Chris said, "Colonel, your son has been doing a good job helping us. I'd like him ahead with us."

Grierson said, "I thought you said that you were certain that we would run into Victorio."

"Got to let him grow up sometime, Colonel."

Grierson paused, deep in thought, finally saying, "So it shall be, Mr. Colt. Sometimes it is hard to be a father."

Chris said, "Sometimes it's hard to be a man."

"True."

Grierson yelled, "Robert!"

His son came riding up from the new position he had just taken with the small patrol. He smiled and touched spurs to his mount's dark-brown flanks, riding up to the CO.

"Yes, Father," he said with anticipation.

"You better stay with Mr. Colt here. You said you wanted to learn how to scout some."

"Yes, sir!" he replied proudly. "You sure you don't mind, Mr. Colt?"

"No, you're doing a good job so far. Let's go."

Man Killer, Colt, and Robert Grierson went out about half a mile in front of the patrol and started looking for sign and for a possible ambush or trap of some sort.

After too many miles of dust, sand, sagebrush, rocks, and deep, rocky slashes in the earth where many could hide, they finally came up out of an arroyo and saw a well-worn rutted road. It passed through Tinaja de los Palmos directly to their front. Man Killer and Robert rode back to the colonel and Man Killer reported.

"The water hole is just there, Colonel."

"Where is Colt?" the commander asked.

"He has gone many miles ahead," the young scout replied.

"But what if he runs into Victorio, alone, by himself?"

Man Killer said, "You have few men. It is much better than if Victorio would run into you and this patrol."

"He would certainly be killed," Grierson said.

Man Killer said, "The great chief of scouts, of all scouts, does not die easily."

Victorio laughed, and his warriors did the same, as he pranced back and forth with his red roan. Chris Colt lay on the hot earth, his shirt several feet away. He was spreadeagled with rawhide thongs tied to each of four stakes. The Apaches standing around taunting him each secretly admired his tremendously muscular torso and all the telltale scars. This man was very much a seasoned warrior. His flesh told the story of many battles against man and beast.

Chris Colt was frightened, more frightened than he had ever been. He was upset with himself for getting caught and being so foolish. Of all things, the way he got caught was most upsetting to him. Colt knew that he was near Victorio, and he was being extra cautious. He had taken his boots off and switched to the moccasins that he always carried in his saddlebags. Colt had even slipped the thonged-leather boots over War Bonnet's hooves so the horse could travel quietly and not leave noticeable tracks.

Before battle, warriors have always had a tendency to void their bodies. It is a psychological need to "lighten the load" in preparation for battle. In the case of ambushes or unexpected attacks, it was universal for all warriors to void after battle, but when a great battle is imminent, it is done before. Chris Colt was no different. He had learned to slow down the excessive pounding of his heart in anticipation of battle, but he could not control the need to get rid of wastes.

Colt had been moving slowly, very slowly and carefully, leading War Bonnet on foot, because he was so close. His eyes searched and scoured every foot of ground, knowing that the Apaches were so skillful that an entire war party could hide in an area where no one else even felt there was cover. The braves of Victorio were smart enough not to look directly at Colt as he approached. It was a trick that most tribes used—and Chris did himself. Animals and those with a better-developed sixth sense could actually feel it if someone stared at them, even when their back was turned. To avoid this, smart braves and hunters would watch the ground next to their quarry and only glance at it directly occasionally.

Colt could not wait, so approaching a stand of creosote brush, he checked in and around the brush to make sure there were no hidden Apaches. There was only sand around him, so Colt decided it would be the safest place to relieve his bladder. He stepped up to the bush and started eliminating his waste water.

The sand suddenly opened up ten feet behind him, quickly and quietly as the Apache warrior sat up, sand falling off the blanket over his face and body. Colt heard the slight sound of falling sand milliseconds before hearing the Spencer being cocked. Apaches, with bows drawn and guns cocked, suddenly appeared from rocks and bushes and crevices all around him. Victorio appeared then on his war pony. He laughed.

The braves all around him quickly closed in. His weapons were seized, and he was grabbed by the arms and ankles and yanked backward, and his shirt was pulled off. His wrists and ankles were spread apart. Stakes were quickly whittled and pounded into the ground, and he was tied off.

Colt knew that he had to use all his mental and emotional powers to not show any fear, pain, or anger. At first, several warriors stood back and shot arrows into the ground all around Colt's head and body and between his legs. Every time another brave shot, Colt would laugh and taunt the man about his poor marksmanship.

Victorio's lips curled back over his teeth in anger. He rode over to one of his braves and yanked the man's bow and arrow away. He drew quickly and released and the arrow stuck into the ground next to Colt's head, putting a slice cut in the lobe of Chris's right ear. Like most ear wounds, it started to bleed profusely. A deep rumble started in Colt's massive chest and shortly evolved into a howling laugh.

He grinned broadly at Victorio and said, "When the dogs among your wickiups shoot things at your woman, I bet they do not miss, Victorio."

Victorio finally smiled. He could not help but admire the bravado of the taunting chief of scouts. They had both taunted each other several times, but now Victorio's blood ran cold when he saw the look Colt was giving him.

Colt said, "You have cut my ear and made me bleed. You and I will fight someday, and I will kill you, Victorio."

"The scout Colt speaks like a mighty bear, but he has his teeth and claws removed."

"The war chief Victorio fights against men whose hands and feet are tied with rawhide bonds."

A little flash of anger. Did Colt detect it on the Apache's face? He was hoping he could shame the man into loosening his bonds, so he could have some kind of chance. Even if he was going to be shot, he decided at least one other brave would go with him, if he could just shame Victorio into releasing him.

Victorio said, "We will sit here and watch you, Colt. I am going to cut off your eyelids and watch you look into the face of Father Sun all afternoon. Later, your skin will come off."

Colt smiled and said, "Good. Father Sun has

smiled upon me many days, and now I can look at him and smile all day."

Victorio came back, "You will not be smiling very long, white eyes."

"I will smile whenever I think of the maggots eating your guts, Apache."

Colt had an idea and said, "I will not cry out even if you would build a big fire to burn me with."

Victorio had been looking for some small sign of weakness, and now he had it. He spoke in Apache to several braves and they immediately started scrambling around. Within minutes, a large pile of brush was stacked up around a piñon tree. The branches of the piñon were hacked off, and Colt was taken from the ground and tied to the tree, his arms stretched up into the air and the thongs pulled over the lone branch left attached. The Apache leader told the men to pile the brush and wood around the legs of the chief of scouts.

Colt was scared but was not about to show it.

He said, "Hey, Victorio, could you set a pot of water on my head before you light the fire. I sure could use a cup of coffee."

Victorio flipped his left leg over his pony's neck, sliding off the right side. He walked up to the scout and reached out suddenly, grabbing Colt's throat and squeezing.

Barely able to talk, Colt muttered, "You are very brave. Make sure my arms are tied very tight."

Then he spit in Victorio's face.

Victorio kneed him in the groin and stepped back. Colt wanted to scream. He couldn't breathe, but he fought with all his might not to show any pain. He also decided he would not cry out when the fire started. His idea was to get Victorio to burn him at the stake.

No matter what the Apache did, Colt knew that he was going to die slowly and painfully. He figured that, at least this way, Man Killer would see the smoke and the detachment would be warned.

Victorio then made a decision that made Chris's heart leap for joy. It was the Apache's idea to make the chief of scouts die more slowly and in more anguish, but in reality, it gave Chris more hope.

The large pile of sticks, logs, and brush was up to Colt's waist, but Victorio gave another command in Apache and a number of warriors built the pile out in a swirling circle away from the main brush pile. It was the Apache leader's thought to light the end of the fire and let Colt watch it slowly burn and spiral round and round him until it finally ignited the large pile that went up around his legs and waist.

Colt thought that he might even have a chance to live now if only Man Killer would spot the first smoke when the fire started. If he could put it together, Man Killer might suggest a patrol to help Colt out. Chris rethought it and felt he was being selfish. He didn't want to wish Victorio's war party on any small cavalry patrol.

He thought about his beautiful wife back in Colorado and wondered if he would ever see her again. He thought about his newly discovered brother. For some strange reason, Colt wished his brother was there. Even though Joshua wasn't really a gunfighter or a scout, somehow, Colt thought, he would know what to do.

Victorio sauntered toward the chief of scouts again, laughing and making private jokes with several warriors on the way, who joined in the laughter. He reached into Colt's pocket inside his war shirt, which had been lying on the ground. Victorio pulled out two of Colt's cigaritos and a couple of matches. Placing one between his own lips, Victorio stuck the other in Colt's mouth and lit both. They both puffed and stared deep into each other's eyes, without either showing any emotion. Even when Victorio stepped forward and stuck the burning end of his cigar up against the flesh on Colt's massive right pectoral muscle and Chris could smell his own burning flesh, he just smiled slightly and blew smoke into the Apache's face.

Victorio said, almost in a whisper, "That is how it is going to feel all over, Colt."

Colt grinned. "Good. I was starting to feel cold."

Victorio struck the other match, and while Colt gulped, he lit the end of the giant spiral of brush.

Man Killer had really started getting concerned when the small patrol dug a defensive position on the ridge line across from the water hole and buttressed each hole with rocks and there was still no sign of the chief of scouts.

The colonel forbade Man Killer from going out after Colt, but the young Nez Perce was not to be stopped.

He said, "Colonel, the Army pays me, but I work for Chris Colt, not you. He is my brother, and I fear something is wrong. If you and your men want to stop me, be fast, very fast with your weapons. I am going, and that is all. I have spoken."

"Be gone and be damned with you," the colonel said angrily, knowing there was no stopping the headstrong scout.

He was heading south and had just topped a rise when he spotted smoke rising from a fire maybe a mile ahead. It was not a smoke signal, and Victorio would not start cooking fires in this country in the middle of the day. Fearlessly, Man Killer kicked Hawk in the ribs. It didn't bother him that he might be riding at full speed into a group with Victorio and more than a hundred hate-filled Apache renegade warriors. Chris Colt was in trouble. The young scout had known it before. He had sensed it. He would get Colt out of trouble or would hunt the spirit bear together with Colt in the afterlife. He did believe that there were spirit bears to be hunted in heaven and spirit fish to be caught.

The flames kept coming closer and closer, and Victorio stared at the great scout watching for some hint of fear or pain, but Chris Colt would not give that satisfaction. Colt kept a smile on his face while he silently recited the Lord's Prayer in his mind. He then asked God to watch over his wife, brother, and Man Killer, and made a final request that God strike Victorio down with smallpox or something horrible.

The flames got closer and closer and were now almost unbearable. Suddenly, he spotted an Appaloosa on the rocky bluff directly in front of him. It was a very large black Appy with a white rump, covered with black spots. It had four white stockings and a broomtail and very little mane. The horse stood more than sixteen hands and was under a McClellan saddle and Army blanket. It was Hawk.

Chris smiled. Directly below Hawk stood Man Killer, Winchester leaning against a rock by him and six-gun in each hand. The flames kept getting closer and Colt could barely see.

Why, he wondered, would Man Killer be shooting with two revolvers? He was far out of range for a six-gun. The Nez Perce opened fire, and Apaches melted into the ground into dozens of hiding places. Many returned fire, but Man Killer ignored it while Colt figured out what the lad was doing. An arrow passed through the lower right side of Man Killer's abdomen and Colt saw the brave wince with pain, but he lifted the Winchester, slowly, carefully, and aimed right at Colt.

Chris saw flame stab out of the end of the barrel and heard a crack overhead as his hands came free.

Colt dropped down into the pile of brush and came up with a stout stick. He crawled on his hands and knees following the space in the spiral out of the trap. When he got to the flames he held his breath and ran.

Coming out of the smoke, Colt almost ran into Victorio, still holding his war shirt. The stick came in a vicious arc from Colt's waist and smacked the Apache chief across the bridge of the nose; the cartilage gave way and blood spurted as Victorio fell backward. None of the Apaches saw this because all eyes were on Man Killer, who kept firing into their positions.

Chris grabbed his shirt and ducked down, pulling it on. He looked left and right and spotted the warrior with his weapons. Colt grabbed the knife from Victorio's sheath and ran forward. He threw it and it stuck in the brave's midsection. Colt jumped through the air and the soles of both feet struck the warrior full in the face as he clutched at the knife in his stomach.

Whistling loudly, Colt quickly put his belt and holsters on and checked the loads in his guns. There was so much firing going on that he still was not seen amid the smoke and confusion. Colt heard hoofbeats approaching and his heart beat with joy. War Bonnet whinnied and leaped across the burning line of brush, heading straight toward his pasture buddy, Hawk, up on the hill. The paint sensed what to do. He swept down on Colt and the scout grabbed the horn and swung up into the saddle as the horse passed by. Staying low, he held the reins in his teeth, while he fired left and right with both guns. Blood blossomed on the torsos of several Apaches, and Colt ignored everything but running full out for Man Killer and Hawk. A bullet hit War Bonnet in the neck, right next to Colt's head. The horse let out a scream of pain, and stumbled, but regained his footing and kept charging, now heading up the hill.

At the top of the hill, Man Killer was already mounted and riding over the crest, where Colt overtook him. Man Killer still had the feather and the last half of an arrow sticking out of his lower right abdomen, but he acted as if nothing was wrong. As Colt pulled alongside and they could hear the beginning cries of Victorio's warriors starting up the hill behind them, he gave the Nez Perce a wink.

Colt hollered, "How bad is War Bonnet?"

Man Killer said, "Just a crease along his neck, but you've been shot bad, Great Scout."

Colt looked down and saw that his entire torso and groin area was covered with spatters of blood. He made a mental inventory of himself and realized what it was.

"It's War Bonnet's blood," he said.

They both slowed their horses to a slow canter and eventually a fast trot. They knew that the two horses could easily outrun the Apache ponies, even the few that were stolen cavalry mounts. There was no need to push too hard; they should hold back now in case they needed to make a stretched-out run later.

Colt teased, "I see you figured out a new way to carry arrows, son. Isn't that a little uncomfortable?"

The teen didn't miss a beat, saying, "Not as bad as the men in Victorio's band who are carrying my bullets for me."

Colt laughed and Man Killer joined in, laughing past the pain, both of them. Colt's pain was more emotional than physical now. He had just been snatched from the jaws of death, once again, by his old young friend.

Chris patted his horse's neck, and the two scouts pressed on toward Tinaja de los Palmos. They barely checked behind them at the growing dust cloud, so little did they respect the mounts of the Apaches compared with the heart and muscle and stamina of their own.

"You okay, partner?"

Man Killer said, "I am good. The arrow went through and is low on the right side. You have told me that is not bad many times. It has not bled much."

"Good," Colt replied. "Let's race the horses now."

Man Killer chuckled through gritted teeth, saying, "Never mind. You won the race."

"Told you I would. That old fleabag of yours can't run."

"But he has no bullet holes in him." Man Killer

glanced at the bullet graze on the pinto's neck and grinned. He then looked at Colt's ear.

"My horse did not have his ear cut either," said Man Killer.

Colt smiled and looked back at the chasing Apaches. They were dropping farther behind, but knowing Victorio, Colt figured that they would chase him and Man Killer into hell.

"Let us go faster, Little Brother," the chief of scouts said. "I think their ponies are just about played out."

In three more hours, they rode into Tinaja de los Palmos and were happily greeted by Colonel Grierson and his men. Man Killer was tended to immediately by a private who had quite a bit of experience with treating wounds.

Colt reported to Grierson and excused himself. He was offered a hot meal and coffee but turned it down, saying he had something to take care of first.

Colt walked out to War Bonnet, grazing with the other horses under sentry. He had gotten some salve from one of the cavalrymen. First he cleaned the horse's bullet wound out thoroughly with water. Next, he applied the salve and fed the horse some oats mixed with barley.

While Colt was captive, Grierson had stopped the eastbound stage and sent word to Captain Gilmore to bring him reinforcements from Eagle Springs. When Colt turned up missing and Man Killer was so vehement about finding him, Grierson knew that Victorio had to be near.

Colt and Man Killer both awakened at midnight when two couriers rode in and informed the colonel that Victorio and his men were in a night position less than a dozen miles from the water hole. The old man sent the couriers to Fort Quitman and summoned A Company, commanded by Captain Nolan.

Two hours before dawn, Lieutenant Leighton Finley and ten troopers from G Company, sent by Captain Gilmore, arrived at Tinaja de los Palmos with the orders to protect and escort Grierson's small patrol to Eagle Springs. Instead, Grierson had the men dig into the ridge line themselves and join the ambush.

He sent two volunteers to Eagle Springs with orders to round up every available trooper from the Tenth.

Chris Colt, despite his earlier ordeal, ventured out into the darkness with a caution to all the troopers on the ridge line not to shoot him out of his saddle. He wanted to give the troops early warning when Victorio was coming.

The sky started to lighten, and a few minutes later, it got very dark again. It was false dawn. Colt waited motionless in his hiding place. He wanted to swat a sand flea but would not move. Motion was what would draw attention to his position more than anything else. How many times had Chris Colt been out and seen hunters ride right by deer which had stopped and stood motionless, watching the people pass by? How many times had he seen Indians appear that had been there but unnoticed moments before?

The most likely place for Chris Colt to maintain a lookout for the approaching Apaches was a small hill overlooking a flat plain in the direction of their night location. Because that was the best place from which to spot them coming, he hid under the branches of a bush on the flat ground at the base of the hill. They would watch the hill with eagle eyes and scour every possible hiding place, but they wouldn't think of glancing at a small hiding place that didn't offer much of a view of the plain. The hill would definitely be one of the possible lookout spots they would watch, because they had no respect for the white man's ability to locate good hiding places. Colt didn't need a commanding view of the entire war party. He only needed to see the dust cloud, as he had already had a commanding view of all the braves—too good a view. War Bonnet was hidden behind the hill, and there was a small depression Colt could crawl through on his belly that would take him behind the hill when he spotted them coming.

Dawn came and the sun started its slow ascent into the eastern sky. Colt lay motionless on his belly and kept watching. He would rest his chin on his forearms and close his eyes for ten to twenty seconds at a time, then slowly, even lazily, open them.

Chris had been through too much in recent days and was starting to develop dark circles under his eyes, but this was not the time to worry about adequate rest. That would be taken care of when he finally went home and could sleep and fish and hunt for several days. He would venture into the "high lonesome," up above timberline in the Sangre de Cristos. Towering over his ranch in the Wet Mountain Valley, those rock sentinels held lakes teeming with cutthroat and rainbow trout wanting to jump into his skillet. Up away from civilization's reach, in the rough but pristine and beautiful mountains, up so high that few dared venture there—that was where Chris Colt could find himself. That was where he could recuperate from anything—at least emotionally and mentally.

Right now, Chris Colt was lying as close to the ground as he could, his body on dusty white sand, waiting for the sun to heat everything up like a giant reflector. It was a dry, arid country, where rains came only occasionally and then in a killing, drenching downpour. It was the land of enchantment, New Mexico, but it was also a land where women could look old before their time, if they didn't heed the baking sun and whistling winds. It was a land that could awe you with beauty or kill you if you didn't respect its power.

Colt saw a cloud of dust rising off the floor of the plain. That was all he needed. It was about an hour after daybreak. He slid backward, his eyes scouring to make sure that Victorio hadn't sent advance riders out too far in front of the main party. The bush between him and the distant dust cloud, Colt spun around and crawled back a quarter mile to his horse, ground-reined behind the hill.

He mounted and took off at a full lope for the water hole called Tinaja de los Palmos. He slid to a stop at the remuda, and a trooper took over War Bonnet for him. He would make sure that the horse was cooled down, unsaddled, fed, and watered.

Victorio gritted his teeth. It hurt very much, especially where his nose was broken. He was still having great difficulty breathing. The chief wanted a scalp badly. He wanted the scalp of brown hair that belonged to Christopher Columbus Colt, the man who had just broken his nose. He was the man who had humiliated him and secretly frightened him when he sneaked into his camp, killed a sentry, and placed the body next to his while he lay sleeping. It was hard for Victorio to believe that a white eyes could do such a thing. His camp was full of Mimbres and Mescalero Apaches, and Colt had performed such a deed. It was rumored that, as a younger man, Colt was respected even by the great Mangas Coloradas of his own tribe and Cochise of the Chiricajua. Victorio had seen Colt some years before when he was there in an earlier campaign against the Apaches, and there were many of his nation who had seen this man and had experiences with him in battle.

A story was even told of Colt leading a cavalry patrol into a hidden canyon, where he found and the Long Knives attacked a Chiricajua rancheria. Colt had gotten separated from the main unit and, wounded, was chased for miles through the rocks by many of the Apaches. During the fight, one of the warriors accidentally shot a girl from their village who had been returning with her family from another rancheria.

Colt had grabbed the girl and carried her many miles trying to find a good defensive position. The Apache warriors slowly crept in on his hiding place and watched as he carefully nursed the girl back to life. She had almost made the spirit walk, but he applied poultices and bandages and healed her. He did not know that these braves watched him the whole time, while he thought they could not find him and had passed him by.

One of the warriors said, *"Inday pindah lickoyee schlango poohacante"*—"These people of the white eyes are wonderful medicine men"—and all the other braves agreed with him.

It was two days before the girl could travel. Colt carried her in front of him on his saddle and delivered her to her village. The whole time, the white eyes scout did not know that the warriors who had pursued him followed him back to the rancheria and watched from hiding places while he delivered her to her parents at her wickiup. He then departed untouched and unspoken to by any Apaches.

Waiting for Victorio and his men to arrive, Colt joined Man Killer at the hiding place the younger scout had prepared for them in the rocks. Knowing they still had a few minutes, Chris rolled a cigarette, as did Man Killer, and they smoked. Neither spoke a word as they waited for the big fight. They were alone with their own thoughts.

The place in the rocks where Chris and Man Killer hid reminded Colt of another hiding place in the Superstitions. Colt remembered the time in his early twenties, when he was scouting the Chiricajuas in southeastern Arizona. He had led the small patrol into a hidden canyon and located a rancheria, but Colt had warned the young West Point lieutenant leading the patrol that there were too many warriors in the village and they were too battle-wise for him to attack. The young officer wanted glory, though, so Colt got many of the Apache fighters to chase him before the main attack took place, leading them far into the mountains. At one point while he fled on his young buckskin gelding, Nighthawk, the warriors fired down on him from higher ground, and a bullet struck a young Chiricajua girl who was walking through the canyon.

Chris had jumped down and bandaged her quickly, then fled with the girl, looking for a good hiding place that would be easy to defend. His other challenge was to be near several roots and leaves he would need for a healing poultice for her wounds. He also had to cut a bullet out of her side.

While he nursed the girl back to health, Colt occasionally caught glimpses of the Apache warriors watching him, but he kept on about his business. After she regained reasonable strength, he would return her to her home. Two days later when he did so, he was followed by the war party, but they thought they were staying out of sight. He assumed they respected him for what he did, but he was too smart to stick around and find out. After he took her to her family's wickiup and gave her to her parents, he got out of there as quickly as he thought he could without giving the appearance of being a scared jackrabbit. He always wondered if those Chiricajua braves ever knew that he was watching them, too.

It was nine o'clock in the morning when Victorio's advance guard came into view. They immediately spotted the movement of several soldiers in the fighting positions on the ridge line overlooking the road and the waterhole.

They turned eastward and headed directly away from the buffalo soldiers. Soon the rest of Victorio's band came into view and followed the point element. One of the vanguard rode back to the main body and spoke quickly to them, apparently telling them about the soldiers spotted on the hillside.

The word was spread along the hillside for Colt to report to Grierson. He worked his way along the rocks without being seen and got to the old man.

"Mr. Colt, hold on, please, until Finley arrives. I

sent for him, too," Grierson said, and both watched as the young officer worked his way up the hill to the colonel's position.

"Gentlemen, run that son of a buck down, attack, and hold him until more reinforcements arrive," Grierson said. "Mr. Colt, I want you with Finley in case that red scoundrel tries to escape into the wilderness. Lieutenant, I'm counting on you to hold him until more men arrive. Take ten men and engage him, pin him down."

Finley was nervous but excited, and his voice showed it. "Yes, sir."

Grierson added, "Mr. Colt, I cannot order you to go with him on this because this is a fight and you are paid to scout and run the scouts."

Colt laughed and said, "Yeah, Colonel, I suppose I could sit up here and catch up on my knitting, because it might be dangerous fighting Apaches."

"Okay, Colt, okay," Grierson said. "I was just trying to let you know that I am aware of the legalities of the limitations of your position in most situations."

Colt said, "I am not like most chiefs of scouts. Besides, I owe Victorio."

Colt made the last statement as he gently touched the bandage on his wounded ear. Finley was already on his way to select ten of his men to lead on the excursion after Victorio.

Colt took off at a run to the horses and signed to Man Killer while jogging what he was doing. Man

Killer would move to Grierson's position to find out what help the commander needed.

Within minutes, the troopers were mounted and were chasing after the Victorio band. Lieutenant Finley didn't even know where Colt had gone, but suddenly he saw the scout on his magnificent paint. They came down off the ridge line to his right while his troops ran up the road after Victorio. Colt charged down the small mountain ridge and headed right at the center of the right flank of Victorio. He had the reins of his horse in his teeth and was firing from the hip with both guns blazing.

Finley was astonished by this show of bravado by the lone scout, and it excited his men as well. The dark-skinned soldiers were hungry for battle, and nervous tension abounded among the tiny patrol.

Finley said, "Well, boys, are we ready to waltz with the Apache killer and his boys?"

A corporal in the rear of the patrol spoke up. "Let's give 'em the what for, suh. Jest like that madman Colt is doing!"

All the men cheered and Finley drew his sabre.

He raised it skyward and pointed it down the road, yelling, "Charge!"

The eleven men charged into the rear of Victorio's war party and actually turned the group as if they were turning a stampeding herd of cattle. Shots came from the Apache ranks, but in the dust and confusion some were yelling to each other among the Mimbres and Mescaleros about shooting their own people. They ran into the rocks and took up firing positions, some of them already grabbing rocks and making the little fortresses as Victorio had trained them.

Finley and his men were amazed by Colt, as he pranced back and forth on his pinto, drawing fire from many of Victorio's people while yelling taunts at them and at the chief in particular. Colt was angry that he had been tortured by these people and that Victorio had sliced his ear with an arrow. He was smelling blood—so angry and so ready for battle. He wanted nothing more than to tangle with the Mimbres leader in hand-to-hand combat, and he just felt that someday they would, someday soon.

Colt and Finley's patrol kept Victorio and his people pinned down in the rocks for another hour. A dust cloud came at the cavalry up the road. There was so much dust and gunsmoke now from the heated battle that nobody could see. The dust cloud had been created by Captain Viele and Company C, but because of the confusion, C Company's trooper started firing into Finley's men. Finley called for the retreat bugle immediately and the small patrol dashed pell-mell down the road toward Grierson's position again.

Victorio did not realize that the confusion was caused by the Americans firing at their own people, so he figured he and his men were routing the white eyes buffalo soldiers. With Colt riding by himself along the Apaches' flank and spilling braves from their ponies' left and right with accurate pistol fire, they chased after Finley and his men, thinking they would catch them from the rear and kill them as they rode.

When the patrol got close enough, the colonel gave the command to open fire. This too overwhelmed Victorio's men, and they backed off their attack immediately.

Captain Viele charged after the Apaches in the meantime, and Colt kept pouring deadly fire in on their ranks. They again sought refuge, as Victorio had so many times before among the natural shields on the hillside, south of Grierson's position. The rocks here were a little more scattered and smaller. Viele's men charged into the fire from Victorio's bows and rifles as though it wasn't even there and dislodged them in short order. Seeing a dust cloud coming from the west, which was Captain Nolan and his men, the Apaches fled from the rocks and crossed the road, then turned south and made a hasty retreat toward the Rio Grande. Viele and Finley chased after them, with Colt actually leading the charge, but he was called back a few miles down the road. It was obvious that Victorio was going to make the border. Viele knew that Colt might be able to catch him, but not his troopers. It was early afternoon by the time they pulled off attack and returned to Grierson's position.

The colonel met with Colt, Man Killer, and his officers. Only one man, Private Martin Davis of C

Company, had been killed. Lieutenant S. R. Colladay had taken a bullet through the shoulder but would be okay. The Apaches had risked their lives to recover their own dead from the battlefield, but even so the troopers counted seven dead from Victorio's warriors, and they knew there were many who were wounded. They also found ten dead ponies near the water hole.

Grierson was both angry and pleased and apparently quite excited from the adrenaline coursing through his body. Colt remembered looking at Victorio with his handsome peaked nose flattened against his face and the dried bloodstains from Colt's earlier action. Victorio had stood up in the rocks when Colt was riding back and forth firing into the Apache positions. Even at that distance, Colt could see the hate and rage in Victorio's glare. He wanted Colt so badly. The chief just stood there, bullets flying all around him, shooting at Colt.

After the attack, when the wounded had been attended to, as well as the horses, Grierson called his top sergeant and directed that night bivouac positions be set up. After dark, officers' call was announced, and coffee was served to Colt, Man Killer, and the officers of the command.

"Smoke 'em if you've got them, men," Grierson said, pacing back and forth in front of the fire. "Gentlemen, I have had the enlisted personnel moved away from the fire, because I want to speak with all of you confidentially. What I am about to say is classified and is not to be discussed except right here around this fire. Do I make myself clear?"

There was a unanimous sounding of "Yes, sir" around the fire.

Grierson went on. "I am absolutely flabbergasted that this red satan Victorio can keep striking, then fleeing across the border. I am going to press as hard as I can and have sent a courier to the telegraph with a message to Colonel Hatch to join my protestations. The scoundrel kills Americans, then flees to Mexico. He kills Mexicans, then flees to America. The politicians in Mexico City and Washington cannot get together and work out a settlement on working jointly or allowing military action to pursue the red bastard and bring him to the ground.

"Well, I publicly want to thank our chief of scouts, Mr. Colt, for convincing us to guard water holes and mountain passes, because we sure are making that son of a pup thirsty. I want to make him hungry, too. There is an old saying that to kill an army, kill its stomach. Many of us commanders lose sight of that, just wanting to figure brilliant tactics and strategies to outfight the enemy. I want to cut him off not only from water but from food and ammunition as well. We are going to concentrate on this in the next phase of our operation.

"Second, I am not a politician, I am a soldier. I'm tired of honoring an invisible line on the ground while a satanic killer rages back and forth murdering, pillaging, and plundering freely. I am prepared to start stretching the rules. Mr. Colt, I need a couple of volunteers among your scouts to cross into Mexico and locate the scoundrel and accomplish that without being spotted by the Mexicans."

Colt didn't hesitate. "Man Killer and I will go, sir."

Man Killer smiled.

Grierson went on. "Good. Find him and let me know where he is. Let's keep track of him no matter where he hides, and we'll be able to prepare a proper reception for him on his next vacation to Texas. I also want to know how many men he keeps with his supplies, where he locates the supplies, and how they are transported. He has a lot of mouths to feed."

Lieutenant Finley added, "And a lot of guns to load, sir."

"Colt, you both can leave in the morning. Don't get caught by the Mexicanos," Grierson said.

Colt replied, "No problem, Colonel, if we get caught. They won't know we are Americans."

Grierson gave Colt a queer look, and Chris winked at Man Killer.

Grierson opened his eyes and saw his orderly standing over him. He blinked and looked at the white ceiling of his canvas tent. He was in night position after the Victorio battle at Tinaja de los Palmos, he thought. It must be around daybreak, but where was reveille, he wondered. It was hard to see the smiling orderly in the dark tent, but the colonel sure could smell the hot coffee he was being handed.

"Don't ya know, suh," the orderly said, with an accent that Grierson had never been able to figure out. "It's Mr. Colt, the mahn ahnd hees friend, suh, Mahn Killer, are ready to leave out on their mission, suh. Colt thought you should know."

Grierson took a sip of coffee and lit a candle by his cot. He looked at his timepiece and saw that it was three in the morning. He sat up, and the orderly helped him find his boots.

A few minutes later, Grierson walked out of his tent and saw two Indians in war paint, one holding a bow and wearing a quiver of arrows and the other holding a Winchester. The horses were familiar. The two men were Chris Colt and the other was Man Killer.

"Well, may the saints bless us and keep us," Grierson said slapping his thigh. "Mr. Colt, is that really you?"

Colt said, "That it is, Colonel, and my friend Man Killer here."

Chris Colt had smeared his entire body with some kind of stain that made his already-tan skin dark copper. His dark-brown hair was braided and a single eagle feather with a beaded-leather base hung on an angle from the back of it. He wore a red breechcloth, a large Bowie knife in a beaded sheath, and porcupine-quill moccasins. His face was painted with black war paint like raccoon eyes, and the red talons of an eagle faced outward on his cheeks and nose. Man Killer had the entire upper half of his face painted black. Both men wore bone hair pipe breastplates and assorted armbands. Colt, for example, wore a beaded armband around the base of each bicep muscle, making those already huge muscles look that much larger.

Both horses wore paint on their legs and bodies in various designs and, as usual, War Bonnet had an eagle feather braided into his mane and another in his tail. Hawk's mane and tail were too short to braid anything into them. Man Killer rode bareback and had a blanket rolled up and hung diagonally across the horse's back. Colt was in a McClellan saddle, but numerous fancy-headed brass tacks had been hammered into it, and it was decorated with dyed horsehair, beadwork, and feathers. It also held four painted Army canteens.

"What about your brown hair, Colt?"

Chris replied, "Colonel, have you not noticed numerous half-breeds among the many legions of Indians you have seen? Have you also seen some Indians with red-streaked hair and blond or brown in their hair?"

"Yes, I have, sir," Grierson replied.

Colt said, "The red, brown, and blond streaks come from poor nutrition with some bands, Colonel. It is not that unusual."

"Very well, I guess, unless Colonel Valle captures

you. No one will confuse you with us," the colonel said. "Godspeed. But wait. You have no saddlebags or bedrolls and only one gun. How will you eat and live?"

"Quite well," Colt said, indicating the land before them in a sweeping gesture. "It contains all that we need to be quite comfortable."

Man Killer said, "We should be back within a week, Colonel."

Grierson shook his head and smiled. He gave them a salute with his cup of coffee and took a long sip as the men disappeared into the night. When the two mounts walked across the rock shelf by his headquarters area, he noticed that the horses' shoes had been removed.

As the two masquerading scouts crossed the Rio Grande, and the Nez Perce scout thought about the white girl of Westcliffe with the honey hair, Chris Colt thought of his own love. His thoughts stayed on her all day as they pushed deeper into Mexico.

That night, as he and Man Killer made camp along Victorio's old trail south and west of Eagle Springs, Chris lay his head on his saddle and closed his eyes. He covered himself with his saddle blanket and thought of his beautiful auburn-haired bride. He pictured her face and her body, her smile and her eyes. He couldn't wait to get home and hold her in his arms once more. Colt wondered if anything had changed between them in the time he had been gone. He wrote regularly but had trouble getting letters from her because of his mobility. He pictured them being parents together of a brood of strong, tough-minded children and thought maybe he'd ask her about it when he got home.

It was about midnight when the loud noise made Shirley sit bolt upright in her bed. She yawned and stretched out her arms. Curling her back in a long, slow stretch, she yawned again. Then she got out of bed, lit the nearby lantern, and walked over to the crib. She reached down and smiled, lifting her son out of the crib and feeling his bottom. He needed changing.

"Boy, is your daddy going to get to do this sometimes when he comes home, Joseph," she said, "so Mommy can get some sleep. Maybe when Daddy finds out he is a daddy, he'll make me sleep a long time for not telling him."

Several states away, a famous chief and orator who had been in the national news on a daily basis sat in a rocking chair smoking a pipe and enjoying a midnight conversation with an old friend.

The friend said, "Joseph, I have news from the home of Man Killer and Colt. They have been in the dry lands after the Apache Victorio. They are gone now many moons. The woman of Colt has had a child, a boy. Do you know the name given to it?"

Chief Joseph took a puff on his pipe and smiled softly. "Yes. They have named it Joseph."

He blew his smoke toward the moon and got a faraway look in his eyes. He was again thinking of his home in the beautiful Wallowa Valley in Oregon. It was the place that the white grandfather in Washington would still not let him take his people to. It was the land where he buried his father, Old Joseph. He had promised that he would never sell the beautiful valley to the whites.

The friend said, "Joseph knows everything. How did you learn of Colt's son?"

Joseph said, "You told me, old friend."

The friend said, "I did? I do not understand."

Joseph said, "You told me with your question. Think of it and you will understand."

The friend looked at Joseph as he again blew smoke at the moon and shook his head as he had done so many times before. Joseph was a poet in his heart and always communicated that way.

Near the Colts' Coyote Run, a group of men with torches in their hands assembled around a large wooden cross soaked in kerosene. They had all ridden out north of Canon City into an area called Garden Park, called Red Canon by some. The Shelf Road stagecoach route took the men right to the place where they headed back into a cut in the canyon wall. The stage road ran up to the western slope of Pike's Peak and led to North Park.

The men of the Klan met here most times, but this time there were more men. They had been summoned from a long distance. The leader spoke before the cross lighting and told them of their humiliation at the hands of the "uppity nigger" near Westcliffe. The plan was made for the riders to cross over from the Black Mountain area and work their way through the big hole back to Long Gulch and take it down to a fording spot across the Arkansas River. The snowmelt from the Sangre de Cristos ended before July, so it was low enough now for them to cross on horseback right at Long Gulch. They would travel the river road up to Texas Creek at night, then head south, slowly climbing uphill a thousand feet to the Colt ranch. Then the wife of Colt and the others were going to die of a sudden epidemic of hemp fever. They would learn, according to their leader, that nobody messes with the Klan.

Colt and Man Killer crawled forward on their bellies, and each slid between twin boulders. They crawled downhill, dragging themselves on their bleeding elbows and knees. The hillock overlooking Victorio's temporary rancheria was covered with sentries, so the horses had been left miles away while the two scouts moved on the ground for a long distance. It had taken hours, and it would take hours more to return to the horses after the scouts had gathered all the information they could about Victorio and his supplies.

Victorio walked toward the small hill, and Colt

unconsciously touched his sliced earlobe, bared his teeth, rose on one knee, drew an arrow back, and aimed at the center of Victorio's chest. Man Killer's hand shot out and grabbed Colt's. Chris turned his head and looked into the young man's eyes.

Man Killer could speak like an educated white man with someone like Colonel Grierson, but with Colt he was more comfortable speaking in the poetic tongue of his first childhood hero, Chief Joseph, the man the great Colt had promised to name his first-born son after.

He said, "The colonel told us, Great Scout, to scout Victorio and report, not kill him and get killed ourselves."

Colt had anger in his eyes, a great deal of it, and Man Killer felt thankful that they were friends and not enemies. Still, with incredible strength, he held the arrow back.

Man Killer whispered, "You have taught me not to hate my enemy for acting like he is an enemy."

Colt suddenly smiled and slowly let off on the bowstring. Victorio pulled his breechcloth aside and relieved his bladder.

Colt started laughing quietly and whispered, "Do you know how much I would love to shoot him right now, Little Brother? You have learned your lessons well, though. We will send him on the spirit journey later."

They made mental notes of Victorio's food and logistical supplies and sentry system, then slowly and carefully withdrew on their bellies. Colt and Man Killer heard some Apache men laughing and talking, and both crawled into a small clump of thick bushes by the trail. One of the men carried a gutted desert bighorn sheep over his broad shoulders. A hunting party. They all stopped at the thick bushes where Colt and Man Killer lay frozen in place. Each scout held his knife handle and his breath. As if Victorio had passed on a telepathic message, the five men stood around the bush and joked in their guttural language and pulled their breechcloths aside, urinating all over the bush and the two scouts hidden underneath. They kept control of their emotions and their breathing until the hunting party went on its way.

There was no way to clean up, nor would the extra noise and movement be wise anyway. Soaked with liquid body waste, Colt and Man Killer blocked it from their minds and crawled on. At last they made it back to the horses without further incident.

Mounting up, Colt joked, "Man Killer, you know how you felt when those Apaches were pouring their water on you?"

"I will not forget the feeling."

Colt said, "Well, if you were a soldier in the white man's Army, you would feel like that every day."

Man Killer started laughing and turned his Appaloosa toward the north, thinking about how good the brackish water in the stream he had complained about earlier would be. His wounded side was very sore from the crawling, but nobody would ever know it was. That was the manner of the Nez Perce. He would suffer in silence. Right now, he wanted to just ride up to that little stream and dive off his horse into the one-foot depth of water. He wouldn't even care if he scraped his face on the rocky bottom.

They were sixty miles into the country of Mexico, due south from Fort Quitman, near the Rio Grande. Colt would push them hard to get to Grierson, but Man Killer knew that his friend would allow them both to swim and bathe in that little stream they had crossed.

Grierson was pleased when the two brought him the news of Victorio. He wondered what the chief's next move would be. He even sent a courier with a dispatch to be wired to Colonel Valle, letting him know about Victorio's camp. He would not let the Mexican commander know how he got the intelligence report but just warned him of the Apache's whereabouts. Grierson was furious two days later when he learned that Valle had moved away from Victorio and headed toward El Paso.

When Colt and Man Killer returned to the command, they were both sent out with patrols almost immediately. Grierson's intelligent order was for each of them to direct the patrols' commanders to the two most likely spots that Colt reasoned they should go. Colt led Captain Lebo and K Company into the Sierra Diablo, the Mountains of the Devil.

Here, Colt easily located Victorio's supply base,

and the unit struck the camp at daybreak. A number of the guards were killed or wounded, and the rest were driven away. K Company captured twenty-five head of beef cattle, several wagonloads of maguey bread, several tons of already-butchered beef that was loaded on pack horses and mules, and dozens of baskets of freshly picked wild berries. The entire supply base was being packed up, apparently to move to Victorio's next location. Man Killer would be the one to determine where that would be.

In the meantime, Grierson guessed that Victorio might try to water at Van Horn's wells and cross over the pass east of there. But Grierson guessed wrong. The Apache chief had crossed northwest of the wells that same day.

The day before, on August 3, an H Company patrol headed by Corporal Asa Weaver had had a fifteen-mile horseback battle with Victorio and his men. During the battle, the only trooper that Weaver lost, Private Willie Tockes, who had been attached from E Company, fell into enemy hands in a most unusual way. His horse started bucking in the middle of the fight, and Willie had to hold on for dear life. In the meantime, the horse bucked and pitched right into the midst of the Apaches. Seeing that death was imminent, Willie Tockes dropped his reins and his hold on the front of the McClellan saddle and drew his repeater, firing over and over into the ranks of Apache warriors on both sides of him. They finally swarmed the mount and dragged

Willie off the horse and beat and stabbed him to death on the ground, but a few Apaches went with him.

Man Killer took a patrol out from Van Horn's wells and found Victorio one valley over, heading northwest at a rapid pace. Man Killer wanted to get word to Grierson immediately, so he came up with an idea when he found a telegraph wire crossing the valley. He suggested to the buck sergeant leading the patrol that he find out if any of his men had been telegraphers previously. Man Killer was too naive to realize that the white man had not let many black men learn such a trade because they thought they were mentally incapable of learning it. But one of the men in the patrol had secretly trained with the post telegrapher when he was with the Ninth at Fort Union and could read and transmit very well. The man climbed a pole and rigged a telegraph key using his pistol and rifle barrel. He sent a quick message, which was immediately given to Grierson, who had tapped in on the same line at Van Horn's.

At three in the morning, the determined colonel had his command mounted and ready for action. He knew where Victorio was headed. Man Killer had had it tapped out over the "singing wires." The chief was trying for water at Rattlesnake Springs, sixty-five miles northwest of Grierson's current position.

Before mounting, he said, "Men, that son of a red devil is headed for Rattlesnake Springs and has a shorter distance and a head start on us, but I think you men can outmarch him. All say that the Apaches can outdistance the cavalry every time, but we are the Tenth. It is sixty-five miles for us, boys. What say you?"

A great cheer rang up among the courageous buffalo soldiers of the Tenth Cavalry, and they started out, alternating between a trot, a hand lope, and an occasional fast walk.

Twenty-one hours later, the men were no longer cheering, but their chests were puffed out. They were at Rattlesnake Springs—and they were there ahead of Victorio.

Victorio didn't arrive until two in the afternoon on August 6. He was greeted by a force of two companies under Captain Viele. The command had arrived the previous night at ten o'clock. The command had had plenty of time to prepare, and ambush sites were well hidden in the canyon. But Victorio felt instinctively that there was a trap, so he stopped his war party. Viele could tell that the Apache chief was going to withdraw, so he had his men open fire. The Apaches quickly withdrew.

Victorio halted them down the canyon and said, "We must have water, and the buffalo soldiers are few. We will ride back in there and attack."

They came charging back down the narrow canyon, the sounds of their yells echoing off the steep rock walls. Grierson sent two companies under Captain Carpenter in to reinforce Viele's men and repel the attack. They charged the charging Apaches and drove them back out the mouth of the canyon.

An hour later, the unit's wagon train, along with Grierson and his command staff, was attacked by part of Victorio's party when they rounded a point in the mountains, heading toward the springs to set up the command headquarters. The train was being guarded by a detachment of cavalry as well as a company of the black Twenty-fourth Infantry. Captain Gilmore counterattacked with a company-minus, and once again Victorio's forces were repelled.

The Apache leader was desperate for water, so he attacked the men in the mouth of the canyon, trying for the springs once more. The return fire by the enthusiastic buffalo soldiers was so intense that Victorio's demoralized force was split into several factions and thrown into complete confusion, unlike a disciplined fighting force. Gilmore chased them for miles.

Victorio had lost thirty more men and many others were wounded. The cavalry killed and captured seventy-five more of the Apaches' horses as well. Private Wesley Hardy was missing in action, and three other troopers had been killed.

As soon as Colt and Man Killer reported back to the unit, they were briefed on all that had happened. While their horses were reshod and rested, Colt and Man Killer selected four stout mounts from the remuda. Each leading a spare horse, the two scouts took off with a promise to Grierson that they would locate the Apaches' new hiding spot. In the meantime, Colt suggested that Grierson guard every possible water hole and mountain pass he could handle. The commander obliged.

It took only a few days for them to return and report that they had found Victorio's trail west of Fresno Spring.

Grierson summoned his commanders. "Man Killer, you go as scout for Captain Carpenter with his company," he directed. "Colt, you lead Captain Nolan and his. I don't care if you have to kill your mounts to do it, you run that scoundrel into the ground. Do you hear me, gentlemen?"

The two units immediately began a forced march, setting a rapid pace. The following day, Colt, now back on War Bonnet, led them up to the night location of Victorio and his people. They had just struck camp and were ready to depart. They were headed south toward the Rio Grande. Nolan and Carpenter's commands charged full out, side by side, against Colt's advice. The horses were tired, and they were too far away to start the charge.

The two captains agreed that Victorio would stand and fight, but Colt knew better. The Apaches would fight only if they felt they had a decisive tactical edge. If not, they would flee to fight another day. Victorio's band took off as if their heels were on fire, and the two units, now committed, kept up the pursuit.

It was several hours later, and Carpenter's mounts started dropping like flies. They had been doing some serious patrolling before the colonel's orders. Colt gave Man Killer a wave from the distance as he and Nolan's command kept chasing the fleeing renegades.

It was mid-afternoon when the first of Victorio's warriors splashed into the Rio Grande and headed across the river. The area was flat, rocky, and sandy, with distant buffs in the background. A determined and angry Colt was now well out in front of the troopers. He didn't want Victorio to slip away once more across the border.

Sliding to a stop on the banks of the Rio Grande, Colt stared at the last of the Apaches as they left the river. The closest troopers pulled up next to Colt. Victorio spun his horse around on the bank and taunted the American, yelling and waving blankets. Several of his warriors turned their backs and bent over, exposing their buttocks to the soldiers while their friends laughed.

Colt yanked off his war shirt and threw it on the ground and handed his gunbelt and guns to the commander.

Nolan said, "Mr. Colt, whatever are you doing?"

Colt didn't answer. He stared across the river while he stripped the saddlebags, canteens, rifle scabbards, lariat, and bedroll from his horse and tossed them on the bank of the international boundary.

Across the river, the wildly grinning Victorio threw his blanket down and gave his carbine to another warrior.

The chief of scouts, wearing only boots, spurs, and striped cavalry trousers, raised his Bowie knife high overhead and yelled at the top of his lungs, "Victorio!"

Across the river, Victorio, who had stripped down to a breechcloth and moccasins, held a war club high overhead and yelled, "Colt!"

At a silent understood signal the two warriors screamed loud war cries and kicked their mounts into action, charging across the wide river at each other. The two horses, both battle mounts, understood that they were in combat once again.

Colt yelled the Lakotah battle cry, "It is a good day to die! Hokahey!"

Victorio yelled a shrill, long, loud war cry.

On each bank, both Apaches and cavalry soldiers yelled cheers and encouragement to their champions.

The two men met in midstream. Such was their hatred and anger at each other that both let out ferocious primal screams as they each dived off their mounts and slammed into each other's bodies.

Colt felt his head crash into something hard; at the same time, he felt his knife tear flesh. He also felt a sharp stab of pain in his left shoulder. He saw everything spin around and felt panic as his world got dark. He could feel himself falling and spinning, falling and spinning, and heard a faint splash as he felt himself hit the cold water. It made him conscious long enough to bring him partially to reality and panic again. He thought, I'm going to die at the hands of Victorio. He has defeated me. Then everything went black again. Colt thought he could hear very distant sounds of gunshots. It was as if they were being fired on the other side of a very thick rock wall.

"Suh! Suh! His eyes are opening."

"Colt! Mr. Colt, can you hear me?"

Colt suddenly figured it out. The voice was Captain Nolan's. He blinked his eyes and saw that he was lying in the shade of a cottonwood tree. His head was spinning slightly. He looked around and recognized the Rio Grande not far away. His fight with Victorio—but this was a different part of the river. Soldiers were standing all around, smiling at Colt. He sat up and shook his head several times.

Things started coming back to him now, and he looked around. His clothes and guns were placed beside him neatly. The chief of scouts accepted a cup of hot coffee from one of the troopers, named Willy. Colt had noticed that a lot of the buffalo soldiers were named Willy. He smiled and nodded appreciation and took a long sip. He built a cigarette.

"What happened, Captain Nolan? He bested me, didn't he? How did I come out of the thing alive?"

"Bested you?" Nolan said, laughing out loud.

All the troopers laughed with the captain.

Nolan said, "You don't know what happened, do you? Why, you were marvelous! You put a slice in that bastard that he'll carry with him to Hades. You two slammed into each other headfirst so hard that you knocked each other unconscious. Your blade took Victorio along his left rib cage and sliced him as clean as a butchered pig. The blood was pouring out of the devil, and I swear his blood was pure black. His war club hit you a glancing blow on your left shoulder."

It was then that Colt noticed that his left shoulder hurt, and he touched it gingerly. He reached up and felt a bandage around his head and yanked it off. He touched a goose egg on his upper forehead and winced from the pain.

Nolan went on, "Willy here went into the water after you, under fire from the Apaches, and dragged you out before the entire river poured into your lungs."

Colt reached out a hand and lay it on the young trooper's shoulder. He shook with him and smiled, then handed Willy a cigar and lit.

"Thanks, partner," Colt said warmly.

Willy beamed at the legendary scout and puffed on the cigar.

"What about Victorio?" Colt asked.

Captain Nolan answered, "His men fished him out downstream and tied him on his pony. He was not moving, but they handled him as if he was still alive."

Colt knew what the man meant. In the midst of combat, wounded men were handled totally differently from dead men. When bullets were flying around, nobody ever seemed to worry about bruising a corpse.

Captain Nolan said, "This is the beginning of the end for Victorio, Mr. Colt. His men did not look like Apache warriors. They looked like a beaten force. I'll bet you we'll not see him back on American soil."

It was the middle of the night when the riders came up to the ranch house. They again wore white robes and white pointed hoods with just eyeholes in them. They all carried torches.

"Nigger! Nigger! Come out here and take what's coming to you, and any of your nigger-loving friends what wants ta join ya can come out, too!" the leader yelled.

Joshua Colt stepped out of the shadows and faced the forty hooded men. He was scared to death, but he decided he would meet his death as a Colt, not as a coward.

Tex and Muley stepped from the shadows, as well.

Tex grinned and said, "Guess I'm one a those nigger lovers ya referred to, boys, an' I'm a gonna take some a ya ta hell with me."

Muley pointed a greener at the leader and said, "My boss ain't no nigger, and you ain't gonna call him that, mister. No matter what happens, I'm giving you both of these barrels."

It was one thing calling people out and being threatened by them, but it was another being singled out of a group of forty and being told you were going to get shot first. The leader was nervous. He had thought that with this many men, they would have a cakewalk this time.

The door of the house opened, and Shirley walked out, holding Joseph in her arms.

She yelled, "We told you once before to stay off our land, you cowards! You make me ashamed to have white skin! You might kill my brother-in-law and our friends, but my husband, Chris Colt, will hunt you down one and all and shoot you in your black hearts. If you kill him, my son, Joseph Colt, will grow up and hunt you down and kill you."

Joshua yelled firmly and angrily, "Shirley, take Joseph and get inside now!"

There was no arguing with his tone, and she started to go but turned at the sound of a new voice.

"My wife's correct, boys. You don't leave, I'll hunt you all down and kill you one by one," Chris Colt said, stepping from the darkness of the road on his big paint.

Man Killer rode up next to him. "And I will help my brother."

Suddenly a detachment of soldiers, all black, rode up and flanked Colt and Man Killer. They all cocked their weapons.

The stocky dark corporal by Colt's right arm said, "Sure glad the colonel insisted we accompany you home, Mr. Colt. I never did like these fellers in the pointed hoods and robes. In fact, sir, I got a lot of friends who would love for me to give them their comeuppance. Why don't you let the patrol and me escort them away from your ranch and explain to them how much the Army likes you and your people, sir, and how the Army wouldn't like for them to ever come back?"

"Really good idea, Corporal," Colt replied, grinning broadly. "What do you think, Man Killer? What do you think, Joshua?"

The entire Colt ranch clan started laughing loudly while the men under the hoods gulped and fidgeted nervously in their saddles.

Colt said, "Corporal, when you men are done escorting these gents out of here, come back and taste my wife's doughnuts and bear sign. Best in the West. Now, boys, start dropping your guns or I start spilling saddles at the count of three."

Colt knew he had to take very strong action or he would have return visits from these men.

He said, "One, two, three."

His hands flashed down and both Colt ivory eagle–snake grip Peacemakers came up and bucked in his hands. The Klan leader and the large man next to him flew backward off their horses, their robes covered with giant crimson stains. Neither moved.

Guns started dropping on the ground rapidly from all the robed leaders.

Colt pointed his guns at several men and looked at the two dead men on the ground.

He said, "Get that trash off my property."

Four Klansmen jumped down and loaded the two bodies on their horses, tying their arms under the horse's bellies. Two more took their reins to lead them.

One hand holding the reins and the other high in the air, the night riders walked into the darkness with a detachment of smiling black cavalrymen holding their Army repeaters on them. Before disappearing into the blackness of the night, the last trooper, the corporal, turned in his saddle and winked at Colt.

Chris slid his leg over his horse's neck and dropped to the ground. Joshua, Tex, and Muley all came over and shook hands with Chris and Man Killer. But he kept staring at the woman with auburn hair on the front porch. She stared back, tears running down her cheeks, and held their son up in the air.

Joshua said, "What about Victorio?"

Colt said, "The Mexican army surrounded what was left of his band in the Tres Castillos Mountains two days ago. Fight didn't even last an hour. Victorio's dead. Most of his people were naked, wounded, and starving to death."

He walked to the porch, and she laughed and

started talking nervously. "I didn't want you to have more to worry about, Chris. I wanted to surprise you. Please don't be angry with me."

Colt swept her into his arms and gave her a long, passionate kiss. He stepped back and smiled down at his son, touching the baby's cheek gently.

Colt said, "He has your eyes, honey. Hello, Joseph, I'm your pa, and you're going to have lots of brothers and sisters."

Man Killer looked at Joshua and said, "Have you heard any news about a Jennifer Banta south of town?"

Joshua laughed and said, "Only every other day when she comes over here and asks about you."

In the Sierra Madres, Victorio's oldest subchief, Nana, got his fifteen warriors ready for battle. They were few, but they would recruit more disgruntled warriors from the reservations in America. He was glad he had left Victorio before the end. He would carry on the fight. Hundreds of miles away, another Apache chief, Geronimo, made his own plans for another attack.

The buffalo soldiers of the Ninth and Tenth Cavalry went back to their dreary existence on their various posts in Texas, New Mexico, and Arizona. Although some were very impressed with their recent campaign, they would be largely ignored when credit was taken for the operation against the notorious Victorio. It didn't matter that the buffalo soldiers had the lowest desertion rate in the U.S. Army or the most medals per capita. They had a different-colored skin than all the officers who commanded the military. They were a different race from the bosses, so they would not be given credit for their accomplishments. But some Klansmen had found out that they were men. The men of the Ninth and Tenth could give each other a wink and a knowing smile. They knew who they were; they were heroes.

"How long will you be home?" Shirley asked, putting some doughnuts in the oven.

"I don't know, Shirl," Chris answered. "How long will our government mistreat the Indians? When will things change?"

Joshua's voice turned them both around. "Maybe never, Little Brother, but this country is made up of people like you and me. As long as people with different colors and backgrounds just keep talking, I think there's always hope."

Chris Colt walked up and wrapped his arms around his older brother, and the two men, one black, one white, gave each other a big hug.

SIGNET

SAGAS OF THE AMERICAN WEST
BY JASON MANNING

☐ **HIGH COUNTRY** A young man in virgin land. A magnificient saga live with the courage, challenge, danger, and adventure of the American past. (176804—$4.50)

☐ **GREEN RIVER RENDEZVOUS** Zach Hannah was a legend of courage, skill, and strength . . . Now he faces the most deadly native tribe in the west and the most brutal brigade of trappers ever to make the high country a killing ground. (177142—$4.50)

☐ **BATTLE OF THE TETON BASIN** Zach Hannah wants to be left alone, high in the mountains, with his Indian bride. But as long as Sean Michael Devlin lives, Zach can find no peace. Zach must track down this man— the former friend who stole his wife and left him to die at the hands of the Blackfeet. Zach and Devlin square off in a final reckoning . . . that only one of them will survive. (178297—$4.50)

*Prices slightly higher in Canada